Martial Artists Elite

Eve of Deception

Disclaimer

This story is fictional. All places, events and names in this story are merely fictitious. Any resemblance to any actual places, events or people, living or dead, is purely coincidental.

ALSO BY SAMUEL E. PERRY JR.

Voices from Within – Serial Killer Novel

www.authorsamuelperry.wordpress.com

https://plus.google.com/+Authorsamuelperryjr/posts

Martial Artists Elite

Eve of Deception

By
Samuel E. Perry, Jr.

ISBN 13: 978-1944051013
ISBN 10: 1944051015

"Mom, second grade's awesome. We saw a martial arts demonstration after lunch," Sammy says, running into the apartment. "One of the boys in the demonstration got hurt. The black belt man carried the boy to the nurse's office. They never come back out."

"I hope the child will be okay . . . Go get your dad. He's exercising down by the water, next to the pier."

"Cool, Dad's finally home from his trip?"

I'm out the door and running across the sand. I see him standing in the middle of some men. Heading towards him, I yell.

"Dad . . . hey, Dad."

Almost there, I hear the men arguing with him, when one pulls a knife and stabs him in the stomach. I watch Dad fall to the ground. I get to him and kneel down next to a puddle of blood on the sand. I start crying and screaming at the men.

"Why did you hurt my dad?" Jumping up, I start hitting the one with the knife.

"He's at the wrong place at the wrong time, kid, just like you."

Pushing me back, he punches me in the face, knocking me down. I fall close to Dad. Crawling to him, I lie on his chest; Dad wraps his arms around me and holds me tight. Looking into his eyes, I can see him dying.

"Daddy, I love you, please don't die!" I slide my arms around his neck and squeeze tight.

Tears drip down our cheeks. "I love you too, Sammy. Protect your mom." He squeezes me too tight to breathe. His eyes close, and his arms fall to the sand.

"Well, kid, looks like you're the man of the house now." They walk away laughing.

"I will learn to fight, one day, I will come for you—kill you all. You killed my dad . . . I hate you!"

Table of Contents

Sammy

The Quest
*** Chapter One ***

Returning from working out at the dojo, I'm excited to show Mom my fifteenth-year training plaque. I reach the side of my apartment building when I hear screams.

"Someone help me . . . please . . . please . . . don't hurt me anymore."

"What the hell—Mom!" Adrenaline rushes through my veins.

Running to the beach side of the building, there's an enormous man, in shabby clothes, long hair and beard smacking Mom's face with the back of his hand. Lifting her off the ground with his massive hand, her eighty-pound body dangles like a rag doll, as he jerks on her purse to steal it.

"Shut up, bitch."

Something overcomes me; my mind goes senseless; a burst of energy fills my body.

"You bastard!" I yell.

Opening his hand, he let Mom's limp body slam to the pavement. He turns towards me, flexing his rippling muscles with the look of death on his face.

"You're going to bleed like . . . this bitch."

Dropping my gym bag, I rush him. Within a few feet of him, I leap into the air. With all two hundred and thirty pounds, I come down driving a punch, breaking his jaw.

"Argh!" he screams, falling to his knees.

Spectators watch the blood squirt out of his mouth, painting the concrete sidewalk red.

Reaching out, I lock my arm around his neck. The crowd jumps back when he stands lifting me off the ground like a small child. I hadn't realized the size of this man. I use all my strength to hold on and squeeze his neck until it snaps. The big man falls to the ground, taking me with him. Becoming trapped underneath, I'm unable to breathe. Using all my strength, I roll him off.

I crawl over the bloody pavement to Mom. "Are you ok?" Placing her head on my lap, I pull the gray hair away from her face. There are black and blue marks across the wrinkles of her aged skin.

"Yes, Sammy. I think you hurt that man bad."

"I don't care. No one hurts my mom. I told you when Dad . . . . I will be here to protect you."

"Yes, you did, Sammy." Giving a painful smile.

Crowds of people gather closer to see what's going on. One kneels down, checking the pulse of the big man.

"I think this one's dead," he says.

Minutes later, police arrive. An officer handcuffs me and puts me in the back seat of a patrol car. The area is now full of people, maybe fifty, trying to get a peek at the big man on the ground. I watch out the car window. Officers are speaking to bystanders and taking notes, when more police and an ambulance arrive. Officers tape off the area with yellow crime scene tape; I begin to worry what will happen. I was only protecting my mom.

An officer I recognize opens the car door. "Sammy, I've known you all my life. We went to school together. I still remember growing up, all the kids looked up to you. I remember you used to look out for me and the other smaller children."

2

"Yeah, I remember protecting you from the bullies. You've sure gotten a lot bigger."

"Sammy, seriously. What happened could put someone in prison for excessive force, maybe for life. That man is dead."

"I went crazy, Paul. He was hurting my mom." I watch the detectives out the front window standing around the body on the ground.

"I spoke to the homicide detective in charge. He's calling it self-defense, no charges against you. You better watch yourself in the future." Grabbing my arm, he pulls me out of the car and removes the handcuffs, letting me go.

I walk over to Mom, who is sitting on an outdoor chair, weeping. "Mom, let's go home." She stands, and we hobble together to the apartment, where I help her to her room to lie down.

"Sammy, make me a promise?"

"What's that?"

"Let this day be forgotten. I never want to speak of it again. I love your dad, but also want what happened to him never to be spoken of. Pain and hate destroy people and their lives—let it not happen to us."

"Someday I will find those men and they will pay for what they did to Dad." I will hold hate until that day.

"Sammy, please, if you love me."

"You will never hear it from my lips again. I promise." Kissing her on the forehead, I leave to my room.

I wake to the smell of Mom's home-cooked breakfast. Jumping out of bed, I dash to the kitchen. "Good morning, Mom," I say, kissing her on the cheek. "The food smells great. Can you make me a quick plate? I need to eat fast, I'm heading to the dojo to persuade Master Bill to let me fight pro. I also wanna check out an apartment across our parking lot."

"Sammy, I thought you're going to live here and take care of me?"

"Mom, I'm a big boy now and need my privacy." She doesn't like it, but I can tell she knows I'm right.

After eating, I'm out the door to the dojo, eager to chat with Master Bill. Arriving, I find the place is empty. I bow, then walk around mats to the back offices. Entering the hall, I hear voices come from Master Bill's office. Stepping closer, I hear Master Bill laughing, which tells me it's a social meeting. I take it upon myself to crash the party; grabbing the door, I swing it open.

The room goes quite and the half dozen students are now staring at me. I ignore them. There is only one thing on my mind.

"Master Bill, I want to go pro."

"Sammy, you have to pass the dojo challenge first. You've been around long enough to know that. Aha, it just so happens we have a couple senior students standing here who would love to knock you out for their morning workout."

"Let's do it." I say.

"Okay guys, get ready. We'll meet at the ring in ten minutes."

Changing into my Muay Thai shorts in the locker room and putting on my shin pads, I have the new kid Timmy wrap my hands and help with the gloves. I arrive on the main floor, Master Bill and the others are chatting by the ring. My buddy Joe, padded and gloved, follows me into the ring.

"Hey, Joe, give Sammy a little punishment for being so arrogant all these years," Tom says and laughs.

Joe springs around the mat like a kid on a pogo stick. "You ready, Sammy?" Joe says.

"Joe, you've always been a boring fighter. Do you plan to stop dancing and start fighting before I fall asleep?"

I think my sweet words piss him off. He comes at me with a flying kick. I side step, causing him to hit and bounce off the ropes. "I'm impressed, Joe." He comes at me again; I wait until he gets into striking range. I spin around, landing a back fist, then spin the other way, connecting to his jaw with an elbow. Down goes Joe for a little nap.

Glancing over at Master Bill. "You're gonna have to send in someone a little better, master." I smile, seeing the anger on his face.

"Tom, get in there, and don't come out with him standing." Master Bill stands and points at me.

"Yes, sir. It'll be my pleasure! I haven't had a chance to put a hurting on Sammy in a while." Tom's padded and gloved before leaping over the ropes into the ring.

Tom's the black belt I met the first day Mom signed me up here as a young boy. I can still remember him showing me around, and watching him kicking ass, taking belts and winning trophies over the years. Gee, I better take this one seriously. I'm sure his goal is not to disappoint Master Bill.

"Feels strange in here with you, Tom, it has been a long time since we played." Moving around the ring, gauging him.

"Sammy, don't underestimate me. I'm not going to be so easy."

"I've learned well over the years from you and the other champs. I know your secret moves." Out of nowhere, Tom kicks me. Feeling serious pain, I drop to the mat, grabbing between my legs.

"Not all my secrets." He's laughing and staring down at me.

"You coward. How could you?" in a squeaky voice.

"I don't recall discussing any rules. Second, I didn't see you put on a cup in the locker room." A big smile crosses his lips.

Master Bill, surprised, falls backward out of his chair laughing. Tom kicks at my face, I block with a forearm, preventing it from connecting, and I grab his leg as it passes my head. I use his momentum to bring him down, by pulling his leg then throwing my weight on it: down he comes.

He's either lucky, I'm in a good mood, or my inner demons are calming down. I could've kept going and snapped his kneecap. The family jewels recover; I jump back to my feet. But the damage I did to Tom's leg makes him unable to stand.

"That's enough, Sammy. You proved your point. You're going pro."

"Thank you, Master Bill."

"Help Tom out of the ring and get changed. I have to go. I'll see you guys later."

"Tom . . . no bad feelings?"

"Not unless you feel them. Welcome to the pros, Sammy!" I get Tom out of the ring and into a seat to rest, before going to change and leave.

Walking home, I stop by the apartments across the parking lot from Mom's building. Stepping to the front, there's a for-rent sign next to the gate, with the manager's number. I call it.

"Hello? Jimmy."

"Hey, looking for an apartment. Whatcha got available?"

"I got an empty front corner apartment, with an ocean view. Interested?"

"You bet. Can I see it?"

"Yeah, one minute, I'll come down to let you in."

Coming out the beachside entrance, he isn't what I expect. Or maybe what I should expect. Instead of some grumpy old man wearing overalls, with a big belly, and half his teeth missing, he looks like the type of guy you expect to be living on the beach, with six-pack abs, long hair, and an Italian look: ultimate babe-magnet.

"Yo, I'm, Jimmy, the manager." He opens the gate to let me in.

"I'm Sammy. I'm staying across the way with my mom, and looking for my own place."

"Cool, follow me." Going inside and up the stairs, we enter the apartment. The first thing that grabs my attention is the enormous front window facing the ocean. I've lived on the beach most of my life but never had an ocean or beach view. Watching the water crash against the shore is an awesome sight.

"Hey . . . handsome . . . up there." Looking down a group of girls, full of smiles, staring up at me.

"Can we come up and visit sometime?" Using their hands to send me kisses.

"Sure, anytime, just yell for Sammy."

"Okay, cutie. I mean Sammy." They laugh.

"Its great man. This really fits my style." Looking back out the beachside window, girls in bikinis fill my view. "Dude, big-screen view of beautiful girls in bikinis. Everywhere!"

"Welcome to the beach front apartments, brother."

Signing the contract I give him a deposit check, and he hands me the keys.

"Welcome to the place everyone wants to be." Waving bye, he walks out the door.

Walking home I'm floating in happiness: I get to fight pro and get a great apartment with a super cool manager.

Entering the apartment, Mom says, "I feel like your secretary. I've been getting calls all morning from recruiters with offers for journalist postions, and I also got a pile of business letters in the mail."

I contact them over the next few days and attend interviews for the ones I like.

"Son, have you picked one yet?"

"The one that excites me doesn't pay much, but I get to work from home, giving me flex time for training. It also starts in a few days and I need the money, so I'm taking it."

The next couple of days I spend moving my stuff, getting furniture and arranging things. With the sun going down, I make hot tea, sit in the beach window and put my feet on the metal plant holder outside. Being bolted to the building, it lets me keep my balance while sitting on the windowsill. Feeling the ocean breeze blow across my face, I look around feeling there's no place in the world like this.

I can hear the kids scream while playing in the sand. The beautiful girls in the bikinis spread across my view. The singing vendors spaced along the walk doing their thing for donations are fantastic.

"Wow, it's so awesome."

There's a sign facing the walk: [Original location of MUSCLE BEACH]. I watch people stop to give muscle poses while having their pictures taken standing in front. It's humorous watching them, as all genders, races, ages, sizes and even teams pose. No one seems to be exempt. Ahh, if I take their pictures, I could create a Facebook account or something. I'm sure I can sell the pictures? But I wouldn't want to embarrass anyone.

Over the next couple of years I work and stash money in a savings account. I use my free time for training and winning tournament fights in martial arts. When one night I receive a call that changes my life forever.

I wake from a dream of being on the beach surrounded by hot bikini girls: It's unfair. Whoever is on the other side of this line will pay for interrupting my wet dream.

"Hello? This better be good. I was in an awesome dream."

"Calm down, Sammy." He laughs. "This is Master Bill. Sorry for calling so late, but this is not only good news—its great news. Drop by the dojo in the morning. You won't regret it."

Waking early, I remember the late-night call from Master Bill. I know he would have waited until morning if it weren't important. Today being Saturday, I'm heading to the dojo for sparring anyway. I'll swing by his office on the way to the locker room. Bowing as I enter the dojo, I walk around the mats to Master Bill's office. Noticing the door partly open, I step up and push it a bit further and glance in. I hear him on the phone in a deep conversation.

He must have heard the door; looking up at me, he covers the phone with his hand. "Sammy, come in, you're just in time. This conversation's about you." My curiosity gets the best of me; I step in, taking a seat in front of his desk.

I silently listen to Master Bill speak into the phone, as my gaze drifts at the pictures on the walls. Many memories fill these walls of pictures of Master Bill and me. We're receiving trophies from my competition fights with most from knockout wins. These memories also bring a reality; I'm getting up there in years. Many fighters hang up their ring gloves in their early thirties. I'm not sure how many good years I have left before Master Bill tells me my time is up.

"Okay, hold a minute. Sammy, we need to talk."

"Yes, sir." Snapping out of my trance.

"I'm on the phone with a long-time friend who happens to be the promoter for the present world kickboxing champ. This is your lucky day; seems the champ's belt fight coming up in thirty days is in trouble. The opponent broke his leg on a motorcycle yesterday."

"What does that have to do with me?"

"With your fight record and present weight, you're one of the possible fits."

8

Stunned. "And?"

"I'm sure I can convince him. You'll be an exciting fight and give the champ a run for his money. Plus this guy owes me a few big favors. If you want the challenge, and will train hard until fight night, I'll lock you in."

"You're asking if I want a chance at the World Kickboxing title? This is either a dream or you're playing a cruel trick on me. If you're on the ups, I'll fight and kick ass and make you and the school proud."

"Earl we have a deal? Great, I'll drop by later this afternoon to sign the papers, thanks." Master Bill hangs up the phone.

"Sammy, don't let us down. I expect you to train hard and eat right. I'm dedicating our best trainers to help get you ready. The fight's in Vegas thirty days from now."

Still stunned, I leave Master Bill's office, bumping into people and knocking over a small stand on the way to the locker room. As I step onto the main floor, Master Bill's voice comes over the intercom.

"Sammy has just accepted a fight with the World Kickboxing champ—for the belt. Let's give him our congrats and help in his success anyway we can."

Everyone's clapping and yelling. "Congrats, Sammy, we're here to help you." Embarrassed, I feel like running and hiding.

Finishing my training, I stop by my job, walking in the boss's office. "Sir, sorry for the short notice, but I quit. I've just been given a chance to fight the World Kickboxing champ and I'm taking it."

"Congrats, Sammy. Your leaving will be a big loss, but I understand and wish you the best of luck. You're always welcome back." Standing, he shakes my hand.

"Sir, I will be the World Champ and my dream will come true. There is no coming back."

Entering the dojo early the next morning to meet up with my trainers, I'm shocked by how many fellow students are there. They want to volunteer as sparring partners and to support me in any way possible. Each day, students come and put aside their training to help me prepare.

9

My day begins by running five miles with our fastest guys, then jump roping an hour with the best jump ropers, next bag training, then to the ring for sparring. When the pain from training gets intense and I want to stop, the teams are there to motivate me to keep pushing harder. I take five-minute breaks between the jump roping and the ring for sparring. This goes on, Monday through Saturday, until three days before the fight.

Two days before the fight, I wake early with daylight coming through the window. Jumping out of bed, I feel more alive then the day before. I pull on my sweats and run out of the building onto the beach, greeting everyone along my run.

"Good morning, chess players." Smiling.

"Good morning, tourists." Waving.

"Good morning, homeless." Shaking hands.

"Good morning, crazies." Keeping my distance.

I continue this to everyone I meet, running on the sand to Venice pier and back. Returning home, I take a shower then kick back with a cup of hot tea and relax. My mind drifts off, thinking of my personality in the ring compared to out of the ring.

Being six foot two inches at two hundred thirty pounds, most people initially fear me due to my size, until they know I'm really a sweet, lovable guy. My kindness sometimes puts thoughts in people's minds that I'm gullible. While having an IQ of one hundred forty does help me quickly catch on to scams or at least most of them, I'm still taken advantage of at times.

My fighting personality is dangerous. I'm not a wild fighter and fight using logic, but I fight for keeps. Climbing into the ring, I become stone cold, approaching opponents with an attempt to take their lives. No one understands why, not even me.

My body and mind go through an adrenaline rush whether it's me inflicting pain on someone or someone inflicting it on me. My ring violence is like a balance of Yin & Yang, as my personality goes to the extremes in both ways. When it comes to martial arts and fighting, I can't get enough of the violence. The bloodier and the more dangerous, the more I crave it.

Finishing my tea, I grab a towel and head down to the sand for the rest of the day: girl-watching. Since living here, I've picked up more hotties off the beach and had them in my place than I can remember ever before. It's so much better to date than having a steady. I'll keep it this way.

After a day of enjoying the sun and the girls playing volleyball in bikinis, I head home to get ready. Master Bill has everything arranged for me to leave tomorrow, allowing me to be there a day early.

Sammy

World Title Fight
*** Chapter Two ***

Excited at being in Las Vegas for the first time, I push through casino-bound travelers on my way to the car rental agents. Finding the rental office, I enter and step up to the counter.

"Hello, I'm Sammy Nelson. There should be a car reserved for me," I tell the big-breasted blonde behind the counter.

"Hello, Sammy Nelson, your driver's license please."

"Here ya go." Handing her the license.

"Oh yes, whoever reserved your car must really love you. Here are the papers and keys. You'll find it in spot 204, just a couple of lanes over. Enjoy, Sammy Nelson." She winks.

"Thank you, have a nice day." Maybe Master Bill isn't so bad.

With keys in hand, I search the lanes for spot 204. "Yikes!" Got to be kidding—Yu-Go. I thought they banned these tin cans? Adjusting the seat all the way back, I crank the toy up. It's off for a quickie at a Thai massage parlor before destination Mandalay Bay Hotel.

Pulling into a strip mall, I park in front a tiny suite with red curtains and Thai writing on the window. Opening the front door, I come face to face with five sexy girls wearing lingerie who run at me, giggling. The granny behind the counter, yells, "Sir, please pick one, or more if you desire."

What a selection! They're all drop-dead gorgeous. Drooling while viewing them in their short nighties and panties, I close my eyes and reach out, taking an arm. "This one will do fine." Opening my eyes, I fall in love with the best one. Holding my hand, she leads me through red silk curtains and down a hall. There are four doors on both sides. She pulls me into the last one on the right.

We enter a small room with a massage table in the center. "Sir, please remove your clothes and lie down on your belly." Being in here with this hottie gives me an instant woody, making me too shy to remove them.

Smiling, her eyes wander down to my bulge. "No problem, sir. I have a fun way of taking care of that." Her hands reach out and unbuckle my pants; she slides them down with my underwear.

"Thank you. I . . . wasn't expecting all this."

With my head facing towards her, she unbuttons the nightie letting it drop to the floor, then slips out of the panties. Climbing over me, she sits her backside on mine and her hands go to work with an awesome massage. My body relaxes. My mind drifts into thoughts of the fight, how convenient to stay in the same hotel as where I'm fighting.

Waking me with a soft slap on my bottom. "Sir, please turn over."

"What?" Forgot where I am, yeah, massage. I must have fallen asleep. "Sure thing." Rolling over, she gently sits back down but on my manhood. It slides between her cheeks.

"Please relax, sir." She moves her hips around to get comfortable.

"Easy for you to say." The smooth skin of her rear cheeks, now wrapped around my shaft, causes a full woody.

How does she expect me to relax with her naked body sitting on mine? She continues to massage, and I relax, going soft and back to sleep.

I wake to her lips and tongue giving a special massage. My God, do they teach these girls this in massage school? Raising her head, she switches to her hand as I shoot off like fireworks on the 4th of July. When my heartbeat slows to normal, we dress and return to the front lobby. Leaving, I pay granny and kiss my angel. "Thanks, the massage was wonderful." Slipping a twenty into her panties, I walk out.

Feeling loose, relaxed and ready to fight, I continue to the hotel. Getting to the room, I hit the bed for a nap. Around midnight, I wake unable to sleep. It's the night-before-jitters that fighters get. Staring at the ceiling, damn, I'll go check out the arena and get a feel of the ring. Jumping into sweats, I head downstairs.

Stepping in the door, I'm overwhelmed. I can't describe how it feels knowing I'm going to have the fight of my life tonight. Looking around at all those seats, I can picture the seats full of people screaming with excitement to see a bloody show full of action. I'm gonna do my best, and I'm sure the champ intends to do the same.

Stepping into the empty professional ring gives an out-of-body experience. Is this real? I feel I belong; I feel I don't. Am I far out of my class? I should leave tonight, leave now. Leave before I humiliate myself in front of thousands . . . millions on national TV or worse, end up in the morgue.

Snapping out of my thoughts, I notice the clock: it's late. Climbing out of the ring, I go back to the room and hop in bed, and drift back into a deep sleep.

After a restless night, I go to a dojo to meet up with my trainer to view some fight videos of the champ. This will allow me to find weaknesses to take advantage of him and strengths to avoid. Finishing the last one, I head back to my room.

Walking around at eight in the evening, my nerves are shot: I can't do this. I want to run, run out the door, get on a plane and go home. But something inside is stopping me, pulling me to the room, where my team is waiting, waiting for me to do battle. At the point of going crazy, I shuffle to the door as my inner self lures me to my worst fear.

I move out the door towards the locker room for warm-ups, last minute briefings and to spend the time psyching myself out. Stepping out of the elevator, I pass hundreds of people in the casino giving it their all to go home a winner. In an hour, I will be doing the same, but not against a clever card dealer. It will be with a highly trained fighter who is going into the ring to hurt me bad or I will him. One of us will walk away with the belt. It isn't my life's savings on the line as with the gamblers in this casino, but this gamble is possibly for my life.

I enter the locker room, it's filled with excited people, all staring at me.

"Sammy, just in time. Let's get you warmed up," the corner man says.

My hands are wrapped and gloved while the champ's manager watches and initials after. The champ's manager says, "Good luck, son." Walking out the door.

I start doing warm-ups on the pads and stretching out while waiting for the undercard fights to end. My fear is distracted with focusing on strikes to the mitts. My team's psyching me out. "Hey, Sammy . . . the champ will be jumping out of the ring or feel your punishment."

Another saying, "Hey, Sammy . . . you're here because you're great . . . not by luck. You're meant to be the new champ." They continue pumping me up as I warm up.

An official peeks in the door: "It's time."

My heart rate jumps, and blood starts rushing through me, making me dizzy. Nervousness returns as I enter the long hallway. My team follows shouting more words to psych me. The screams get louder as I see the arena entrances. I'm hearing the spectators and feel their energy.

I shuffle into the arena with my head up high, the spectators begin to chant. "Sammy, the new worlds champ." People on both side of me reach their hands out to grab me. The security do their best to block them.

"Go home! You're not in the same league as the champ," others say.

"Hey, wannabe, you're going down in the first round." They laugh. My mind and eyes stay fixed on the bigger-than-life ring directly in front.

It's like I am walking forever to cover the short distance to the ring. Climbing through the ropes I continue to psych myself pacing in circles around my corner. I can't believe I am in Las

16

Vegas in a ring, and in moments will be in a fight with a world champ.

The crowd screams—sounds like millions of people as the champ strolls to the ring, waving and shouting. It's hard to avoid getting intimidated as he climbs into the ring.

I stand in my corner listening to the announcer come over the microphone, introducing the judges and the referee. He then turns to me.

"In this corner in white and brown shorts. The challenger, with one lose and seven wins all by knockout—Sammy Nelson." I become overwhelmed, unable to focus or move. I force myself to relax, to focus.

The announcer turns to the champ. "In this corner in red, white and blue shorts, the defender with 21 wins all by knockout and no loses,, the undefeated and present World champion, Joe Fitzgerald." Screams and chants fill the arena. It's so loud I feel like the roof of the building is going to come off.

The announcer comes back over the microphone with the famous "AND NOW FOR THE THOUSANDS IN ATTENDANCE AND MILLIONS WATCHING AROUND THE WORLD—LETS GET READY TO— RUMMMBLLLLE."

The referee calls us to the center of the ring. "I want a clean fight. You've been instructed in the locker room, abide by the rules, touch gloves and let's give the spectators a good show." I'm staring into the pitch-black eyes of the champ—seeing death once more. The champ looks into my eyes speaking in a low, deep voice. "You're out of your league, son."

Hearing the champ doesn't scare me but pisses me off.

"You're going down, this fight's mine." We pound gloves before going back to our corners to wait for the bell. I no longer have fear. He'll be the one going down, and I will be the victor.

"Ding—Ding—Ding—Ding." Leaping off the stool, I attack the champ, determined to take him out quick. Swapping blows, this guy's fast and hits hard. Of all my fights, no one has ever caused so much pain as the champ is doing now. Strikes are coming out of nowhere, pounding on my face. I gotta pull my gloves and arms up in hopes of blocking this upper body and face assault. I gotta go offensive, before he destroys me.

The champ changes his targets, seemingly by reflex.

He's now tearing up my legs and lower body, I feel pain throughout my body and legs, damn, it's overwhelming. The pounding his kicks are putting on my legs, they're trembling. I'm about to fall. "Ding—Ding—Ding—Ding." Watching the champ walk back to his corner, I stumble back to mine.

I sit on the stool. My legs tremble. I focus to get my mind and body in sync.

"Sammy, if you ever needed to pull your inner demon out, it's now," Master Bill says.

Remembering what happened to Dad and images of the assault on Mom, hatred fills my mind, but something inside screams. "No." I don't know why, but something, I believe from Bruce Lee, pops into my mind. 'Fear is your enemy; forget about winning or losing; the most dangerous weapon is your will'. An inner calm overtakes my fear, and the pain becomes bearable. The champ is no longer a threat.

"Ding—Ding—Ding—Ding." The champ and I move towards the center of the ring. He begins an aggressive attack of both hand and leg combinations. Dodging his strikes and at the same time delivering mine, my art now flows. I hit the champ with a brilliant uppercut; he wobbles back and falls against the ropes.

Screams and cheers echo the arena, and hearing them excites me. "Sammy—Sammy—Sammy." I attack to finish him off, but he recovers and moves quickly, avoiding my assault.

Charging in for another attack, the champ counters by leaping into the air, striking with a knee to the chin. Flying back and bouncing off the ropes, my head's spinning. I can't believe his skill.

My mind starts to clear; with blurry vision, I see the champ coming to finish me off. It must be for a knockout. His strikes are hammering directly at my body, leaving his head unguarded; this is my chance to survive. I throw a left kick to the side of the champ's head. As my kick is in motion, I see him throw a body kick with his right leg. My kick's so hard it causes my body to turn far to the right, leaving my back open. The champ's kick, having a tremendous amount of power behind it, strikes my back, causing us both to hit the ground at the same time.

As I lie in pain the arena goes silent. Lifting my head, I glance; everyone's leaning forward watching us with expressions of suspense. In a low tone, the announcer comes over the intercom. "Ladies and gentleman, who will be the one to stand, if either?"

The champ is an arm's length away. He isn't moving, possibly knocked out. Trying to stand, I fall back to the mat with extreme pain shooting through my back. Dragging my body to the ropes, I grip them and pull with the last of my strength to stand.

The announcer screams. "The new world champion . . . Sammy Nelson." Everyone in the arena stands, stomps and roars. "IT'S UNBELIEVABLE . . . A LAST-MINUTE UNDERDOG TAKES THE WORLD BELT."

My team runs over as I fall back to the canvas unable to move. Medics rush over and carry me away on a stretcher; I see the champ on one too. I'm carried to an ambulance and rushed to the hospital.

After running multiple tests throughout the night, by early morning the doctor allows medication for pain and to help me sleep. Later in the day, the lead doctor visits.

"Mr. Nelson, the tests are complete and results back. There's good and bad news. What do you prefer first?"

"Give me either, Doc, I'm ready." I'm trying to sit up but can't.

"You'll live an ordinary life . . . but will never fight again. Your back is damaged beyond repair. If you ever get hit again with a powerful kick, you'll end up on crutches or worse. Paralyzed from the neck down." He frowns while placing his business card on the table next to the bed. "If you have any concerns or questions, give me a ring."

"Thanks, Doc," I say, watching him leave the room.

Gee, what a day. Here is my Yin and Yang again: I am the world champion, but will never fight again. What should I do, cheer or cry? Wait, what happened to the champ? Is he okay? I'm laying here feeling sorry for myself not knowing his condition, so selfish.

"Can you tell me the condition of the champ?" I ask the nurse taking my pulse.

"If you're speaking of the other fighter, he is hurt bad, but is stable and will recover."

"Thank you!" Ouch, still calling him champ, guess it's because of the great respect for him.

Master Bill comes in. "How are you, Sammy?"

"I'm happy. I've done what I thought was the impossible, something only dreams are made of. Master, I did it. I'm the World Kickboxing champion. How many people can say this? With the belt now laying on the nightstand next to me, I'm beyond emotions."

"What will you do now?" He sits at the end of the bed.

"Well, the doc said I can't fight anymore."

"Yes, I heard. Sammy, I was so scared seeing you lying there on the mat. I feel it's time to tell you."

"Tell me what?"

"Do you remember when you were seven and the dojo did the demonstration at your school?"

"Yes, but —"

"Remember a student was hurt and I carried him to the nurse's office?"

"Yes."

"He was my son. He died that day in her office." Tears form in Master Bill's eyes. "I've always thought of you as a son. Seeing you on the mat brought back memories. I started praying. 'Please, God, don't let me lose another son!' When you pulled yourself up the ropes, I thanked God."

"Master, I'm okay with giving up fighting. I'll retire the champ."

"And do what?"

"I still enjoy journalism, I'll give up fighting and go back full time being a journalist."

"Stand proud! The whole dojo and world are proud of you." Master Bill stands, moves up the side of the bed and pats my shoulder before walking out.

Returning to my old job is fun, but I'm not happy. After a while, I quit and go into freelancing. Again finding I'm not happy. I go into a partnership with a skilled organizer and fund raising genius named Frank: a magazine for journalist, with both of us battling for the editor-in-chief position, it doesn't work out either. So, I go back to freelancing.

One night I'm sitting in Mom's kitchen having dinner. "I'm tired of freelancing, and the workload's slow. I have money stashed from the fight and what I saved over the years. I want to do something special."

"What do you want to do?" She pours us hot tea.

"Take some time off and fulfill my life dream."

"If you can, then you should. What is it?"

"To bring groups of martial artists from different countries to compete. Although there's been these types of competitions, this one will be special—yeah, unique."

"How's that?" Mom stands, collecting dishes off the table and puts them in the sink.

"I want to bring together the deadliest and most secret martial arts in the world. I'll select them from only a handful of countries, creating teams of five from each country picking one for team lead. It will be the greatest martial arts tournament ever."

"Good luck, Son." She wipes the table using a wet cloth from the sink.

"Thanks, Mom." Yeah, don't think she believes me.

Excited, I dream all night of scary-looking warriors lining at my door to join the competition. This dream is going to cost plenty, and I don't have near enough savings to do it. Lying in bed, I wonder whom? Yes! I remember my old friend Frank who always found ways to come up with funds for projects. I want to do this on my own but need Frank's money connections. Frank and I were business partners for a while, but separated and went our own ways after one too many arguments. The good thing is we've remained friends.

Grabbing the cell, I call, hoping to catch his interest. I haven't spoken to him in years, so I'm not sure what he's up to. "Hey, Frank, this is your old buddy and former business partner."

"Sammy, how could I ever forget your voice? What a shocking surprise. What are you up to?"

I describe my plan in detail. "So, what do you think?"

"Hey, great idea, give me a little time to make calls and come up with the money. I need to check what contacts are still good."

"Great, I'll be waiting." Lying back in bed, I think that life can't get any better than this. I doze off into dreamland with my new adventure about to come true.

I was unable to sleep with so much excitement on my mind, feeling that Frank will find the money somewhere. I get out of bed and do my daily routine of opening the front window, letting the morning ocean breeze freshen the room and I spend a few minutes looking out the window watching the people exercise. I have a lot to do to get ready for the project. I'll need to visit multiple countries, requiring airline tickets, passports, maybe visas, hotels, rental cars and possibly more.

I need to research the different martial arts from the different countries. I need to find countries having martial arts skills, awesome, enough to be considered elites. Making a hot cup of green tea, I sit behind the computer. First I open a blank document and create a list of different martial arts from Google searches.

I stop my list. I know there are still many more martial arts out there that can bring cheers from the spectators. It feels like a sin. But looking over the compiled list of seventeen arts, I need to end here. We may even need to cut this list of great arts, due to time and possible lack of funding. I'll save this list and worry more tomorrow.

Waking, I go for a run along the water from Santa Monica Pier to Venice Pier and back. It helps me get my blood flowing and mind alert. Returning I shower, have breakfast, then flop in my chair. Opening my notes, I begin what I enjoy, studying different styles of martial arts. From the top, I run the list, evaluating each one and create separate folders on the iMac, then fill the folders with data. Finally, I bookmark the Google sites for reference.

I wish Frank would call, saying he got money from a large investor and we can start now. I'm at a dead stop, until I find out how much money so I can narrow my choice of teams. I start getting frustrated when my cell rings.

"Hey, it's Frank. Got with an old connection and he sounds interested, but hold off spending until we get a contract signed."

"Frank, you're the man! This is great, you've brought happiness back to my life."

"Signed contracts bring joy to mine. Talk to you soon." We drop the connection.

Frank

Third World Adventures
*** Chapter Three ***

"Sir, here's your passport, enjoy your stay in Bolivia," airport security says.

I move between the powered glass doors finding a short, stocky man carrying a sign "Welcome Frank Capper" I step up to him. "Hi, I'm Frank."

"Hi, I'm Jim Peterson's guide Ricardo. Welcome to Bolivia. Please follow me." Ricardo escorts me to another part of the airport where we board a private helicopter.

After flying awhile, I say, "Hey, Ricardo, this is a beautiful view."

"Yes, it is. I take this trip often picking up and dropping off clients."

"I've never been in a jungle. I hope we live through all this."

"Well, my friend, you're about to get the chance. Our camp is just below."

The helicopter swoops to a tiny opening in the large trees, landing, it bounces off the ground, causing my head to slam the top a few times. The propeller slaps the tree limbs sticking out as Ricardo grabs my sleeve, pointing to my bags, then the door.

After we hop out and clear the propeller, the chopper takes off, sailing out into the sunset.

"I hope you enjoyed your flight. Shall we find the camp?" I follow Ricardo into the jungle finding a tall, skinny man standing by a campfire. Moving to the fire, I'm surrounded by tents just beyond an area cleared of brush.

"Mr. Peterson, I have brought back Frank."

"Excellent, welcome, Frank." He extends his hand, we shake.

"Glad to meet you, sir." He has a powerful presence about him and a strange uniqueness.

"Make yourself at home, Frank, we'll be leaving in the morning . . . Ricardo, set Frank up with a comfortable place to sleep."

"Yes, sir. Frank, follow me."

I cross a dirt path to a four-foot-tall, two-man tent. Ricardo waves to me to go inside, there's one green military cot to the left. Putting my things on the right side, I return to the fire.

"Frank, enjoy some coffee. Those cups on the table are clean," Jim says.

Sliding on the mitten, I lean down to the fire and grab the grey metal coffee pot. I pour a cup. The strange noises coming out of the jungle give me the creeps; I move over and sit close to where Jim is standing. He looks deep in thought, drinking his coffee.

After dark, I return to my tent when moments later Ricardo pops his head in. "Frank, remember to zip your tent door, unless you want unexpected company joining you." He laughs

"Sure will. Thanks for the heads-up." I zip the door closed seconds after he leaves and hop onto the cot.

"Bang—Bang—Bang." Rolling off the bed, I slide under it and peek out. "What the hell?" Crawling to the door, I look under the opening. It's Ricardo hitting pans together. "Let's get up everyone and ready to go. We have a long but fun day ahead," Ricardo says.

Local natives pack all our stuff while we eat. "Ready to go? I'll take the lead," Jim says. We follow him into the jungle with the natives right behind, carrying our things. Walking a few steps from Jim, I watch him cheerfully check everything out as we go along the paths

Each day Jim gets excited, and I get scared as we find wild creepy stuff: snakes, bats, ants as big as my pinky finger, raccoons and more wandering in our path. After a week, my legs hurt, and my body's sore from all the hiking. But I don't complain, seeing that the weight these natives are carrying would break my back.

Two weeks into our adventure, I wake climbing out of the tent. It's more beautiful and peaceful than ever. Maybe because it's the last day. Or I'm getting used to it. But this place is as comfortable as home. Everyone's sitting around the campfire drinking coffee.

"Good morning, everyone." Walking over, I sit next to Jim.

"Good morning," most say.

Laying folders on my lap, I turn on the video camera. "Jim, may I show you a brief of the video and documentation?"

"Sounds great, let's see what you have?" He grins through all ten minutes of a short clip of the video. "This is excellent footage. Well done, Frank!"

"I'm going to create photos of the coolest scenes for you."

"I'm impressed with the documentation too. Please pull it together and send it to my office."

"Give me a week. If you're happy with the results, please pass my name around." I gather my things back together.

"I'll pass your name around, one way or the other."

Hours later, Ricardo and I are on the helicopter, flying out of the jungle. Getting home, I finish my project and send the results to Jim's office. A few days later, the phone rings. "Frank, this is Jim's assistant. He's excited with the results and will pass your name and number to friends."

"Tell him thank you, please."

With his referrals, it's hard keeping up with the workload. Documenting expeditions for the rich has me traveling the world to different kinds of crazy and dangerous places. It's fun and adventurous, and the pay is great.

Five years later I'm sitting in a small cafe in South Africa, sweating and guessing it is time for a change. I have a new plan: writing international travel guides from a firsthand perspective. I'll travel to different countries, one by one, living off their economy. My books will be written with facts I'll gather, not like other books. Here is as good as anywhere else to start.

After finishing the book in South Africa, I spend the next year jumping from country to country. Sadly book sales are down. People tell me not to worry, but the problem is my savings: they're starting to run out. The fun is over, and I've got to go back to the U.S.

Landing in San Francisco, I decide to hang out a bit in hopes of picking up local work to earn quick cash. I find a boarding house near the famous Chinatown. After checking in, I take a stroll around town. Signs are posted everywhere advertising the San Francisco Writers Conference; it's held each year and goes from Thursday until Sunday. I've attended in the past and know it is a great opportunity to socialize and pick up work. Going back to the room, I redo my portfolio and make copies for the conference.

Arriving on Thursday with a dozen copies of my portfolio, I'm amazed at how it's grown over the years. So many more people, booths, professional writers and more. I begin checking out the booths, going aisle to aisle socializing. This place has everything from how-to books and software for preparing outlines, to anything a writer will ever need. I direct my focus to the stands with writers' book signings: from how-to-write books, fiction to nonfiction novels and more.

I come up to a booth with a sign reading "Open to all writers, join our local writers club" on the table, with pamphlets that say "This is one of the oldest writers clubs in the nation. We have over fifteen hundred members". This is a good place to start.

"Hello everyone, I'm Frank Capper, a freelance writer."

"Welcome, Frank," they say.

Pouring on the charm, I begin to fit in, as everyone is friendly. We speak in the same writer's vocabulary, so I start chatting and sharing my recent adventures when a big, fit guy walks up to the table smiling.

"Hi everyone, I'm Sammy Nelson."

"Hi, Sammy," they say. He shares a bit of his past and indicates his present status is freelancing.

"Hey, Sammy, I'm also freelancing and search of work."

"I have money put up and am thinking of opening a journalism business."

"Are you interested in a partner?" I ask.

"It'd sure help having two setting up and building clients. Pass me a copy of your portfolio, I'd like to read it over and confirm its information."

"Sure, I understand, here ya go." I hand him a copy.

"Great, I'll check it out and give you a call." We part ways.

I'm wakened by the cell: "Frank, it's Sammy. I checked you out, and I'm impressed. What surprises me is you're not up there with the elite. You've had many awesome adventures. Anyway, welcome aboard partner, that's if you're still up for it?"

"You bet!"

We do well and end up filling our bank accounts with profits from our business. But partnerships don't always last, and six months later I get an offer in New York. Sammy and I agree to stay friends, as there is no bad blood between us. He takes me to the airport, and I'm off to the Big Apple.

A year into the new company, I realize it's being run badly as my paychecks begin bouncing. When I arrived at the Apple, I moved into a low-rent apartment across town, in case something like this happened. I guess I did something right. I sit at my favorite bar blocks from home in New York's Bronx, drinking to my recent unhappy life. What is a man weighing two hundred pounds at five-foot six-inches with cash running out to do? Then my cell rings.

"Hello?"

"Hey, Frank, this is your old partner," comes a familiar voice from the past.

"Sammy." Spilling my Bacardi and Coke, I sit up on the barstool.

"Frank, I'm not sure what you got going on, but I got a crazy idea for a project and there're big bucks in it for you."

"Sammy, perfect timing. My present project finished days ago and I'm ready for action." Finally, a way to make some money. I love you, Sammy, I thought.

"I'm in this to fulfill my life's dream, not for money."

"No problem, Sammy. I will keep the change." I laugh.

"The reason I'm calling is this one will be expensive, and I don't have enough money. I know it will make a profit and need to get the upfront investment. We can both gain: for me, a dream. And you, a bank full of cash."

Sammy explains the project in detail.

"My savings are gone, Sammy. But let me go through my connections. I'm confident I'll find someone to sponsor us. I can see how there's money to be made."

"I believe in you. Don't disappoint me."

"One last thing, if this happens, we're travel buddies. I need to make sure the money isn't wasted. Whoever sponsors us will be holding me responsible. There's reason to be nervous."

"I'm okay with it. In fact, I think it'll be fun having a companion," Sammy says.

"Bartender, another Bacardi and Coke please, I'm now drinking to good times." Picking the spilled glass up, I hand it over to him.

"Happy to hear it, Frank, just keep spending money on drinks and tips. I'll help you make up more reasons as the day goes on."

I sip the fresh Bacardi and Coke. Yum, it tastes delicious. I run names of rich guys who have hired me for expeditions in the past. I focus on the ones with good attitudes, who won't interfere with my project or put pressure on me to complete the project sooner than needed. I go home and sleep off the alcohol.

Four hours later I wake, take a shower and eat slices of cold pizza before going through my client files.

Setting up two documents side by side on my screen, I create a naughty on the left and nice on the right, referring to people I will hate asking and those I would enjoy working with. The nice list comes up short. Well, I only need one of these to agree. One after another I dial, leaving messages with secretaries, spouses, servants or whoever picks up the phone. Not getting returns, I remember the guys with big bucks are hard to get with unless they want something from you.

Fixing a Bacardi and Coke, I flop down on the couch and turn on the TV to catch a Jay Leno episode.

Calls come in as the days come and go, with a few interested and a couple of requests to meet. It's not happening; I'm unable to convince them of a good financial return on their investments. Regretfully, I start on the naughty list and get the same results. I'm feeling hopeless and ready to give up when I receive a call from the worst of the naughty list.

"Hello?" I say, hoping for luck.

"This is Andrey Baskov's secretary. Mr. Baskov wants to meet with you to discuss your ideas. He will meet with you two weeks from today. Don't be late or your meeting will be cancelled."

"I'll be there on time." I give her my home address so she can mail a formal meeting invite.

I can't believe I'm stuck with Andrey (the arrogant jerk). He's the last guy in the world I want to work with, still remembering his rude and belittling manners. On our adventure, I thought someone was going to end up killing him. With no other options, it's him or nothing and we need the money. I'll have to make a deal with the devil: there's no choice.

The day of the meeting's here, and I'm ready to put on a Grammy-type performance. Pulling in front, I wait for the attendant to open my door. I give him a couple of dollars before he drives off, in hopes there're no scratches when the car's returned. I bought this Audi A8 series for cash a few years back when the money was good, and it is still in mint condition.

Coming through the doors, I tell security about my appointment with Mr. Baskov. She validates then escorts me to the elevator, opens it with his key card and presses the button for the top floor. The panel light glows on each number as the elevator passes each level. When the light gets to PH, the door opens.

I see a single door with a small intercom box on the wall next to it. When I hit the button, a voice says, "Mr. Capper, please pull the door when you hear the buzzer."

A speaker above the door sounds: Buzzzzzz. I pull the door and walk into the reception area.

"Good evening, Mr. Capper, please have a seat." About ten minutes later she returns. "Mr. Baskov is ready to see you now. Please follow me."

She leads me to closed double French doors; opening them, I'm led into a room the size of my studio apartment, triple the size of the last office I remember him having. He also has the whole top floor now. I'm amazed at how luxurious this office is and the money spent to furnish it. Andrey looks up from his desk. "Take a seat, Mr. Capper."

He's so formal after we spent quality time in our adventures together. Taking a seat, Andrey continues staring at documents and ignoring me. I gaze at the elegant and luxurious furniture and paintings throughout the room. It is like something seen in a Donald Trump biography video. Andrey's made major jumps on the wealth ladder from the last time we met.

Andrey looks up. "What's on your mind, Mr. Capper?"

A bit nervous knowing this is a one-shot try, I look at him, acting confident, taking a deep breath and clearing my mind. I begin.

"Andrey, my partner Sammy has a martial arts background, and we want to organize a martial arts competition like no other. Sammy's goal is to search for the most deadliest and dangerous fighters to compete. Even though the fights will not be to the death, fighters with these skills can easily cause death or permanent injury."

"I'm impressed. You may have something here." He sits up, putting his arms on the desk and leans forward.

"Andrey, these type of fights are illegal in most countries, if not all. Finding a venue may be a concern. The good side is the wealthy will gladly pay big money to see these types of events. We can sell seats for almost any price. Second, live streaming video over the Internet makes it a globally viewed fight, also allowing huge profits."

Andrey turns his chair to the side and scans out the window as if in deep thought. A few minutes later, he turns back, staring directly into my eyes.

"I need a little time to think it over. If I agree to fund your project, sixty percent of the net profit is mine." His look scares me.

"Mr. Baskov, if you agree, I am good with the split." I sit up and lean forward.

"Good evening, Mr. Capper. I will let you know my decision."

Leaving his office, the secretary says, "Mr. Capper, I will call security to bring your car to the front."

Stepping towards the elevator, I say, "Thank you." When I exit the building, my car is waiting. I give the Audi a quick once over and drop a few more dollars in the attendant's hand before hopping in and driving off.

Waiting on Andrey's call, I hang out at the local bar drinking and shooting pool for the next few days, until one morning I wake to my cell ringing.

"Hello?"

"Good morning, Mr. Capper, this is Mr. Baskov's secretary. He wants to speak to you, one minute please."

Andrey

Coming To America
*** Chapter Four ***

I'm raised in poverty due to loser parents, who waste their lives working for beggars' salaries and cause us kids to go for days without eating, or at least my siblings. Why they decided on five kids, when most days they're unable to feed themselves, is beyond me. But that's how it is in this family. With parents always working and our bellies always empty, the streets have become my escape for now. It's not my destiny. I was born into this world for greatness, and it will happen one way or another.

Hanging out in the streets, I master self-reliance from street kids and thugs. They've taught me well on how to make money off suckers. There's a world full of them waiting on me. Embedded in my brain is that no one succeeds in life unless they're only looking out for number one. This means I'll step on whomever I need to on the way to the top. At sixteen, living by my philosophy, I take advantage of anyone I can; young, old, homeless, well-off, even the food money Mom hides to feed us. I show my family favoritism, (I laugh) yeah right.

While working the streets, I notice houses being abandoned and families disappearing all over the neighborhood. Concerned it will cut into my revenue, I grab a neighborhood kid by the throat.

"Hey, first, where's my protection money?"

The kid gives me the money I told him to steal from his mom.

"Good job, keep it up. Second, what is going on with all the neighbors disappearing?"

"Mom told me we are stashing away money to pay for us to ride on a boat to America. We are going there for a better life," she says. "That is where all her friends are going. We're leaving soon."

"What the hell. Your family and others stashing money and telling me they can't afford my protection fee? I'll have a not-so-friendly talk with them."

All these are neighbors holding out on my cut of their savings; I just can't get any respect around here. Well, I'll have a yard sale with the belongings left behind. It'll help make up for my lost wages.

"Kid, one last question. Why leave everything behind and run off in the middle of the night?" I ask, squeezing, then releasing his neck a little more to watch his face turn colors.

"Honestly, I don't know. Please don't hurt me!"

Letting the little kid go and grabbing the throat of an old man walking by, I think I like this throat-grabbing thing; it gets me immediate attention. I smirk.

"Old man, why are people leaving everything behind and running off in the middle of the night?"

"Because if they are caught leaving the whole family will end up in prison or a work camp for life."

I didn't realize living in a communist country is so scary. I wonder what is this America? What kind of better life does it have to offer that they'll leave everything behind and risk their fate to go there? I decide America is the place for me to get rich. After choking out a few more neighbors, I learn the contact names to make the trip and where I can find them.

"Argh." I need to find money to pay for this trip. Got it. I go to the bedroom all of us kids share, finding my twin sisters doing their school homework. "Girls, your loving big brother needs a favor." Sitting down in between them, I give each a kiss on the forehead. "I am going to America to get rich, but need money to get there."

"We don't have any money . . . now leave us alone."

"Can I pimp the both of you? I promise to give you girls five percent of what we make." Giving them a big hug.

"Leave us alone or we're telling dad." Giving me a mean glare they push me away, yelling. "Dad . . . Dad."

Oops! Not a good idea. I run out the door. If they tell dad I'm trying to pimp them, I'll end up in a coffin, not America. Plan B, selling the things in the homes of families who left for America.

Finally getting the money, I befriend a sweet family who helps arrange my trip. I leave with them late at night. We're out to sea riding along when I realize I need start-up money to get my business going. Hmm, my pockets are empty.

All these people must have money stashed to help them once they arrive. I'm sure they'll find more money some place. I'll just find and withdraw their money each night from its hiding spots. What's wrong with them investing in a good cause, me? I'll collect more than enough to get started.

Awaking late at night I'm ready to go, but first need to find a hiding place to keep my investments safe and to prevent getting caught if searched. Finally, I find a secret spot. Okay, who will be my first investor? It's only fit to take the life savings of the family who trusts me and is helping me get to America. Easily finding their money hidden in the woman's backpack, I take and secure it in my spot. I get back in my sleeping bag feeling good. I fall back asleep.

Waking to the sound of crying, I find it to be the family who is my first investor. Wandering over to them, the wife says, "Andrey, all our money is gone. We don't know what to do, and we don't know anyone in America."

Not wanting to be a party pooper and mastering the art of crying while growing up, I decide to join in and sit down next to the kids.

Tears begin pouring down my face. "This is terrible. How can someone be so cruel?" Squeezing the children in my arms, I say, "If it's the last thing I ever do, I will find this evil person who took your money." The whole family circles around hugging me (this is a Kodak moment) telling me what a sweet boy I am. Waking the next night and every night after, I visit each person or family taking what little money they have.

On the last night sneaking up to a cuddling family, I see the money pouch between a woman and a little girl—she looks about three years old. This is going to be a tough one; the daughter and mom are sleeping close together. I slip my hand between them, grabbing the pouch and slowly pull it up. Got it. Opening the pouch, I find only a small amount of money, but hey, every little bit adds up.

Dropping the pouch back between them, I feel a hand grab my wrist. I freeze in place, then realize it is a small hand. Looking down, it's the little girl with her sleepy eyes looking up at me. She moves her other hand down, digging into her pocket, and pulls out a small coin. With a shy smile, she reaches out, handing me the coin, before moving to the safety of her mother's arms and shutting her eyes.

Heading to my sleeping bag, I stop. "Damn it! The little girl." Turning around, I stroll back to where she's sleeping and kneel down. I pull their money and a little more from my pocket, dropping it between the girl and mom. I don't understand how, but this little girl got the best of me. Anyone who can soften old Andrey has a bright future. "Good luck in the new world—little one," I whisper, patting her lightly on the head.

Before leaving, I hide the coin the little girl gave me in my wallet. I'll keep this coin forever: in remembrance of the one and only time someone got the best of me: a little girl at that. Stashing my earnings from the night, I walk to my sleeping bag and moments later am dreaming of riches.

Stretching in my sleeping bag, I feel the morning sun hit my face. "What the heck is that?" I yell, seeing a huge statue of a woman holding a torch and a crown around her head.

"It's the lady of freedom," people yell.

As we get closer to land, our tourist guide starts moving us into large metal containers. Grabbing my investment money from its hiding place, I then collect my things together.

The guide says, "The next time these doors open, there'll be white vans waiting. Jump in quickly with all your things, or you will be left behind."

I suddenly stop. "What? Left behind." I wait for everyone to climb into the container making sure I'm the last one, so I'll be the first out ensuring a good seat in the van. Climbing in, he closes and locks the doors behind me.

After I get on shore, everything goes well in a city called New York. My first business is loan sharking. I learn this from one of the guys on the boat. He is fleeing to escape being put in prison for loan sharking in Russia. During the long boat ride, I learned a lot from this guy and other hoodlums escaping prison time. Okay, who will be my first customer? I know; the family I came with needs my help. I'll start with them.

Saving all my hard earned money over the years allows me to change businesses. This one will let me take advantage of people without the risk of going to jail. Great idea. I become good at being a venture capitalist and now rolling in the dough. I love that phrase: it fits me. I knew my new career would make me a rich man, and a rich man it did.

Sitting at my desk, in a midlevel office of a skyscraper in the heart of Manhattan, I'm now worth millions of dollars and getting bored of hustling people. It is time for a break, but what shall I do? Talking to friends, one suggests an expedition, which they all do for fun. I'm told this is a new trend for the rich. One of these friends recommends a guy named Frank Capper to go along and document my trip for me. Maybe have him write a book about it. It's an excellent idea, I think, hitting the intercom.

"Arrange for a scuba diving adventure in shark-infested waters of South Africa. Hire this Frank Capper guy and make sure he is at the right place at the right time."

"Yes, sir."

I feel the sharks won't bother me, as we both have the same personalities. I smirk: it's so true. Hitting the intercom again, I say, "Just thinking, I don't want to be in a shark security cage. Make sure I'll be able to dive and swim right up to these beautiful beasts. Validate that Frank Capper knows how to dive. Let him know if not he'll be in diving class with me in South Africa. Also, he'll be right along side me under the sea, to meet my comrades, the great white sharks. I want this underwater experience documented with photos."

"Yes, sir."

She knows to arrange what I want no matter the cost.

The day is here. Arriving in South Africa, Frank and I do our dive training, then meet up with the team my secretary pulled together.

"Mr. Baskov, we'll be heading out in the morning," the captain says.

During the evening, it's hard to sleep with the sound of thunder and rain pounding the tin roof all night. In the morning, I step out glancing at a sky full of white clouds while the cool breeze puts goosebumps on my arms.

"Everyone ready?" the captain says.

"Captain, we're good with this weather for sharks, right?" I say.

"Shouldn't be a problem, sir."

"I paid good money and better get what I paid for!"

"Please board, sir."

We all board and are off to sea. A few hours later, the boat stops. I watch the crew drop anchor and get excited.

"Where are the sharks?" I shout.

"Our sonar detection system picks up large fish movement, and it's finding it here. So let's go diving."

It takes me about twenty minutes to suit up; I'm ready to go along with everyone else.

"Are you sure this is a good idea? Maybe the crew should go first to make sure the sharks aren't biting. Or even better, I can stay in the cage!" Frank says.

40

"Frank, you'll go in now and be right next to me the whole time. Or I will leave you here, and sue you for every penny you get for the rest of your life. Understand?"

"You know, Andrey, you're . . . a lovable guy. I'm so happy I came."

"Me too. Now, let's get in the water and have fun. Captain, I'm ready."

"Everyone stay close to me and watches for my hand signal directions," the captain says. "I don't want to bring back any dead bodies or feed the sharks."

The captain falls backward off the boat into the water first; I'm right behind him. Aha, there's his fin. It's a bit cold down here, but catching up to the captain warms me up. Wait . . . where's Frank? I look back, finding him behind me.

We move deeper into the sea. A little water seeps into my mask, but I can still see. What looks like a thousand fish comes our way. I'm unable to see the captain or Frank with all these fish surrounding me. Yee-haw! Sharks everywhere. I almost choke on the water attempting to scream for Frank.

Feeling pressure on my back, I look up seeing the head of a great white over me. I'm scared yet excited. What an awesome feeling. Watching the sharks around me, I grab the fin of one passing and go for a ride. I see the captain watching and Frank taking pictures. He gives the single to go up, but having too much fun, I ignore him. Frank's waving and pointing behind me, what? Looking back, there's a great white inches from my leg, with its mouth open.

Using the shark's fin I'm holding, I quickly jerk myself to his other side, putting distance between me and my hungry friend. Pushing the button to fill my jacket with air takes me up. The damn beast comes after me. Pushing the button harder quickens my ascend to the top, but I'm getting dizzy. My head's spinning.

The captain is waving his body around in the water, trying to distract the shark to his direction. The shark turns and swims off. Getting on the boat, I lie down, feeling sick.

Lying on deck resting, I watch a large boat pass with a miniature submarine on it. "Hey, Captain, what's going on with that boat? And where's it going?"

"I've overheard people on the dock and in the seaport bars talking about it. They say it's full of scientists doing deep-sea expedition, in search of creatures no man has ever seen. And other things scientists like to do."

I think to myself, that sounds like a fun adventure and one I can't pass up. "Captain, how can I ride with them?"

"I'm told it's impossible because of the many dangers. The sponsor doesn't allow the scientists to take anyone down with them."

I call my secretary once back to the hotel. "I want to go deep-sea diving in the submarine I seen today. Do whatever it takes to get me on that boat. Bribes are fine, even fifty million dollar research donation ones."

"Yes, sir," she says, hanging up.

Any size bribe is fine; I have no plans on paying it, I laugh. It's helpful to have excellent lawyers who know how to break contracts. I hang up.

Calling my secretary back, I add, "One more thing. Make sure Frank is on the sub too. I want this trip documented and photographed as well."

I don't know how and don't care, but my secretary is able to make the arrangements; I knew there's a reason I've kept her around for so many years. She's never let me down.

The trip is on, with Frank to boot. But the sub owner has conditions: signing forms, attending classes, undergoing an in-depth physical, and taking tests. They say it's to see if our bodies and minds will adjust going down possibly as much as seven miles under the sea. We sign documents understanding the danger and accepting all the risks, including the possibility of not making it back up.

I'm more excited now than with the sharks; I bet Frank is too. We pass everything they give us without problems. We're on our way to the bottom of the sea. It's an adventure none of my buddies will ever be able to top.

Peter, the lead scientist, walks up. "Andrey, even though you're donating a great sum of money this trip, isn't just a joy ride. My scientists will conduct their research; we're all putting our lives on the line: agreed?"

"Whatever."

"The boat's leaving in the morning, Pack for a five-day trip. It'll be a long boat ride."

Up early, I grab my bags, head to Frank's room and knock. "Hey, Frank. Let's go." I need my main man for this adventure. Frank and I walk down the hallway to the dock.

On the boat, Peter briefs the crew and soon we're off. After a couple of days on the boat, it slows down and the motors stop.

"We've arrived," Peter says.

Arriving at our destination, after two days of boring seas, I decide a boat trip back isn't an option. I need to get the grid location of this place in order to have the secretary arrange a helicopter to pick me up.

"Peter, what's the grid location here?"

"We're at Mariana Trench, having a grid of 11°22.4′N 142°35.5′E. It's about two hundred miles of the coast of a country called Guam."

Using the satellite phone, I call my secretary. "I want a helicopter on standby at Guam to pick me up from this boat when I come up. It'll take me to Guam where my jet will be waiting to take me home. I'll call once we surface. Tell the chopper pilot, 11°22.4′N, 142°35.5′E, he'll pick me up off a small boat."

The scientists finish loading and doing last-minute safety checks before lowering the sub into the water. "Everyone going down, hop aboard. It's going to take about ninety minutes down and seventy up," Peter says.

Taking a seat I find a stack of fiction novels on the table. "Don't know who owns them, but they're excellent choice." It'll be a pleasure to read one when there's no action outside.

The submarine descends. I look for the best seat. "Hey, Bud, you need to move. I'm taking that seat." The guy gives me a "who in the hell do you think you are" look before moving. Peter calls off names of the creatures as we spot them—anglerfish, viperfish—and continues the whole time. Some of these, if not all of them, are very scary-looking creatures. Frank stays busy taking pictures and writing the whole time.

Getting to the bottom, the scientists spend several hours doing their research. I read Samuel Perry's novel, *Voices From Within*, causing time to fly by and catching glimpses of weird fish swimming by the window. On the way up, Peter continues pointing to fish and calling names. Frank documents and takes many pictures of me as proof that I took this journey. I do notice Peter taking a few pictures of Frank with Frank's camera.

Back on the boat, I call my secretary, "Get the helicopter here now." Within an hour, a chopper is hovering overhead. "Mr. Baskov, we're here to pick you up. We're lowering a harness. Strap it on. When you're ready, give us thumps up," comes from its speakers.

"Peter, overnight the rest of my stuff to my office. Frank, make sure you get everything to my secretary within the month if you want to get paid."

Grabbing my small backpack, I strap in and give the crew a thumps up. Like James Bond, I'm off swinging in the air as the chopper pulls away and reels me up.

"Frank, take my picture. Hurry!" I scream.

A few weeks after I'm back, my secretary comes in handing me a FedEx package from Frank Capper. Opening it, there's an enormous amount of great photos, including one of me hanging from the bottom of the chopper and material from both expeditions. I hadn't planned to pay him, thinking I'd let him try to sue me, but after seeing his great work, I tell my secretary to cut him a check. Looking over Frank's package reminds me . . . I hit the intercom. "Cancel the sponsor agreement with the scientist. I'm sure they'll find someone else to donate.

Andrey

Pleasures Of The Rich
*** Chapter Five ***

Looking out my penthouse office window of a Manhattan skyscraper, I watch the boats pass the Statue of Liberty. With a greedy smirk, I listen to the pleading voice coming over the phone.

"Mr. Baskov, please! I just need some more time?"

"Guy, I don't care if you invested your life savings into developing this dream building of yours. There's someone offering double for the land. And you missing a payment voids our contract. That's all that matters."

"Gee! It's only one late payment."

"Sorry, bud, you best give your workers the address to unemployment. They're going home Friday without a paycheck. Your funds are being cut as of today."

"Wait. Please . . . Please! Just one more—"

I hang up. I don't have time for weak-minded people.

I answer the intercom.

"Sir, I received a call from Frank Capper. He's asking to set up a meeting to go over a big international investment deal."

"Isn't this the guy we hired awhile back?"

"Yes, sir."

"This guy's been around. I'll give him a few minutes of my time. I'm curious to see what this international investment is. Set up a meeting."

Days later while chatting with an old friend on the phone, he says, "Andrey, I bought an island out in the middle of nowhere in the South Pacific Ocean. I had big plans for it but don't have time to play with it: I'm looking to sell. It's small but perfect for a single guy like you. A hideaway when you need a break. Interested?"

"Why would I want to hide on an island in the middle of the ocean? Unless the IRS was after me." I laugh.

"It's a place you can fix up and bring your sweethearts out there for some fun."

"Well, maybe. Tell you what. I'll do a fly-by to see if I like it. If so, we might do business." It'd be kind of unique having an island.

Hanging up, my secretary comes over the intercom.

"Sir, Frank Capper's waiting."

"Bring Mr. Capper in and close the door behind you."

I watch Mr. Capper step into the room. His eyes are bloodshot with bags under them.

"Mr. Capper—please sit."

Leaving him sitting, I finish going over the island documents. Done, I look at him. "Mr. Capper, what's on your mind?"

He throws a sales pitch about some kind of global kung fu competition he and his buddy want to do. I let him continue and listen carefully, while running possible scenarios to see if there's money to be made. These guys just may have something. But how can I get maximum gains while cutting Frank and his buddy out of most of the profits? I need time to think and to do some homework, before agreeing to put money out on this project. I'll toss him a bone.

"Mr. Capper, I need time to think it over. If I'm game, I'll sponsor the whole thing, and we'll make it happen."

"What cut?" Frank says, staring into my eyes.

"I'll play fair and only take sixty percent off the top. If you're done, I'll speak to you soon. Goodbye, Mr. Capper."

46

Watching him get up and leave, I decide to call it a day and go home early.

Hitting the intercom, I say, "Get my limo pulled out front. I'm going home. You take off too."

In deep thought on the way home, my conversation with Frank Capper is eating at me. What is it that I'm missing? I'll let it go for now but will rethink it in the morning. I don't want to miss an opportunity if there's one. Getting home, I jump on the treadmill before taking a shower and off to bed.

While eating breakfast, I decide to drive in. I want to stop by Starbucks to chat with a few friends. Coming through Starbucks' door, Ted and I make eye contact. He's one of my favorite guys to chat with having the same corrupt or devious mindset; I smirk. He waves as I walk up to the counter and order a French Latte. Getting my drink, I stroll over, sitting at his table.

"Hey, Ted, how's life?"

"The best, and you?"

"Interesting. I've run into an opportunity to buy a small island. I'm thinking of using it as a retreat."

"Wow! If I had an island, I'd fill it with sexy girls like a harem-type deal. The girls will do the labor wearing sexy outfits, like cooking, cleaning, gardening, even female guards. Their outfits will make a grown man cry." He grins.

"Not a bad idea, Ted."

"Now that would be the life of luxury." We both laugh it off while finishing our drinks.

"Well, Ted, guess I better get going. Later."

Arriving to the office, I hit the intercom, giving my secretary the grid location of the island and telling her to arrange my jet to take me there this evening. It's a distance, so I'll sleep during the trip.

"Good evening, sir. I've picked up a change of clothes from your servant and confirmed your jet. It's waiting."

Climbing in the limo, we speed to the private airstrip where I hop aboard the jet. We're airborne within a few minutes. In the morning, I'm awakened by my flight attendant, climbing out of my bed to prepare breakfast. Mmm, I've always enjoyed the flavor of these blond bombshells with big tits.

A short time later, she returns. "Sir, your breakfast is ready." Climbing out of bed, she comes up behind me, slipping a robe over the back of my naked body. Reaching around, she lowers her hand and gives it a squeeze. "Sir, you're hard again." She continues to play with it until there's a need to change the sheets. After dressing, I go out to the main cabin take a seat and have coffee.

Seeing the landing strip as the jet flies over the island, I tell the pilot to land. Sitting on the airstrip, the pilot lowers the door; I exit. It's different world from Manhattan. Roaming around, there are groups of little huts spaced throughout the island; I wonder if there are groups of families that are living or lived in them. I decide it's best to leave them alone for now; don't want any crazies attacking me. Finishing my tour, I kick back in my favorite chair on the jet and hit the intercom. "Pilot, take us home." Airborne, I look out the window, thinking that this island's size is perfect for my plans.

Arriving at the office I feel a bit jet-lagged from the two-night round trip to the island. I finish my morning emails and messages before going over the day's agenda. Okay, first I want to review notes for the island deal and begin to think about what Ted said about having it full of girls.

Next in the stack is the note for the martial arts competition deal. Something clicks in my mind as I put the island deal and the martial arts deal side by side. Aha, what a great idea; having Frank and partner pick up girls from these different countries they visit and bring them to the island. The only problem is the girls' expenses. The costs for feeding and other stuff will be high. I'll file it in the back of my mind for now.

During lunch, I think of what Ted said again. It comes to me. I can pimp girls on the island, but unlike the small money pimps make in Russia, I'll have only rich clients. Now how and where will I get these girls? Looking at Frank's proposal sitting in front of me, I think this might work. If I can persuade Frank to get girls during their travel, I can build a harem of international girls in a short time. That would be great, and I'm sure none of my rich friends own a harem of international girls, except the Saudi ones.

How to get Frank to do my dirty work? Let's see, he's way too kind to agree with the pimp thing. I'm not sure how but I'll think of a way to trick him. Okay, let's get the island.

I call my friend. "Hey, I did the fly-by of the island; not bad. Let's negotiate an offer. I'll have my secretary call yours. They can arrange meetings between our lawyers, accountants, real estate people and whoever else to work out the details. If there's an agreement, I want to close ASAP."

A few weeks later, everything goes as planned and the island is mine. Time to work on the second half of this plan: the girls.

I decide to swim some laps in my pool to clear my mind. After swimming, I have the servant heat up the fireplace and pour some wine. I just want to relax.

"Joyann, come back in here."

"Yes, sir?"

"I'm feeling tense tonight, come over here and get on your knees in front of me."

"Sir, please, I'm not like that."

"Now, Joyann, you like feeding your family with the generous salary I provide. Yes? Don't ruin my mood."

"I understand, sir." She kneels down, opening my robe.

Reaching out, taking the back of her hair, I guide her to the treasure. She opens her mouth, putting her hands on my knees. Feeling her tongue give a full massage, I say, "Joyann, you're awesome." She speeds up her bobbing. "Don't forget to drink the juices of life." Her eyes widen as she takes the load.

Wiping her lips, she asks, "Sir, did I do good?", looking up with puppy-dog eyes.

"Yes, you are wonderful. I will give you additional practice later." I grin. I close my robe after using her tongue to clean me up.

Standing, she grabs her purse. "Good night, sir, see you in the morning." Tears slide down her face as she walks out the door, heading home to her husband and children.

Finishing my morning routine at work, I get back on the island project focusing on getting girls. I'd better close this deal with Frank before he changes his mind or finds someone else. I'll find a way to trick him into gathering these girls. Hitting the intercom, I say, "Get Frank Capper on the line."

Moments later: "Sir, I have Frank on line one."

Hitting line one's button: "Mr. Capper, I'm still not one hundred percent convinced, but we have a deal. Once the attorneys draw up the legal contracts, my secretary will schedule a meeting with you and your partner to come review and sign off."

Hitting the intercom: "Have the contract lawyers in my office after lunch."

Just after lunch, over the intercom: "Sir, the lawyers are waiting."

"Well, bring them in."

The lawyers come in, taking a seat and wait for me to begin. Tossing each a copy of Frank's proposal, I give them a few moments to study the proposal before I start. Each reviews the documentation then looks up and patiently waits on me.

"Let's begin. I want hidden clauses allowing us to easily break the contract. Just in case it doesn't go the way I want. Second, I want sixty percent of net profit."

"Yes, sir."

"In addition, Frank and his partner will be fully responsible for the fighters: from finding them, to getting them ready and on time for the competition. They will be responsible for setting up the venue to include the cage, staff, judges, ring announcer and whoever else is required."

"Failure to comply with anything in this contract will cause it to become void. Requiring a refund of all investments spent up to that point, if unable to pay the full amount. All monies invested, and any personal or business assets owned by Frank Capper or Sammy Nelson will become the property of Boskov investments Inc."

Looking down at the lawyers, I grin. "If I missed anything you guys better make sure it's added. Send me a copy of the draft once complete."

"Yes, sir."

"Oh, and get it done quick. I'm eager to get started."

Approximately a week later, the secretary brings in a FedEx envelope. Inside is the martial arts competition draft from the lawyers. Looking it over, I'm pleased.

Hitting the intercom: "Call Frank Capper and arrange a meeting to sign the contract."

Leaving for the day, the secretary says, "Mr. Capper agreed for Thursday next week. Mr. Capper's partner Mr. Nelson will also be joining."

"Perfect."

"Sir, I faxed them a copy of the contract so they can review it and make a list of any concerns."

"It's been a fine day. The only thing that can top this day is getting some Joyann when I get home."

"Sir?"

"Nothing. Going home."

3rd POV

Let's Make A Deal
*** Chapter Six ***

Sammy's cell rings. "Hello."

"Sammy, I received a call from Andrey Baskov's secretary. He's an old contact with plenty of money. He's interested in the project and wants to meet us at his office."

"That's great!"

"The secretary will fax over the contract, so we can look it over before the meeting. Let's go over it together before then."

"Frank, I'd feel much better having an attorney look over the contract with us." He knows Frank's excited and maybe too eager to sign without investigating. "Frank, I'd rather lose my life dream than to sign into some shady deal."

"Ah, you're right. Let's have an attorney review the contract with us. I'll arrange for one, but there's a problem—you're in California, and all of us are in New York."

"Geez, Frank. I'll hop a red-eye flight if you'll pick me up at the airport."

"I'm good with that. I'll fax a copy of the contract so you can read it on the long flight. I'll also arrange a meeting with the same attorney I worked with multiple times in the past."

Sammy steps out of the security area of JFK Airport, finding Frank waiting. Shaking hands, both men smile.

"Sammy, after all this time, you still look the same."

"So do you," Sammy says, grinning.

"Shall we go?" Frank asks.

They leave the airport, walking to Frank's car.

"Sammy, I'm sure I can find room for you at my place."

"Thanks, but I've arranged to stay at a hotel in Manhattan." After loading the bags in the car, they're off to drop Sammy off.

"Your hotel's about sixteen miles and maybe twenty minutes. Traffic's light late in the evening."

"Late night? More like morning, it's three o'clock." Sammy stares out the window in amazement, seeing New York for the first time.

"If there's time, I'll take you for a little sightseeing," Frank says, thinking he hates the thought of traveling through Manhattan's heavy traffic home and back, but for Sammy he'll sacrifice this one time.

Frank drops Sammy at the hotel, then speeds off for his two-mile journey to the Bronx happy; being late will make the drive only ten minutes. Tomorrow will be a different story. He'll have to pick up Sammy, making the same two miles in one or more hours, due to daytime traffic. Well, it's all for a good reason, so he should stop complaining.

Sammy wakes to a beautiful morning and feeling good. He enters the restaurant; smelling the hot food coming from the buffet tables is awesome. The best is the aroma of the fresh fruit. After enjoying breakfast, he goes to the room wanting to finish reading the contract. Opening the briefcase, he pulls it out and begins. Without much experience, he's limited, but he finds sections that concern him. With a yellow marker, he highlights these sections, making sure to get all hidden clauses. Then he reviews the document a few more times.

Over in the Bronx, Frank's ready to do the same. While kicking back, he pulls out the contract and goes through it. Frank doesn't realize he's underlining the same things Sammy's highlighting as concerns with the contract. He downs, a Bacardi & Coke is a reward. Sitting back down in his favorite chair with his drink, he turns on the TV just in time for Jay Leno.

In the morning, Frank picks up Sammy and walks the few blocks to the attorney's office. Entering the receptionist says, "Welcome, Mr. Capper." Then looks at Sammy. "You must be Mr. Nelson? Welcome, sir. You're right on time, please follow me to the conference room."

Moments after entering, Mr. Ward steps in, shaking both their hands. He checks if both have copies of the contract, then says, "Gentlemen, shall we begin?"

Mr. Ward also caught the sneaky words in the contract and reads them out loud.

"Sammy and I have the same concerns you found," Frank says.

"The contract was fine except for this clause, through which you two men could end up losing everything you have if there are any issues." All three agree: with the size of this project, things will happen, as they always do. "I recommended persuading Mr. Boskov to remove this clause, or at least give a sixty-day grace period to come up with the money. If he refuses, it'll be best for you guys to walk away from the deal." Both men thank Mr. Ward while leaving.

Stopping at a little sandwich shop on the way back, they discuss the meeting, then Frank calls Andrey's secretary.

"This is Frank Capper. I'd like to arrange a meeting with Mr. Boskov for tomorrow if possible. My partner's here and flying home the following day."

"I understand. Can you both be here at nine in the morning?

"Yes thank you," he says, hanging up.

The next day, they arrive at Mr. Boskov's office ten minutes early. A temporary secretary is sitting in for the day but is aware of the meeting. She offers them a cup of coffee, and they accept. While waiting, they discuss New York and going on a tour.

The secretary returns saying, "Mr. Boskov is ready, please follow me."

She Leads them to a large conference room, a man in a grey suit is reading documents on the table in front of him.

"Good morning, gentleman. I'm Mr. Boskov's senior attorney responsible for this contract."

Andrey walks in as the attorney finishes talking and takes a seat at the head of the table.

The attorney starts the meeting. "Everyone has a copy of the contract?"

Frank and Sammy shake their heads yes.

The attorney goes over the contract, then asks. "Any issues or concerns? Are you guys ready to sign?"

"Sammy and I have a major concern with the clause covering failure to comply with anything in the contract will make it void. A full refund of any investments up to that time is immediately required. If unable to pay, anything owned by either Sammy Nelson or Frank Capper, including investments, will become the property of Andrey's company."

"Frank, you're lucky I'm even giving you a thought."

"Watch your manners . . . sir." Sammy stands.

"Sammy, please," Frank says, pulling on Sammy's arm to sit him back down.

"Andrey, as written, this is unacceptable for us to agree on."

"This is needed to protect my investment, which will happen to be a large one."

"Is it possible to modify it allowing for a one-year grace period to repay?"

"Tell you what. I will, if you agree with a twenty percent APR interest during the grace period. If the loan isn't paid in one year, I'll come for everything both of you own, down to your underwear."

Frank sees the fire in Sammy's eyes and grabs the back of his shirt. He looks at Sammy with begging glance.

"Andrey, I need to step out into the hall to speak to my partner for a moment, in private," Frank says.

"I understand, take your time. Once the contract is signed, there is no backing out. Oh, and put a harness on that meathead partner of yours." Andrey snickers.

Frank grabs his arm and pleads with him to follow. Sammy being a huge mass of muscle, Frank is unable to pull him. Sammy gives way and follows.

Stepping into the hall, Sammy says, "Should we deal with this contract? Or kick his ass and leave?"

"What happened to your dream, Sammy? I'm willing to lose everything along with you to see this dream come true. To be honest, at first I only cared about the money. But now I feel I'm part of this dream. I'm excited as this will be the biggest thing I've ever pulled off, too."

"It will be tough holding back from smashing that . . . Let's do it, Frank."

"Let's do it," he says, giving a high five.

"I still may kick his ass before this is all over. But for now, it is his game." They walk back into the conference room.

"We have a deal," Frank says, sitting back down.

The attorney excuses himself to modify the contract to meet the new agreement. Ten minutes later, the attorney returns with the revised copy. Frank, Sammy and Andrey go over it line by line with their copies to make sure it matches as agreed. Once done, all parties sign them before the attorney notarizes them, then gives each party their copy back.

"As noted, I'll loan two hundred fifty thousand with five installments of fifty thousand deposited into an account. This will ensure the project is progressing, so I don't take a total loss from the get-go."

"Thanks, Andrey," Frank says.

Frank and Sammy walk back to the hotel.

"Sammy, let's meet up early tomorrow and I'll take you out on a grand tour of New York."

"Can't wait."

Frank goes down the hotel elevator to the garage and Sammy back to the room. Powering up the iBook, he opens Apple Pages and downloads his working copy of the martial arts list from iCloud.

List of country and Arts:
Brazil - Capoeria
Cambodia - Bokator
Canada - Combato
China - Dim Mak
Germany - Nindokai
Greece - Pankration
Hawaii - Kajuenbo
Hawaii - Kapu Ku'ialua
Israel - Krav Maga
Japan - Ninjitsu
Kerala - Kalarippayattu
Korea - Muye24Ki
Peru- Bacom
Philippine - Eskrima
Spain - Keysi
Thai – Lerdrit
Thai - Muay Boran
USA - Bojuka
USA - Jeet Kune Do

Looking over the list, he realizes he'll need descriptions of each art to help narrow the list down, due to funding limits. What a shame this list is only a small amount of the great arts, he thinks. There are so many more arts; this will be the most stressful part.

Scanning over the list, he keeps jumping between arts. They're all awesome; he's unable to force himself to eliminate any of them. Frank has no knowledge of martial arts, but he'll have to pick. Each is unique: whichever Frank ends up selecting will work.

Sammy's cell rings.

"Hello."

"Are you ready?" Frank says.

"Ready? I'm excited. I will meet you in the hotel coffee shop."

Frank is watching a rerun of Jay Leno on the widescreen TV and drinking coffee when Sammy arrives. While eating, Frank tells Sammy all the places he wants to show him, which will be fun.

After eating, they're off.

"The best way is by cab because finding parking spots suck. And worse, when you do find one, it's about twenty-five dollars an hour."

Surprised, Sammy nods his head in agreement. On the tour, they visit the Statue of Liberty, Central Park and so many more places. Over the course of the day, they become chummy hanging together. They sit outside a coffee shop watching the sun go down.

"I'm starting to get comfortable being around you. I think it'll be great traveling together," Sammy says.

"I was thinking the same thing."

Returning to the hotel Frank takes off, and Sammy goes to his room and packs.

In the morning, Frank arrives and takes him to the airport. "Frank, I'll continue working the teams if you're okay with taking on the task of arranging all the travel? I'll send you a list of countries in a few days."

"That sounds fun, partner."

Cramped in economy seating, he decides to ask Frank if they can budget at least business class. The long hours traveling from country to country in economy with his large body will be unbearably painful.

Sammy

Who Are The Elite
*** Chapter Seven ***

Before unpacking or working on the project, I drop my bags; it's time to hit the waves. Grabbing the surfboard, I'm out the door running across the hot sand. Dodging girls in thong bikinis lying out getting a tan, I make it to the waves. Man, it's great being back on the California coast, even with the chilly waters.

With only two-foot waves and choppy water, I understand why I'm the only one out here. But who am I to complain, having the ocean to myself?

After a few hours of boarding, I peel down the top half of the wetsuit and stuff the board under my left arm, before forcing my stiff legs to move. Getting to the outdoor showers by the bathrooms, I wash the sand off the board and myself, before finishing the fifty-foot walk to the apartment, where I shower and finish unpacking.

Powering up the iMac, I decide to call Frank to check on the budget and how many countries we can afford to visit for our recruiting.

"Hello?" Frank says.

"I'm getting ready to pick martial arts styles. I need to know how many counties we can budget for?"

"I've been working on the budget and estimate no more than five."

"Okay, I guess five it is. Oh, one more thing. Being a big guy, economy seats are painful riding domestic. International will be even more of a bummer, can we do business class? Please?"

"We can. But it will affect money availability for your teams. I will work it in."

"Thanks!"

Opening the martial arts list, I search online for descriptions on each art, then copy and paste them into my document. This'll help me in deciding the five. It's sad being limited, with so many beautiful arts. How am I to pick between them? Finishing I read over the raw list of countries and arts:

1) Brazil (African) - Capoeira
2) Cambodia - Bokator
3) Canada - Combato
4) China - Dim Mak
5) Germany - Nindokai
6 Greece - Pankration
7) Korea - Muye24Ki
8) Hawaii - Kapu Ku'ialua
9) Israel - Krav Maga
10) Japan - Ninjitsu
11) Kerala - Kalarippayattu
12) Lima - Bacom
13) Philippine - Eskrima Serrada
14) Russia - Systema
15) Spain - Keysi
16) Thai - Lerdrit
17) USA - Jeet Kune Do

I email Frank the list, then call.

"Frank, you should have the list now. I'll wait for your reply." I hang up.

Waking from a nap, I check my email, finding Frank's reply. When I open it, there's the five he picked. I would have picked a couple of different ones, but I can live with these:

1. Brazil – Capoeira
    This martial art was born in the slave ghettos of Brazil hundreds of years ago. Originally, it was meant to be a technique by which runaway slaves could defend themselves against attackers. But before long its practice came to be outlawed due to its "dangerous nature".

2. Thai – Lerdrit
    Lerdrit is combined in sparring practice with Navy SEALs being trained in some of their lethal and crippling takedowns. The combination can be rather nasty because Lerdrit can slip into someone's defenses and block counterattacks. Lerdrit tends to be a bit slow but powerful, which can be used for an unpredictable change-up into a crippling strike and clinching moves that turn into grapples. Cut kicks are also pretty nasty, which is probably why they like to teach Lerdrit to the SEALs and some ranger units.

3. Israel - Krav Maga
    Not surprisingly, the world's most effective and dangerous martial art comes to us from one of the most conflicted regions of the world. Developed for use by the IDF or Israeli Defense Force, Krav Maga is a non-sport martial art, meaning it doesn't concern itself with the opponent's well-being. In fact, it generally assumes no mercy or that your opponent intends to kill you. For this reason, the brutal techniques of Krav Maga have been developed with the sole intention of rapidly and efficiently inflicting as much damage as possible. Very often this includes deliberately ending the life of your adversary.

4. Japan – Ninjitsu
    Practiced by the shinobi, or ninja, in feudal Japan, this martial art focused on unconventional warfare,

espionage and assassination. Its practitioners were even sometimes referred to as Hinin, or non-humans.

5. Philippine – Eskrima
Sometimes called Arnis or Kali in the west, Escrima is a Filipino martial art that was outlawed by Spanish invaders, as a result of its being "too dangerous". Like some others on this list, it only exists today because over the next several hundred years it was disguised as a dance.

Okay, here we go. Spending the afternoon focusing on these and a few more (in case any of them doesn't work), I get a lot accomplished before bed.

The phone ringing wakes me like an alarm clock.

"Hello."

"It's almost time, Sammy. We need to get our passports. Luckily, with the length of stay at these countries, there aren't visa requirements. I emailed you a list of dates for each country, using the express at the post office. It will allow you to receive the passport in days."

Knowing I'll miss my mom, I decide to take her out before hitting the blue skies.

Calling her, I say, "Hey, Mom, let's go out tonight. I'm leaving on a project and want to see you before going."

"That will make me happy. Tonight?"

"Yes, at seven," I say, hanging up.

After our joyful evening, we walk from the pier down the ocean-front-walk home. We don't speak but listen to the ocean waves crashing against the shore. I feel edgy leaving this peaceful place on a journey, which for me is bigger than life. Am I stupid for even thinking I can do something like this? Looking to the sky.

"Dad, if you can hear me in heaven, please help me survive this. And watch over mom while I'm gone."

"Son, you're a good man. I know your father will look over you. I will pray each night for God to bless you." She squeezes my hand as her eyes begin to water.

I arrive home just as Frank calls, "We have tickets to leave tomorrow."

"I'm ready."

Excited, I rush getting packed for the long journey. Lying in bed, I get very little sleep thinking of the things gonna happen. I wake early; my mind is still racing. Maybe this will change my life forever. I use the morning to check everything, then call mom before I'm picked up at noon.

The shuttle arrives. I grab my stuff and run for the door, almost forgetting the iPad. Grabbing it, I'm off to Bradley International terminal. Upon getting to the airport, I drop a five to the driver and I'm off to ticketing, then the torture of security. Happy getting to the boarding area, I find the VIP lounge; I grab a hot snack and tea, then kick back until my flight boards.

Frank

☯

Yippies Aren't So Bad
*** Chapter Eight ***

Dropping Sammy off at the airport, I swing by my favorite bar to celebrate the new wealth coming soon. It's unbelievable how well this day has gone.

Pushing open the bar door, I say, "Time to celebrate, drinks are on me."

The only customer in the bar says, "Thanks, mister, you're awesome." Sliding to the right ten bar stools, he sits next to me. "What's your name?"

"Frank and yours?"

"Joe."

"Bartender, two Bacardi 151 shots, and two Bacardi and Cokes." Joe and I down the shots and chase them with the rum and Coke.

"Hey, Frank, this place has a new pool table want to play?" He points at a tournament size in the back of the room.

"Sure, haven't played in a while." Joe follows me to the table.

I rack the balls, then walk over to the stick rack hanging on the wall. All the sticks are new; picking a size twenty-one, I chalk it up and wait on Joe to break.

"Bartender, two Bacardi 151 shots, two Bacardi and Coke."

We do shots and shoot pool until eight when the Yippies pile in to sing karaoke and drink. Normally these Yippies and their karaoke get on my nerves, but not tonight. Tonight I'll make an exception; in fact, I buy them all rounds.

Swaying side-to-side, a bit tipsy, I take over the microphone and sing my favorite song—"Jazzman" by Carole King. It reminds me of New Orleans. I'm a hit: the Yippies sing along with me and clap their hands.

Before handing back the mic, I yell, "Next round of drinks is on me." Two sexy Yippie girls hop on bar stools on each side of me.

"Hi, what's your name?" the girl on the left asks.

"It's Frank and your names?" I reply, checking these blondes out.

"Oh, we're twins. I'm Mary, and she's Terry," the one on the right says.

Wow, the girls are a bit chubby, but what big boobs. They're wearing short dresses with low-cut fronts. I can almost see their nipples, as they're not wearing bras. I can see their matching panties, as their dresses had slid up when they sat.

"Bartender, another round for the ladies and me, please." I drop a twenty on the bar. "How old are you, girls?"

"Today is our twenty-first birthday," Terry says.

"Happy birthday, girls. Tonight the drinks are on me."

"You're so sweet, Frank." I feel their kisses to both my cheeks.

I keep them laughing with my best jokes when Mary says, "Frank, you're giving us a fun birthday. Thank you!" The girls are kissing my cheeks and neck when I feel a hand between my legs.

"Mary, I found a toy for us to play with for our birthday?"

"Let me check!" She tugs on my zipper. "Terry, hold the top of his pants so I can unzip."

Shy, I reach to pull the girls' hands away when Terry says, "It is okay, Frank, we won't hurt you. We'll make you feel real special. Promise." The girls have my pants open and each have a hand playing with me.

"It's smooth and hard," Terry says.

"Frank, I bet this feels wonderful, doesn't it?" Mary says. I hear their breath as they suck on my earlobes. I feel the softness of their hands, as they take turns stroking me.

"Girls!" I lose it, shooting my first non-self induced cum ever: on their hands, their legs, my lap, the floor and the bottom of the bar. Mary and Terry grab napkins, laughing while they clean up.

"Thanks for such a good time, Frank." Standing, they walk over to a group of girls huddled by a snack table eating.

After drinking and singing a few more songs, I call it a night and stumble home.

My eyes gently open, my head is pounding and a desire to drink an ocean full of water. Rolling off the bed, I wobble into the bathroom. I get the tub's water pouring and add a little bubble bath. Off to the kitchen, I pop a couple aspirins and down a Bloody Mary, then back to the bathroom. I drop my shorts and hop in the warm water for a short nap.

Waking refreshed, I climb out of the tub and get dressed. Man, them girls were fun last night. Okay, focus on work.

First on the agenda, I go downtown and open shared international bank accounts for Sammy, Andrey and myself. I call Andrey's secretary I give her the bank information so she can have the money transferred.

A few hours later, I receive a call. "Frank, this is Andrey's secretary. Fifty thousand dollars has been transferred into the shared account."

"Thank you."

It has been a long time since I've had access to this kind of money. I'd love to withdraw the fifty thousand and vanish, but I'm too honest. Second, Andrey would hire a hitman to hunt me down. It's time for a break. A walk to the park is what's needed to clear my mind and get rid of this jelly belly I've built over the years.

When I step outside, the sun warms my body as I walk the eight blocks to the park. It sure is a beautiful day; feeling alive, I arrive at the park.

The dirt jogging path around the park is full of young women, some pushing strollers. Starting off slow then picking up the pace, I feel my heart beating faster and legs tighten. My eyes are locked on all those sexy butts in front bouncing. I'm able to complete five laps before wearing out. Tired, I sit on the benches realizing I'm the only male; I'll keep this my little secret.

Walking away I hear, "Bye, sweetie." The moms wave and yell.

"I'll catch you next time, moms." They noticed me?

"Catch us if you can." They laugh, waving bye.

"What?" I didn't realize they heard me. Embarrassed, I speed home.

Getting into the house, I clean up and eat. Then I focus on travel, with the nearest countries first. Okay, the logical first stop is Brazil. While booking airline tickets for Sao Paulo-Guarulhos International Airport, it occurs to me that Sammy and I are on the opposite sides of the U.S. I decide it will be best if we meet in Sao Paulo. This brings up another issue, access to money. I call RBC Wealth Management and have them send Sammy and myself credit and ATM cards to our residences. Best I call and give Sammy a heads-up.

"Hey, Sammy, you'll be heading directly to Brazil. I have the bank FedExing you a credit and ATM card overnight, keep an eye out for them. I'll see you in Brazil."

"Thanks. Don't forget to email me all the travel info. By the way, how are we going to keep in contact?"

"Good point. Cells suck for international. Got it! Let's do satellite?"

"That's a great idea. FedEx me one before I leave."

"Will do." Hanging up, I order satellite phones on the Internet and have them sent overnight to us. Tired, I take off the rest of the day.

The day of the flight is thrilling: after much planning and prep, I'm eagerly on my way. Pulling up to JFK International terminal, I slip the driver a few bucks and head to the door, expecting long lines at the ticket counter and worse for security line.

I finally get up to security, two airport police nab me when I'm exiting the metal detector.

"Sir, you need to come with us."

I'm led through a secured door and put in what looks like an interview room. Not knowing what's going on, I get paranoid. I've never even had a traffic ticket in my life.

A man's face peeks through a little window in the door, then he comes in. Wearing a blue suit with an airport police badge pinned to the left front pocket, he says, "Sir, remove the contents from all your pockets, and put them on the table, please." I empty everything from my pockets. He picks up my driver's license and passport. "Someone will be with you in a moment." Leaving the other items, he steps out the door.

I keep glancing at the wall clock, it's about thirty minutes when a guy wearing a grey suit, with a detective badge, comes in and shuts the door behind him. Sitting across from me, he says, "Mr. Capper, I'm Detective Joe Friday, and you're being held for questioning in an investigation."

"What, What . . . investigation?"

"Scanning your bags at security we found large quantities of hidden money, causing a need to detain you for further questioning. Checking, we found the bills are marked by the FBI in a Brazil drug cartel case."

Now getting angry. "You guys are crazy and better let me go now!" He gives me my rights before continuing.

"I'm sorry, sir. You're being transferred to the FBI central building downtown for an interview by special agents handling this case." Airport police come in and handcuff me. They lead me out the rear door to an unmarked black sedan.

When we pull up to the rear of a building, a metal garage door opens allowing us to drive in before it shuts. I'm led through a secured door and up an elevator to another interview type room. My right handcuff is removed and connected to a metal ring on the table. A while later, a short, skinny and beautiful woman comes. She sits across from me. I notice her FBI badge before gazing into her eyes.

"Mr. Capper, my name is Agent Starling with the FBI. We found marked bills hidden in your bags. They're linked to one of our investigations."

Her words blow any hope for love between us. "I don't know why you people are trying to frame me, but forget it. I didn't do anything and have nothing to hide."

A tall, skinny man wearing an FBI badge over his pocket walks in carrying a large luggage bag; he sets it on the table.

"Sir, the money was found in your bag here," he says.

"Hey, this isn't my bag, you morons."

"Having an attitude isn't going to resolve this any faster," he says.

"Okay, what needs to be done?" Frank says.

"If this is not your bag then you agree to be fingerprinted? This will allow us to match them against the bag and its contents," Agent Starling says.

"Let's do it now and get it over with. You people already made me miss my flight."

"Sorry, sir, but you need to understand this is for national security. The safety of our country."

"Whatever."

"Mr. Capper, an officer will print you in a moment," Agent Starling says, as both Agents leave the room.

After being fingerprinted and returned to the room, Agent Starling returns in what seems an awful long time later.

"Mr. Capper, we just caught the guy and he's in custody. You've been cleared and will be release. We apologize for your inconvenience, but this had to be done. We've booked you on a flight leaving in two hours."

An airport police officer picks me up, and we return to the airport. He escorts me through security up to my gate, where another officer is waiting with my bags. He hands me a plastic bag with my wallet and other items. Not seeing my passport.

"Hey, where's my passport?"

The officer who escorted me gets on his Mic starts talking and walking way. Standing there I watch one-by-one of the long line step-up and scan their tickets then walk down the corridor to board the plane. Watching the last one pass the security door it closes.

The officer standing with me, says, "Sir, we are unable to locate your passport or driver's license."

"Damn, this is not my day."

"Sir, be assured we will find them and get you on the next available flight once we do."

The officer takes me home in a police cruiser. When we get there, he says, "Sir, we will put you on the very next flight once we find your passport, I promise."

I call Sammy and explain what happened, then tell him to start without me, that I'll be there soon.

It's been two days when my cell rings. "Hello?"

"Mr. Capper, we have recovered your passport and driver's license. There's a flight leaving in three hours, can you make it?"

"I'll be ready."

"An airport police cruiser will arrive to pick you up, sir."

The cruiser comes and gets me. The officer escorts me all the way to my gate; Agent Starling's standing at the corridor entrance to the airplane.

"Mr. Capper, I, personally, wanted to come apologize and see you off." She gives me a sexy smile.

"Thank you, Agent Starling." I hand my ticket at the gate and step up to the aircraft-loading entrance.

I'm finally on my way. Once in the air I hit the buttons, changing my seat into a bed, order a Bacardi and Coke, then start the feature *Silence of the Lamb* and take it easy.

When mealtime arrives, I find out it is a three-course meal, not the bag of peanuts and a cup of soda like I'm used to in economy class.

Sammy

Danger In The Dance
*** Chapter Nine ***

Stepping into my hotel room, I flip open the laptop and start googling. I'll travel anywhere in Brazil to build this team if that's what needs to be done. Good isn't enough; I need secret societies of deadly fighters, possibly mercenaries.

The satellite phone rings.

"Hello?"

"Hey, this is Frank. I ran into some problems."

"Where are you?"

"I'm still in New York." He explains what happened to him.

"That's a crazy story, Frank."

"Yeah, maybe it sounds crazy. But it's true."

"Okay, call me when you get here." Think I'll call this satellite phone the S phone for short. I laugh.

"Okay," Frank says.

Getting on the S phone in the hotel lobby, I begin calling schools on the list I created, and I ask if I can drop by. Just showing up may be considered rude and end up pissing someone off. I also want to ask if they'll give a demonstration or two. After setting up visits with a half-dozen places, I'm on my way. Flagging down a cab, I give the first address and we're off.

Entering the first school a black male approaches me wearing only shorts; sweat is running down his face,

"I'm called Mestre, translates to senior instructor. Just finished training hard, so you'll have to excuse the sweat."

This guy's a big man. He must be close to seven feet, with muscles bulging from every part of his body. The twenty-pack abs are intimidating.

"Follow me."

He takes me over to a set of benches where we sit; I go into more detail of what I'm looking for.

"Mr. Nelson?"

"Please call me Sammy."

"Okay, Sammy. I'm interested but want a little time to think about this."

"I understand."

"Would you care to see a demonstration of what Capoeira's about?"

"I'd love it."

"There is a lot more to it than just the fighting, but the kickass is there too." He chuckles.

"I've done some studying of the art, but excited to see it in action."

"Take a seat over in the training area." Excitement floods my mind as I sit down.

Moments later, the gym fills with guys wearing white pants, with long cords of different colors around their waists. Some in oversized shirts and others with no shirt. These must be the fighters. Others sit behind musical instruments along the far wall.

"Mestre, what's going on with those instruments?"

"It is part of Capoeira."

"They look like an oversized bongo drum and a tambourine. Not sure of the other ones."

"They are the music of the dance: Berimbaus, Pandeiros, Agogo, Reco-reco and Atabaque. Once we begin, you'll understand."

76

This is going to be exciting, listening to the culture's music before the demonstrations start. The musicians begin playing some really cool sounds. As I kick back listening, the sound controls my mood.

"Okay, let's get started."

All the ones with the color belts gather around the circle in the center of the room when Mestre grabs my arm.

"Come, my man."

He pulls me up to the group. One jumps into the circle and starts stepping widely forward and backward in rhythm to the music. Moments later, he begins what looks like a dance. His legs stretch out as he spins in circles, sometimes low and others high. Next he's doing handstands and cartwheels while kicking his legs out. I'm enjoying this dance when a second guy jumps in the circle and begins doing the same type of moves.

"What do you see, Sammy? There is more than what meets the eye," Mestre says.

Now watching more carefully, I begin to realize the dance's hidden martial arts. Each dance move is now a strike of the hand or foot. The acrobatic abilities of these guys seem impossible, as they flip into handstands allowing them to kick the other in the face, or triple spins in the air and ground to catch the other off-guard. This is amazing. I realize how deceptive and deadly it is, but also the beauty of this art.

"Mestre, I'll tell ya. I hold the belt for the world kickboxing title, but these guys scare the hell out of me." I laugh.

"My man, never underestimate anyone on the streets, they may just surprise you in a deadly way."

I gotta have a team of these guys doing battle in my competition. After seeing them in action, I'm now determined to search and find the most dangers and skilled fighters in Capoeira. This is great. Leaving I thank Mestre and give him my S number.

"I'll need to have a serious talk with some of my best students. If they're interested, I'll call you."

Walking out, I yell to the guys, "Hey, guys, thanks for the demonstration. Every one of you is awesome."

"You're welcome, sir," they respond.

Then, I say to the musicians, "Hey . . . do you guys have a CD, I'd love to have a copy?"

77

They laugh, waving goodbye.

I draw a line through each school on my notepad as I visit them. Some of the students at the schools give me the numbers of independent fighters. ones who do battle in underground tournaments. Hmm, these underground fights got to have some real bad dudes competing. I smell a team coming on and snicker.

My only concern is who's going to control these crazies; I need a team-lead. Got to check out an underground fight to see how deadly Capoeira really is and if so, pick up some fighters. Before crashing for the night, I call the numbers and leave messages for the independent fighters.

The sun hits me in the face through the open curtains; I wake up thinking I should have closed them last night. When I get up, the red light's blinking on the S phone. I play back the recording, it's some of the fighters I left messages for. I decide to call one of them.

"Hey, this is Sammy. I'm returning your call."

"Sammy, I here you're looking for street fighters?"

"Yeah, happen to be one or have any in mind?"

"I may be able to help you."

"Well, let's meet up at a public spot for both our safety?" I say.

"Works for me. Where?"

"Let's do the lobby at the hotel I'm staying, say tonight at seven o'clock."

"I'll be there."

At seven, kicking back in the lobby, I call the guy's number and hear a phone ringing a few feet away. Looking over I see a man putting a cell to the side of this head.

"Hello?"

I'm hearing in stereo from across the room and the S phone.

I walk over. "Hello, I'm Sammy Nelson."

He looks over at me smiling.

"Hello, I'm Fabio Santos."

We sit and begin chatting, he says, "I've been training and fighting since a young boy. My father was a champion Capoeira street fighter, as far back as, I can remember until he died. I've followed in his footsteps, and I'm now considered the best around here."

"Fabio, I'm looking to pull together a team of dangerous Capoeira fighters who have no fear of death. It's for a one-of-a-kind tournament, competing against fighters from other countries just as dangerous."

"Sounds awesome, tell me more."

"One problem is I need a way to keep them under control. They must do what they're told and not cause problems."

"Sammy, with what you're looking for there better be a big bucket of money."

"Yap! Fifty thousand dollars to split for the winning team."

Fabio laughs. "You have got to be joking. Even for deprived people, it's not near enough to risk death. Now fifty grand per fighter and one hundred grand for the team-lead is what will get you the elite."

I realize he's right, but three hundred thousand is double our budget. If this guy is as awesome as he's bragging, I've got to find the money.

"Fabio, if you can pull the kind of team I'm looking for together, with a good team-lead, with a demonstration to see how elite they are, we may have a deal."

"Get the money, and I'll not only get the team but will lead them."

"Works for me."

"I'm sure the fifty grand will keep the fighters from getting stupid, but if it doesn't, I will."

"Deal." Standing, I head back to my room.

Shutting my room door behind me, I call Frank.

"Hey, you here yet?"

"Yes, I just arrived."

"Need to chat. I've got something important to discuss. I prefer we do it in person."

"If that's the case, we should meet at the bar, where I can get a drink."

We both get to the bar at the same time. Frank orders Bacardi & Coke, and I'm thirsting for a chilled glass of green tea. Getting started, I lay it out straight.

"I met up with an elite fighter name Fabio, who tells me it takes a three hundred thousand purse to pull a team of the best together."

"Sammy . . . you crazy? I'm sure you can find a team much cheaper."

"I'm serious. The three hundred thousand makes sense. These fighters are not just jumping into a cage. They could be looking at death." I'm eyeing Frank. "Can you get the money?"

Frank grabs his drink, emptying it in one gulp and looks back at me.

"What! Three hundred grand winner's purse and expense for the teams, plus our costs? This makes me very nervous." His face turns red. "I'll call Andrey in the morning, but no promises." He shakes his head. "Remember we're dealing with the devil."

"Relax, guy, it will work out in the end. I'm going to my room to crash." I get up and leave.

The S phone rings, waking me from an exciting dream.

"Hello?"

"I spoke to Andrey. He gave verbal approval for an increase up to one million, but he has additional demands that are not negotiable. His secretary will send a new contract for us to sign."

"It's no problem, Frank. If you're scared we can back out now, not much of the money has been spent. Together we can pay it back."

"Damn, let's make this competition happen. Hopefully, we'll beat the devil."

"You're the man!"

Back in the room turning on the tube, the S phone rings.

"This is Fabio. I've got a team that's kickass. Did you get the three-hundred-thousand-dollar purse approved?"

"Sure did."

"I have the meanest, dirtiest, skilled fighters in the world. I know what you're thinking. Don't worry, I'll keep them under control because I'm the worst of them." He chuckles.

"Can't wait to see them in action."

"Meet me in front of your hotel at nine tonight. I'll take you to an underground fight to see them in action."

"Don't let me down," I say, getting a woody.

Stepping out to the street, I see Fabio standing by a car.

"Let's go. The team will meet us there. They've been fighting underground at this place for years."

We pull up to an old abandoned building with the front surrounded by people. Dodging cars through a full parking lot, we get to the door, where a few big guys stand questioning people trying to get in. We step up to these guys, who tower over us.

"Hey, Fabio, fighting tonight?" one says.

"Not tonight, Mac." The big guy puts his arm around Fabio and escorts us in.

"Man, this place is packed," I say.

Crazy looking guys in street clothes stand around a large open area in the middle; I bet that is where the action will happen. I follow Fabio as he walks towards the building, we approach four guys.

"Sammy, I'd like to introduce you to the deadliest dudes on the face of the earth and your new team."

"Hello, team."

"Team, this is Sammy, the one who is looking to sponsor fighters for the deadliest competition in the twenty-first century."

"This may be a match made in heaven or maybe hell."

A voice comes over a loud speaker, "Ladies and gentleman, quiet. We are about to start the night's events; have you all placed your bets? We have some great fights tonight. We also have our long-standing champ, Fabio, here tonight."

Fabio waves his hands over his head as the crowd cheers. The announcer continues, "Unfortunately he won't be entertaining us with his skill this evening. Sorry. Let's get started."

The crowd takes their seats on wooden bleachers and folding chairs, set up around the painted circle in the middle of the room.

"Sammy, follow me," Fabio says.

I follow him to the front row, where we take a seat.

"The front row is for fighters only," the man wearing a security shirt says, "but being the honored guest, Fabio has special privileges."

Over the speaker comes, "Okay, the fighter match-ups are on the chalkboard to my right, and will be updated after each fight. I will call "next" as each battle ends. If it's your turn, jump in and get started. This is not formal. Got it?"

"Fabio, this guy's weird."

"Yap."

"Let's get started. Guys for the first match jump in and fight," the announcer says.

The music plays when two fighters, one in Blue and other in Red, jump in the circle, doing the same dance of the schools I visited. But these guys aren't looking very friendly toward each other.

They're flipping and spinning around, barely missing each other. The moves are so fast, it's hard to tell what's happening when Blue kicks Red in the chest with both feet while doing a handstand on one hand.

Red's hurled backward by the impact. He does a backflip in mid-air, landing on his feet: the crowd screams. Blue's acrobatic skills help dodge the flow of kicks and punches. Red's throwing, using combinations of flipping and spinning.

Red drops to a handstand, kicking his legs out, catching Blue in a scissors-type move, throwing him backward and slamming his head on the floor.

Blue jumps up bleeding from the back of his head, which only seems to piss him off. Blue does a triple spin in the air, kicking Red so hard he comes off the ground flying five feet into the front chairs, knocking fighters backward out of their seats.

The fighters throw Red off them and jump up yelling. Two of them jump into the circle attacking Blue. All of a sudden this place turns into a free-for-all with everyone fighting.

My new team's not only kickass; they're watching each other's back, giving me respect for them. Fabio laughs while knocking people out with single strikes as they come at him.

Getting hit in the back with a chair, I turn around to a midget punching me in the legs. Picking him up I sit in a chair and turn him over my knee spanking him. Some huge guy steps up, knocking me out of the chair with a punch to the face.

"What the hell you think you doing to my little buddy?"

The big man reaches down grabbing my throat. I grab him by the balls, squeezing tight. Screaming, he lets me go. I jump up, nailing him with an elbow to the jaw and head to the door. Fabio is still laughing. He follows me out with his team right behind.

"Fabio, this sucks, I didn't get to see these guys fight in the tournament," I say once outside.

"We can go back in if you like."

"No thanks, from what I've seen tonight, I am sure they will do just fine."

We all start busting up laughing.

"Guys, I'm going to drop Sammy off, then will meet you at the club to decide on this." Fabio drops me off at the hotel.

I get a call from Fabio in the morning.

"We have a deal," he says.

"Sounds great. I'll have my sidekick Frank call to arrange everything with you. I'll tell ya, I like this martial arts and the team. So keep everything under control. I'd hate replacing, anyone or the team."

"No problem, Sammy. Just have the money ready when we win." He chuckles.

"You got it."

Hanging up, I just chill out in the room waiting for Frank to call. Mid-afternoon, he does.

"Sammy, I just finished my part."

"My part's done too. Hey, call Fabio, the team-lead of the fighters, to arrange the details." I give him Fabio's number.

"Sammy, get ready to go. Next stop is Israel."

"Yap, Krav Maga. Let's do it." I pack my bags and get ready to go.

Frank

Should I Trust The Kid
*** Chapter Ten ***

Exiting the terminal, the afternoon heat of Brazil causes my head to spin. I quickly hop into the nearest taxi.

"Damn, it's hot out there." Sweat is dripping off my forehead.

"Must be your first visit here. Yes?" He laughs.

"Ya, question if you don't mind?"

"Sure," he says, glancing at me in the rearview mirror.

"Where can I find party spots and . . . sexy girls?" Staring down at my shoes.

He drives off, saying, "Oh, Moca! Your luck you picked this taxi. Been driving here twenty years and know everything you need. Here take my card. I can find you girls or if you want party club. Call me day or night. I'm your number one man." He hands me a business card with his cell number on back.

"Here you go, senhor." We pull in front of a fifteen-story, pink hotel.

"Thanks for the lift." I pay him with a little extra.

"Hey, don't lose my card and remember to call me, day or night for anything," he screams out the window.

I smile without saying a word, rushing to escape the heat. Walking into the hotel lobby a cold breeze hits my face, giving instant relief. The walls are full of Brazilian art, giving the place a touch of class.

A man wearing a pink uniform and hat directs me towards a row of receptionists also in pink to include makeup and costume jewelry.

"I'm Frank Capper checking in, please," laying my passport on the marble counter.

"Welcome to Brazil, Mr. Capper." She gazes into my eyes like she's reading my mind.

"Are there any messages for me?"

Checking her computer. "Yes, Senhor, from a guest named Sammy Nelson. He said to call him once you arrive."

"Thank you."

"Senhor, here is your room key—the elevators are over there." She points to her left. "Enjoy your stay and please call if we can help with anything," she says, winking.

Stepping into a large room with two twin beds, a small TV, and aged furniture, I lay my stuff on the bed nearest the window. I pull the curtains to the side and peek out. From my previous travels, I know this is going to be fun. My belly is making hungry noises when the mobile phone rings.

"Hey, Frank. The receptionist said you were here."

"Yeah, just arrived."

"I need to discuss something important about the fighters with you. Think it would be better in person."

"If that's the case let's meet at the bar where I can get a drink and eat."

While digging into a steak and chasing it with a Bacardi and Coke Sammy explains our money problem.

"Sammy, I'll discuss this with Andrey and let you know."

Sitting on my bed, I call Andrey. "Andrey, this is Frank. Things are going well, but we've run into a problem that we need to discuss."

"And that is?"

"The prize money isn't enough. Sammy told me when he interviewed the fighters; they said to get quality fighters willing to die, it will require a three-hundred-thousand-dollar payout for the winning team to split."

"Frank, what the hell? You're requesting an enormous amount of money. You sure you can pull this off?"

"Andrey, seriously. Sammy and I can do this. I promise we can make a bundle for everyone."

"Okay, I'll approve one million, max. But for this kind of risk I'm going to demand something additional in return. I'll think about it while my lawyers rewrite the contract. I'll have it sent to the hotel's front desk."

"Alright, hurry, please. I don't want to spend any more until I see the contract." Damn, what is this guy up to now?

Setting my phone on the bed, I unpack and set up my computer on the small desk at the window. I search the Internet after powering up the laptop, when my mobile phone rings.

"Hello?"

"Hello, Frank. How are you, partner?" Andrey says.

"How are you partner? Andrey, either you're on drugs or you're up to something. We both know this is not your normal cheerful sarcastic personality." Did I just say that?

"Enough! Here is the deal; in each country, you will find five young, beautiful and poor girls. They will be homeless with no family. You will hire them."

"What are you trying to pull on me?" Standing, I walk over and look out the window.

"Listen, I'm telling you what I want. If you don't agree, we can call the deal off. One million is a big investment. I need to make sure I find ways to get maximum returns."

"I'm listening, but there better not be any funny stuff."

"We'll use these girls for multiple tasks, largely for the contest promotion and marketing. I want professional pictures taken of them in their street clothes. We will use the pictures on marketing posters. We're going to promote how we care and sponsor the poorest of these countries. Second, each of these girls will be assigned to a fighter from their country, to do cleaning, cooking or anything else the fighters need or want. I want them there early to help prepare for the guests and fighters."

"Go on, I'm listening." I don't trust him but have to hear him out.

"That's it. Do we have a deal?"

"I like the idea. We have a deal." Hmm, It's not as horrible as I thought.

"Wait, let me finish. At each country find a local assistant to manage these girls until we are ready to transport them. Find one location for each group to stay that fits it into your budget. Better make sure you keep track of them."

"Okay, it all makes sense."

"One last thing, Frank. I'm hiring an investigator to do spot checks on these girls. And if any of them doesn't fit my demands, our contract becomes void, canceling the project. That means the money spent will need to be returned as agreed to in the contract. You need to take this seriously." He hangs up on me.

I speed-dial the mobile phone. "Hey, Sammy, just spoke to Andrey. Let's meet for lunch, so we can go over the new contract." During lunch, I explain the new requirements letting Sammy know I'm okay with it.

"I agree it makes sense, but who will be the one to find these girls?"

"Andrey's demands will make it difficult to find them," I say. "I will take the responsibility for finding them. I'm sure there are thousands of girls who will qualify. So, do we agree to take the risk?"

"Let's do it. Oh, just let me say. I feel your pain having to search for beautiful girls." I laugh.

"I'll call Andrey and let him know."

"Seriously, I know you'll have to search the shady parts of town. If you run into any problems, please call me and I'll get there in a hurry."

"Thanks, I will." I put his number in my speed dial. I call Andrey. "We signed and I faxed the contract. I'm on the way to start looking for the girls."

"Great news. Remember as you find the girls, put them all together in a boarding house, with all meals supplied. So we can keep track of expenses and the girls."

"This is a good plan, Andrey."

"I'm working on the venue. I want the girls there early to train them and help us set up."

"Once I have them in a boarding house, I will send you the names of the girls and personal info with pictures. Then you can start working on the marketing."

"Frank, let the girls know the job comes with a salary of minimum wage for their country. Plus free room and board from the moment they're hired, until the contest is over. Also, if they last until the end, a bonus of one-month salary for each."

"It will certainly help in recruiting what you're looking for." I hang up.

I take off my watch, rings, and dress down for the occasion. Before heading out. The cab driver gives me a strange look when he drops me off.

"Be careful, guy. It's dangerous in this area."

Strolling down the sidewalk, a boy about ten years old is sliding a broom handle along the chain-link fence, skipping towards me. I stop him as he gets to my front.

"Hey, are you from around here?"

"Yeah, why?" stepping back as if getting ready to run.

"You interested in making some money?"

"You one of them foreigner perverts?" A grossed-out expression comes across his face.

"No. I need someone from the local area to help me with a project." I smile.

"What kind of job, how much pay, senhor?" He pokes his stick at the sidewalk.

"I'm looking for beautiful girls in their late teens or early twenties to work as helpers on a project."

"What's my pay if I help you?"

"It's twenty-five U.S. dollars per girl, but they must meet my needs."

"Okay, maybe I trust you. I'm Mike and lived around here all of my life. I know everyone and everything that happens this town. How many girls you want?"

"First, my name is Frank, and I'm looking for five girls." Giving him my phone number, I say, "I'll be looking too, so you better hurry."

He gives me a challenging look. "I will be the one to get them all. Make sure you have my money ready." He runs off.

Searching the streets all morning and afternoon with no luck, I get tired; I decide to stop at a bar for a drink. I spot a small club with the door open. Walking into a dimly lit room, I sit up at the bar near the door and order a rum and Coke.

Sipping my drink, I see a shadow of a girl in the refection in the mirror behind the bar. She's sitting alone in the far back corner in the dark. She must have seen me look, because she comes up behind me, puts her arms around my waist and rubs between my legs.

"Buy me a drink and I will make you very happy back where I'm sitting." She gives my shaft soft-squeezes.

Hidden behind me, I can't see what she looks like in the mirror, but her voice sounds sexy.

"Bartender, please bring us both a drink to the back table."

"As you wish." He smiles.

Climbing off the stool and turning around she's already going back to the table. I follow her checking out the cute ass. When we reach the table, the bartender was right behind us and sets our drinks down. This girl has my zipper down and is stroking me before I can sit.

Looking over to tell her how good it feels, I now see her face up close. She looks mid-twenties but aged fifty years from substance abuse. She smiles; half of her teeth are missing. She lowers her head and goes under the table, working her tongue. But the vision of moments before are hunting my brain, causes me to go soft. I gently pull her away, down my drink in one swig, throw enough money on the bar for the drinks and tips, and run for the door.

Looking for a cab, my phone rings.

"Hello?"

"Its Mike, I have some girls interested, what should I tell them?"

I give him the address of the fast food restaurant next to the hotel, saying, "I preferred to discuss the salary and benefits with the girls directly. Bring all the girls you have and call my phone once you arrive. I can be there within a few minutes of the call."

"That won't be a problem. I have seven girls now. You can have some extra to choose from."

"That's great work, Mike. I hope they're the sexiest ones in the country and meet my needs."

"These girls will make your winnie hard, Frank."

"Not if the girl I was with is still in my memory." Still grossed out.

"What's that?"

"Nothing." I laugh. "See you soon."

I wave down a taxi and go to the hotel. In the room, I search for boarding houses with enough available beds. Calling an old mansion on the edge of town, I explain my needs to the keeper.

"This will be a temporary place for five girls until our project starts."

"I'll give you a discount, since you'll be renting all my rooms."

"I'll call to tell you when they're coming."

Lying down, I fall asleep.

Waking in the morning to my phone ringing, I answer, "Hello?"

"Hello, it's Mike. I now have ten sexy girls. What you want to do?"

"You did a remarkable job. Let's meet for lunch at noon. I'm buying for everyone."

"I'm hungry. I'll call you from the restaurant," Mike says.

Going in the bathroom, I shower and get ready to go. At noon, I get the call like clockwork and leave for the restaurant. Entering, I see Mike with a group of girls sitting at a large wooden table in the back. These girls are looking super hot from here.

"Mike, bring the girls to the food counter," I call, waving my hands over my head.

I let the cashier know I'm paying for everyone in our group. Getting the food, we sit at the same table and eat. I watch the girls squirm around excited when I go over the details of the project and perks. Feeling I have them hooked, I do one-on-one interviews.

I select five hotties with great personalities with ages under twenty-three. The kicker is, they all live on the streets with no one in their lives. I have the selected girls sit at a different table. I release the others, letting them know I may need them later if there still interested.

"Girls, we're going to a boarding house where you'll stay until the project starts." I tell Mike, "I'm leaving the country and need you to keep an eye on these girls. If you take care of their needs and keep them at the boarding house, until I send for them. I'll give you an extra one hundred dollars. Deal?"

"Deal," he says.

Getting to the street, we wave down multiple taxis and take the girls to the boardinghouse. Once the girls are happily settled in their rooms, I pay Mike for his services.

"If you do a good job there'll be an extra one-hundred twenty-five dollars, and maybe an additional bonus to boot."

Returning to the hotel, I call Sammy, "I've got my girls. They're staying in a guesthouse."

"Cool, I have my fighters. I need you to get with a guy called Fabio. He's the team-lead for the fighters and the one to work the details out with." He gives me Fabio's phone number.

"Sammy, get ready to go . . . next stop is Israel."

"For some Krav Maga? Let's do it."

I meet with Fabio in the afternoon then make arrangements for morning travel to Israel.

I call Sammy. "Everything's done. We're heading out in the morning. Get packed." The next morning we eat, grab a taxi and are off to the airport.

Andrey

Designing Paradise Island
*** Chapter Eleven ***

"Frank, I don't know anything about this fighting business, however, I do understand putting one's life at risk does need enough incentive." I hadn't thought about the prize money, but I need to find a way to put a twist on this before taking a risk on increasing the funds. "I'll get back to you soon." I hang up.

One way to save on expenses is using the island for the venue. I can also show off my greatness by inviting friends to watch the fights.

Let's see, if the fights become popular, I can expand by opening a resort for the rich. Ugh, it's too small for a fantasy type Grand Five Star Hotel or Family Fun Park. My island needs to cater to singles and couples from the elite class. But what'll attract them to pay huge money? Mmm, what will do it? Aha, global enjoyment among the rich has always been girls. A small tropical island full of girls servicing the rich: will do the trick. Better yet, a one-stop shop.

That's it. A variety of girls from different countries: men, women, couples, or even groups of guests. I'll make the girls do whatever my guests want, from mild to extremely kinky. We will discreetly cater to the rich and famous. My girls will never tell. Because once they arrive on the island, they'll never leave. This island is something that tops any of my friends.

Okay, need to find these girls? I know the girls for the fight. I'm sure Frank and partner will bring the first batch of girls. One problem. These guys are too kind-hearted to support my good cause. I need to discover a way to fool them into thinking it's for their project. Should be easy. I'll give Frank a buzz.

"This is Andrey. We have a deal. I want girls from those countries you're visiting for promotional/ marketing for the tournament. Do you agree?"

"Andrey, what are you trying to pull?"

"This will be good for both of us. Will use five from each country. I want them homeless with no family. It's a good way to get cheap labor and to use as promotional items. Everyone wants to help the needy. Right?" Thinking, I'll wait to tell Frank about using the island for the venue.

This island is getting my juices flowing: me, having a playground of submissive girls, to sell for crazy amounts of money. It's time to design the island for an awesome competition and plan for my one-stop sex shop for the rich.

Hitting the intercom, I say, "Research and find architects and designers. I need experienced ones in undeveloped islands or resorts. I want to meet with at least a half dozen if you can find that many."

"Yes, sir."

"Don't let me down. I want this to be the best get-away island in the world. It's urgent. I'm putting on a competition there soon."

"I will never let you down, sir. I'm getting right on it."

These fights will be the kick-off attraction for the island's grand opening. Timing for the fighters and island completion will be tight.

Seeing those huts set up around the island makes me wonder if there's running water or electricity. I could put in solar or backup power generators or even windmills. I've got a lot to discuss with the architects and designers. I didn't realize stress could be so much fun. My plan is coming together or at least in my mind.

While the secretary works on doing her part, I'll work on collecting information on beautiful girls around the world. Who knows, my island plan could become famous. This search engine is giving millions of pop-ups on my screen.

It's an eye-opener how many countries have beautiful girls and all of them unique. Geez, I may have to build floating rooms off the island to house them all. I'll prioritize from the poorest countries, as it's less likely anyone will be looking for the missing girls. I bookmark many web pages.

Okay, what else do I need? Yes, make a staff list. There's much more to this than I expected: cooks, waitresses, bartenders, maintenance, housekeeping, groundskeepers and front desk. Maybe it'll be too much for one person to organize. I'll need to hire someone to take care of all this prep-work. Also, I need to prevent my great idea from getting out. I need someone I can trust; too many spies of my friends out there.

I've been busy on the project the last few days when the intercom lights up.

"Sir, I've found companies to renovate the island. I've arranged interviews with all them, at the same time. It'll save time and the need to repeat yourself. They'll arrive in the morning."

"That's great news! I'm sure you left my calendar open."

 The next day her voice fills the office.

"Sir, the architects have arrived. I've put them in the conference room."

"Great. It gives us a large table to spread out drawings."

On the way to the room, there's a vendor pushing a cart with coffee, juice and snacks in the same direction. I allow him to enter first to drop the cart and get out. I have my arms full of the island's aerial maps, enough for each person, to help explain my ideas. I pass them around before opening one on the table.

I'll have them all take their copy with them to do a personal write-up and overlays. Each can do independent work and submit their best. I'm hoping to get some awesome designs to pick from.

"Men, first let me say, there are two phases of the project. One a temporary setup for competition fights and the other an island paradise resort." I give them time to take notes.

Taping my map to the whiteboard, I give a visual of my ideas and explain how luxurious I want it.

"There's already a functioning airstrip on the island. The landing strip will allow ease of bringing in materials," I say, pointing to it on the map.

"Sir, what we need to know is how the island is set up. Are there water, electricity and plumbing? How deep is the water off the island? Is it deep enough to allow yachts to dock? Or is the island only accessible by air?" one says.

"Is there working telecommunications? Is there an island close by we can tap into if needed?" another says.

"We need all these answers to complete cost estimates. But we can work on the designs in the meantime," another says.

"Fine, I get the point already. Get started working on my designs. I will take care of all these questions." What a pain in the ass these guys are—so demanding.

Walking past my secretary's desk after the meeting, I hand her the list of demands from the team.

"I need the answers to these questions. Get right on it."

A few days later, I'm kicking back in my office chair thinking what a day when the secretary strolls in.

"Sir, the airstrip is five thousand, four hundred feet long and sixty feet wide, which will allow for small to mid-size jets. But it won't allow large airliner passenger jets. Second, the island has everything on your list in place and working, including deep enough water for small yachts."

"That's great!"

"More good news. I'm receiving meeting requests from the designers. They want you to come to their offices. They say the model island designs they built are too big to move."

"That's fine, tell them I agree to meet at their offices. Set up appointments quickly." I want this now.

Attending each meeting, I'm presented with these miniature island paradise models, drawn to scale of the island with tiny buildings. They are all so lifelike, as if they shrunk the island. In the end, these models don't excite me enough but give me some good ideas.

I decide to do my own, using one of the groups to build it. I tell Island Custom Architect Inc. (who did the best model) I'll hire their team to build an Andrey custom model. It will be done out of my office, if they're interested. I plan to dedicate a large conference room for this project, which will allow me to work closely with them: ensuring I get even the smallest details flawless. After we agree, it's back to the office to start setting things up.

The team arrives the next day ready to start. I take them into my new war room; I had my secretary set up for this project. We begin working side-by-side, sharing ideas. After long hours and hard work, it's built in only two weeks. We complete two models, one design for the upcoming matches and one for the resort. I give the go-ahead to start on the first one right away. I'll give them a heads-up when to kick in with the second objective.

Thanking the design team for great work, I sign the contracts allowing the architects to move full ahead with construction.

"I want a double workforce. I want this project done quick."

"Yes, sir," the project manager says.

"If I catch any corner cutting, it will be your balls. This needs to be perfect . . . like me." I hope I'm getting my point across.

I stay business making money while waiting on the contract proposals, when I receive a call.

"Sir, stage one is days from completion. Please come over to inspect it."

Man, this is great. First part's done.

Getting on the intercom, I say, "I want the jet ready for a flight this evening to the island. I'll possibly be staying a couple of nights."

In the evening, I'm on the jet, leaving for blue skies.

Sammy

Israel's Secret Weapon
*** Chapter Twelve ***

Waking to the sunrise, I stare out the window, watching land approach, when a voice comes over the intercom.

"This is your captain speaking. Welcome to Israel, the land of milk and honey. We will be landing in Jerusalem in approximately twenty minutes."

I've never been to Israel but heard many stories over the years. My understanding of this a small country is surrounded by many larger countries, all wanting to wipe them off the face of the earth. Yet it continues to survive and protect its people. It's said that Israel is one of the most dangerous countries in the Middle East.

Rumors are they pay back in triplicate as an eye for many eyes; kill one they kill three or more in retaliation. Their survival depends on having the most deadly weapons and the most well-trained and fearsome commandos. These commandos are trained in an art called Krav Maga. Its purpose is to destroy: to destroy quickly, without mercy.

"Hey, are you an American?" an old man to my left asks.

"Yes, my name's Sammy."

"Mine's Joe, I'm also an American. I'm here on company business."

"This is my first time here."

"Well, Sammy, let me give you some advice. Be careful while here. Israel is under attack almost daily from its neighbors."

"Thanks, Joe. I've read about Israel and I don't know who's right or wrong and don't care. It isn't my business. I just want to pull together a team from here for a project, then get out alive."

"I don't blame you. Be careful." He goes back to reading a magazine.

Looking from the sky, Israel's breathtaking. I could spend a lifetime visiting all the wonderful places I've heard about. I feel the plane's wheels hit the ground, and this breaks my stare. Landing, I get through customs and rush to the hotel with excitement. I come through the hotel's door. Glancing around, it's beautiful. Checking in, I go straight to my room, make a hot cup of green tea and open my computer.

I begin researching local Krav Maga schools, military posts and any other places these elite fighters may be hiding. After building a list of training locations, I start calling them hoping to arrange visits and view some sparring if possible. Capoeira has its own uniqueness; I'm sure Krav Maga does, too. I'm more than ready to see it in action.

After spending the day on the phone, hoping to hit the lotto of great fighters, I decide to power down, relax and watch some TV. The TV's broadcasts are mostly in Hebrew. But like Brazil it does have a couple of English channels, which happen to be news. Rolling through channels, I find a romance movie in Hebrew with English subtitles, catching my mood. But I fall asleep halfway through.

Waking early I get ready for the day. Not wanting to wake Frank, I eat alone. Finishing, I hit the streets of Jerusalem. Yeah. This is awesome, an exciting new place, hearing people speak a language I've never heard. Some people may feel out of place, but I'm enjoying it. I guess this being the second country, I'm sure it will even get easier as I go.

100

Waving down a taxi, I hop in and give the address for the first place. The taxi stops in front of the school. Hopping out, I go in the building. The only man in the room approaches as I walk in the door.

"Hello, my name's Adam. You must be Sammy?"

"Hi, Adam, glad to meet you."

"I'm the senior instructor here. Please follow me."

Following, I glance around, noticing the layout is like Capoeira, but there are no musical instruments. I do notice in back there's training equipment like our dojo at home. It kind of gives me a sense of bonding with this art.

Adam takes me into the office, giving a rundown on the history of the art and his training layout. He's done around the same time a senior class is about to begin. He invites me to watch. We walk out to the main room. I notice there aren't any training mats at this place either. The instructor steps in front of the class.

"Class we have a special visitor named Sammy. He's searching for skilled fighters to enter an international competition. If anyone is interested, get with me before you leave."

While everyone stares at me, Adam says, "We're going to give him an exceptional demonstration this morning."

An expression of excitement comes over the students' faces.

"I want the senior students on the floor."

Fighters wearing street clothes and no protective gear move next to him.

"Sammy, this is real-life training for combat or street defense. We teach that a good offense is an excellent defense. With that in mind, let's begin." He looks at these seniors. "Run through our unique demo."

Students come out from a back room carrying foam benches, bus signs on poles, stop signs on poles and boards to simulate store fronts. They set up what looks like a mock street.

"This is to simulate real-world self-defense environments. When students train like this, they seem to take it more seriously," Adam says.

A girl sits on the bus bench reading a paper when a guy walks up, ripping the paper out of her hand and sticking a

101

(training) knife to her throat. He demands she follow him to his car. She reaches up, knocking the knife to the right while sliding to the left, standing. Slipping around behind him, she grabs the back of his hair and slams her knee—like a dozen times—between the legs. Simulating pain (or maybe it's real), he drops to the ground and she takes off running.

I continue watching these training exercises. Each one gets more brutal than the one before. One thing I learn is that everything is a weapon or a shield, including an attacker's partner.

"Man, this is great stuff." I try to remember as much as possible.

"If you like that, you'll love this. Okay, guys, pad up. It's time for our weapons demonstration. It covers disarming opponents—armed with knives and guns," Adam says.

Watching them go at it one-on-one and one-on-many tells me this training is dangerous, even wearing protective gear. Their combination moves while using the attacker's momentum against them are pretty awesome. It's thrilling watching these demonstrations; I would love to spend a year cross-training here. But I want to and will complete my dream.

Finishing, Adam offers me the floor. I step out, telling the students what I'm looking for and what is being offered. I then say, "If you guys want to do this and can pull together a team, with a leader who's willing to accept full responsibility, let me know. I'll have my partner contact you to make the arrangements." Leaving, I continue through the list of schools enabling me to see some great demonstration at each.

Next on the agenda is an attempt to enter a commando military post and persuade senior officers to let me speak with their elite soldiers. The taxi stops about a fourth of a mile from the gate.

"This is as close as I'm getting, fellow. If you're crazy enough to approach that gate, I hope you're wearing body armor. Tell ya what. It's a long way back to town; I'll give you a break and wait thirty minutes. But if you're not back by then, I will take it you're dead."

"Thanks, I'm nervous enough. I'll be back."

"If you don't mind paying before you go, sir? You know . . . just in case." He reaches his hand out, smiling.

"I'm going to do it. Here's your money and extra to wait." I pass him the money.

Climbing out, I walk up the dirt road, passing signs written in Hebrew. I guess they're warnings for guys like me. Getting about twenty feet from the gate, I stop to calm my nerves. Someone grabs me from behind, and I feel a knife cutting into my throat.

"Please! I'm an American and come to speak with your boss." I feel the back of my leg being kicked; I fall to my knees.

A soldier from the guard shack comes running. Getting to me, he grabs my nose and pinches off my airway. When I open my mouth to breathe, he puts the barrel of his pistol in it.

"You've got five seconds to explain yourself," he says, pulling the pistol out of my mouth.

"Please, I beg you to let me speak to the man in charge." I reach into my pocket.

The gunman pulls the hammer back on the pistol and says, "Slow and easy."

I hand him my papers and school checklist.

"You think we're stupid?" The guy with the gun grabs the papers.

"No. It's an elite martial arts competition. Check it out."

They speak in Hebrew for a few minutes then the gunman makes a call. Hanging up, they continue talking in Hebrew and looking at my papers. It seems like hours boiling in the hot sun until a jeep pulls up. The gunman salutes the jeep's passenger and hands him the papers. The knifeman keeps the blade to my throat.

"I'm Lieutenant Segal, security commander. Sergeant, bring him."

The one behind me with the knife grabs my hair, helping me up. They handcuff me behind my back, and I'm put in the back seat of the jeep. After a ten-minute ride through the desert, the jeep stops in front of a compound. The lieutenant escorts me towards buildings, past a field full of soldiers training with knives and guns. The moves look similar to Japanese Jujitsu.

We enter the back of a building and into an office. I come face-to-face with a general sitting behind a mahogany desk. I'm explaining my plan when the general says, "Stop. It isn't possible to allow my men to be involved in this type of activity. But I do know an ex-general who used to command elite forces before retiring. He now runs a private security force, hiring out to diplomats or wealthy executives who visit Israel." He hands me the retired general's contact info. "Lieutenant, promptly escort this man off my base."

I'm dumped back at the gate where I was found. I walk the dirt road, finding the taxi still waiting and hop in the back.

"Let's go."

"Glad you're still alive." He starts the car and we drive off.

On the way back I wonder how badass this ex-general and his team are, given that these elite forces protect the rich and diplomats. It's getting late, so I'll call him in the morning.

Back in the room, my curiosity gets to me. I do a Google search on this general to see if there's a military history or anything on his present security firm. I'm interested in learning as much as possible before meeting him. It's not every day I go into contract with someone like this: it's intimidating. My search comes back with nothing out of the norm.

Getting up in the morning, I meet Frank for breakfast then return to my room to make calls. I'm able to get a hold of the ex-general: Ori Lev.

"Sir, this is Sammy Nelson. I got your number— "

"I know who you are. The general called giving me a heads-up and a quick brief."

"Great. Can we meet?"

"How about coming by for lunch at noon. There's a small restaurant next to our building. We can eat before walking over to my office to discuss your needs. I give special clients a video presentation."

"Sounds good. I'll be there."

"Ask the restaurant doorman for Ori's table."

Arriving at noon to a small but luxury type restaurant, I walk up to the doorman.

"Ori's table please."

"This way, sir."

Getting to his table, I sit across from him. We chat about living in the U.S. while eating. Finishing, we head to his office. Ori hits the button for the top floor; on the ride up I notice cameras on the ceiling, guessing they are there to prevent any surprises. The elevator door opens, and I'm taken to a conference room, where there's a small group, looking deadly serious.

"Have a seat. I decided to present a high-security level briefing. Our standard meeting doesn't introduce our elite teams, but I'm making an exception for you. You'll be allowed to ask questions before leaving."

"Thank you."

"Please sign the non-disclosure agreement in front of you. The information you're about to see is highly classified."

I sign the forms and they start a video.

A suited man steps out of a hotel towards a limo; there's a sound of a gun. A man comes out of nowhere, knocking him to the ground and climbs on top of him, shielding him from any bullets shot in his direction. Two motorcycles race up and screech to a stop; the passengers jump off and rush towards the guy on the ground.

Four guys charge out of nowhere and attack the two guys now wielding knives and using martial arts. Within what must have been moments, it was over. I'm amazed at how their fighting skills are so unbelievable and awesome. They're quick at getting things under control. The bad guys are on the ground not moving, possibly knocked out or even dead.

Ori looks over at me. "These videos are only shown to selected clients. This action is real."

"I've seen this stuff on movies, but never thought it happens in the real world."

"This video happened to be taken by a bystander. Luckily one of the team members noticed the filming during the rescue and confiscated the tape. We paid the man for his inconvenience. I'm sure you understand the need to keep it for the safety of my team and our clients."

"I understand."

"The teams' training includes keeping a 360 watch around them while in action to prevent any surprises. This allowed them to notice the filming. Keeping a 360 is important as you never know if the bad guys are hiding in with the spectators."

"Never thought of that."

"We've completed the presentation," a team member says.

"Sammy, I went over the documents you provided. I like this competition. It'll give my team a little workout between jobs. I'd let my team fight for free, but these guys are expensive with their salary and perks. Sign us up. We'll be happy to take the prize money at the end."

Ori hands me the bio of each member, minus their names and any information that can be used to identify them, then opens the table for any questions.

"What other teams will be fighting, and what arts are they trained in?" one says.

"I'm not passing that information out to anyone, as it will give an unfair advantage. I want the element of surprise for all teams to allow for a better show. But what I will tell you is that the teams are from different countries. All will be elite fighters, the same as your team. My advice: it will be best not to underestimate the other teams."

Ori walks me to the elevator where we shake hands. I head down and back to my room.

I wake early and call Ori. "We have a deal. My partner Frank will call you to arrange everything."

"Great, I will be looking forward to meeting him."

Hanging up, I wonder if Frank not being a fighter, he realizes that there needs to be something in the contract excluding us of liability for any injury or death for this competition. It isn't a Ping-Pong tournament. I'll bring it up to him the next time we speak.

Getting back from breakfast, I start documenting all the information I have up to now. I haven't taken the time to finish Brazil's either. Kicking back the next couple of days, I finish documenting; it feels good getting it done.

106

Frank calls in the morning. "Sammy, I got the girls."

"That's great. I've got my team. Hey, do we have a liability clause in the contract?"

"It's covered, don't worry."

Meeting Frank downstairs for tea, I hand him the team's info to close the deal. A surprised look comes across his face.

"Really, Ori Lev?" Frank says and tells me his story. We both have a good laugh. "Take today and tomorrow off. I need to make the arrangements for the next trip."

"That sounds great, Frank."

Going back to my room, I take it easy until time to leave. The morning of the flight we both meet for breakfast, then turn in our room keys at the lobby desk. Stepping out the door, we hop in a cab and off to the airport. I look over at Frank and smile.

"Here we go, off to Thailand to find some Lerdrit fighters."

Frank

Behind The Metal Door
*** Chapter Thirteen ***

I slide the keycard into the door and step into a small room with ugly green carpet, a king-size bed and fifty-two-inch plasma when the phone rings.

"This is Andrey. I'm calling because I want your contacts' names and numbers for the girls in each country. If I want to add or replace girls on the island, I need that info in front of me."

"No problem. I'll email it."

Feeling my throat a bit dry, I leave the room and down the elevator to the hotel bar for a Bacardi and Coke. Entering the bar, it takes a few minutes for my eyes to adjust. The only lights are coming from the big screen TVs on every wall. Sitting on a dark brown wooden stool, I glance behind the bar, where hundreds of different kinds of alcohols stack the shelves.

"I'll take a Bacardi and Coke, please."

"Yes, sir."

Alone except for the bartender, I sip on my drink and watch football and news on the many screens, trying to decide. I pick football when the bartender tosses a basket of popcorn in front of me.

"Hey, bartender. I'm here on business. Maybe you can help and make a few dollars for your troubles?"

"Yeah, and how is that?" he says.

"My partner and I are putting on a martial arts show and need to hire help. My part is hiring five Israeli girls willing to travel internationally," I say, handing him a business card with my mobile number. "These positions are to help the fighters and promote the show."

"It's a marvelous idea. I'll keep an ear open and pass the word around. I do charity work in the community during holidays and know quite a few shelters. Give me a minute and I'll jot down a few you can visit." He hands me a list of local homeless shelters.

"Thanks . . . this will help."

Swallowing the last of my Bacardi and Coke, I drop a tip in the big glass jar at the end of the bar, walking out the door.

I wake lying in the middle of the bed feeling comfortable; I watch the sunrise through an opening in the curtains. Business cards and advertisement are a must if I'm to be taken seriously, and not as a rapist or pervert.

Leaving the business center with a pocketful of cards and handful of fliers, I climb into the first taxi of the three parked out in front of the hotel.

"Good morning, please take me to these shelters." I hand her my list, hoping to catch homeless girls during breakfast hours.

"I need to stop by a store and pick up a digital camera and a notepad."

"No problem, sir." A few minutes later, she pulls into a small outdoor mall and parks in front of a drug store.

"Here we are," she says.

Getting my needs, the taxi drives slowly down a small street. The window view goes from beauty to tent cities and graffiti as we drive deeper into the slums. I watch the female driver through the rearview mirror. She winds up her open window and starts biting her fingernails.

"No . . . No . . . No!" The screams from a woman come through the glass. Two young guys covered in body tattoos are punching this woman in a torn-up dress with dirt covering the rest of her body. The taxi driver speeds up. I'm surprised; one minute there's people standing by a Bentley chatting and the next people digging in garbage cans.

"Here you are." She stops in front of a shelter. "I'm not waiting. You're on your own. This place is too dangerous for me to stick around."

I'm not sure this is a good idea, but I'm here now, strolling the line of people that continues halfway down the street and around the corner. I hand out fliers to a couple of girls who catch my attention, but the rest are just too far out there. Most are scared, full of body sores, yellow eyes—maybe hepatitis—and full of tattoos.

"Sir, what you doing here . . . and with are those papers?" a young, cute girl yells.

"Looking to hire some girls for a project."

She and her friend are surprisingly clean, with no signs of living on the street long.

"Hire us?" They cheerfully step up to me.

"Here, fill out these, then I'll take your pictures." I hand them pens and forms. They sit on the grass between the sidewalk and the street filling them out.

"Mister, what's this you're doing?" an old woman says spitting out chewing tobacco.

She grins, half her teeth are missing and the others are black. Putting her arms around me, she tries to kiss my lips, I quickly push her away before the nasty deed.

"Just having these girls fill forms."

"I heard you, mister, it's for a job. You think I'm not good enough for your job?"

Her smile changes to a mean smirk. She pulls a small knife out of her pocket and jabs at me. I jump back, falling to the ground. Feeling pain, I look down seeing the front of my shirt ripped and bloody. I pull it open, finding a small cut.

With the sun in my eyes, I can hardly see her coming down at me with the knife; I begin saying my last prayers when a shadow comes over us. Behind the crazy girl, a massive man stands, wearing all black, to include his hat, with a long grey beard.

"Rina! What is the meaning of this? Hand me that knife."

Turning towards him, she stands rigid, handing it to him. "I'm sorry Rabbi, but he wouldn't give me a job." She drops her head staring at the sidewalk.

"Go get in the food line and don't cause anymore mischief."

She skips off like a child.

"Forgive her, sir." He turns and walks back into the temple.

"She's crazy, sir, but please don't take it out on us," the girl says, handing me the completed forms.

"It's okay, let's get pictures of the two of you." I take their pictures and pass them my card. "Call me tomorrow."

I finish the day off by visiting the rest of the shelters on the list. Sitting by the window in a small coffee shop, I drink hazel latte and organize my work. When this began Sammy had the cool job, but now I have the coolest job. Who wouldn't want a job waking each day to search for beautiful women?

When it gets dark, I flag down a taxi. Getting back to the room, I call the bar and have a glass of Bacardi & Coke delivered, then hit the power button on the computer. I connect the USB cable between the camera and computer then create a folder called Israel; for each candidate I create subfolders. I copy the photos for each girl into their own folder. "Damn." I forgot to take photos in Brazil. I call my little buddy Mike and have him email the girls' photos.

I call taxi companies to get a lift back there. They all refuse to take me to the slums after dark. I end up calling a private chauffeur company that specializes in bodyguard services. I arrange for a driver who's a bodyguard so when I go back tonight I will be protected.

I step out of the hotel to find, a black 750 series BMW with tinted windows parked with the rear door open. A tall, well-built man stands next to the open door wearing a black three-piece suit.

"Mr. Capper?" he asks, speaking in a deep voice.

"Yes, sir," I say, stepping up to the car.

"I've been sent to escort you this evening." He glances at the open door. "Please."

Pulling out of the hotel parking lot, I say, "Good evening, my name's Frank. Just to let you know, I hired you because I'm visiting places in a shady part of town, and I'm scared of getting hurt."

"Don't worry, sir. I'm trained to protect clients in all environments including terrorist areas. I've always kept them safe."

Staring out the window, I'm comfortable knowing I have an armed bodyguard behind the wheel. If this was a taxi, I'm sure the driver would run off without me if something bad happen. We enter dark, narrow streets. I call women's shelters on my list and speak to senior staff members, confirming my request for thirty-minute group meetings with the girls.

Stopping in front of the first shelter the driver gets out and opens my door. There are three girls standing out in front smoking, one says, "Hi." Another opens the building door for me. Looking back I see the driver get in the car and open his window. Knowing he's listening, I turn towards the entrance feeling safe.

Stepping inside, I approach a grey-haired woman covered in costume jewelry seated behind a desk. "Sir, may I help you?" Her big round glasses slide down her short nose.

"I have an appointment."

"Sir, your ID please?"

Reaching into my front pocket I pull out and hand her the passport. Watching her computer monitor, she taps on the keys. While waiting, I look around, glimpsing security cameras along the ceiling and doors. There's a small one-way mirrored window on a steel door between two men in guard uniforms.

She hands back my passport. "Thank you, sir." She hits a button. "Mr. Frank Capper has arrived for his meeting."

The metal door opens and a tall, slender woman dressed in name brand clothes walks out. "Hello, Mr. Capper. I'm May. Sorry for the trouble, but we need to protect our guests from crazy boyfriends and ex-spouses. Unfortunately they're always trying to get at the guests and it happens more often than you would think."

"I completely understand."

I hear a beep before the old lady says, "Johnny, open up." When the door opens, May takes my hand and leads me in. It's an old basketball court with the baskets and bleachers still in place. Cots filled with women and children are spread out across the wooden floor. Boxes, suitcases and garbage bags full of things surround them.

Walking in, the place goes quiet except for a couple babies crying. All eyes in the room are now staring at me. Stepping up to the podium, their attention stays on me. Nervously, I give an ad hoc speech on opportunities I have to offer.

"Does anyone have questions?"

I scan the room for sexy, young girls waiting for someone to speak up. When no one responds, I set fliers and cards on a table next to the podium.

"Anyone interested, please take one of these and call me tomorrow to set up an interview."

May and I walk to the door, and she opens it to let me out. The next thing I know I'm looking up at the ceiling. I realize I'm on the floor with May lying next to me. Sitting up I feel a hard object poke me in the back of the head.

"You move you're dead," a voice comes from behind.

Scared, I peek over my shoulder finding a crazed face staring down at me with a gun now to my ear. He reaches, putting an arm around my neck.

"Stand slowly, no funny stuff." He keeps an arm around my neck and gun to my head while I slowly stand.

"Becky . . . Becky, I know you're here. Come now with Billy and Suzy or I'm going to shoot this man. Now . . . I said!" My head's jerking around in his shaking hand. "No one else moves. I swear . . . I'll kill him."

Hearing a loud pop, a splash of wetness hits the right side of my face. I too terrified to move, when the arm around my neck lets go and a thump comes from behind.

"It's okay, Frank." It's the voice of my bodyguard.

I force my head to look right, he's standing at the door with a scope-mounted pistol pointing behind me.

I hear a woman screaming and children crying as I step forward then turn around to look. A kid about nineteen wearing a business suit lies with blood gushing out the side of his head.

"Bill," screams a young girl running up.

114

She drops to the floor putting his head in her lap crying. A boy and girl no more than three years old run up. Falling to their knees, they hit him.

"Daddy, please, please, wake up." Blood is smeared across their faces from kissing their dad.

The bodyguard hands me a handkerchief to wipe the blood off my face and puts an arm around me, nudging me towards the door. Leaving the front receptionist is lying on her keyboard, bleeding from the hole in her head. We step over the dead bodies of the guards and walk out the door.

Coming out the front door, the bodyguard opens the car's rear door, setting me in. He hops in the front seat, and we speed off.

"I've had enough for one night, please take me—"

"I understand, sir," he says, looking in his rearview mirror. "I'll drop you off, then come back to take care of this mess."

Climbing out of the car back at the hotel, I shake his hand. "Thank you for saving my life tonight." I slip him a generous tip before heading to the hotel bar.

Many calls come in over the next few days from the girls at the shelter; I arrange a group meeting at a fast food restaurant near them. Scared to go back alone, I call the security firm asking for the same driver. Getting to the restaurant, I buy meals for the girls before a quick briefing to separate the ones I like from the group. Once photos and data sheets are completed. I explained I'd notify those picked within the next twenty-four hours.

Back in my room, I pick through the data sheets and photos to find the awesome ones and take care of getting the boarding house. I have the girls I've chosen picked up by taxi and brought there.

In the morning, I call Sammy. "Morning, got my girls and ready to go."

"That's great, I'm done too. Let's meet for breakfast."

During breakfast, Sammy hands me his team's info so I can make the arrangements. Looking it over, I'm stunned.

"I can't believe this. Your team is from the same firm I hired my driver from." We both laugh.

I never told him what happened.

"Sammy, take tomorrow off. I need to arrange for the next country."

The day of the flight, we meet for breakfast, then turn in our room keys and head out to catch a cab.

"Thailand, here we come, in search of Lerdrit fighters," Sammy says.

Andrey

Inspecting My Pride And Joy
*** Chapter Fourteen ***

Waking on my jet at thirty-five thousand feet, I hit the intercom. "Prepare my bath and have breakfast ready; I'm getting up." Within minutes, my personal flight attendant steps into the room.

"Sir, your tub's ready at your instructed seventy-five degrees."

Naked, I follow her to the Jacuzzi, climbing in. Dropping her robe, she slips in, sitting behind me. I wonder if my staff can read my mind, for the most part, they know what to do without being told, but that would be a bit scary. The secrets I hide could put me away for a hundred lifetimes, or more. What a horrible thought!

Relaxing in the warm water, I feel her smooth hands caress my neck and back. Enjoying my spoils, I watch international news on the flat-screen TV built into the wall.

"Sir, please stand and turn so I can finish."

Standing, I turn to find her with a lustful smile. She reaches up, taking hold of my rod, licks her lips then slides it in, bobbing on it; her tongue massages the bottom. Ah, her tonsils are tickling the top; I can't hold it. Grabbing the back of her head, I shove it all the way: her eyes pop wide open when my stream shoots.

"Here's a little treat for being sure a good girl." I give her the full load down her throat.

I love this feeling in the morning, it puts me in a good mood all day.

When I release her head, she coughs. "Sir, thank you for the treat."

I can only imagine how many married men wish they had this kind of power over their spouse.

I'm shaving when the attendant comes over the speaker. "Sir, your meal is ready." Grabbing my red silk robe, I decide to eat before dressing. While eating, my curiosity gets my mind wondering what the island will look like after the changes.

"We will be landing in twenty minutes," the pilot says.

I down the last bits of toast followed by the coffee before going to dress. Coming back to the main cabin, I take a seat and watch the jet soar over the island. Picking up the high-powered camera off the table, I zoom in on the island and snap pictures. I brought the camera to build an aerial map; I'm able to get a few good angles before landing.

Walking from the main cabin, I open the door and glance into the cockpit.

"Hey, I'll have someone escort you and the crew to sleeping area shortly."

"Thank you, sir," comes from the cockpit.

I step to the door and down the ladder, a group of people are at the bottom. One says, "Good morning, Mr. Baskov. I'm Mr. Abdella." He reaches out to shake my hand.

"You're the guy I hired to watch over the construction." I ignore his hand and continue, "and my eyes to ensure everything is done according to my demands?"

"Yes sir. Everything is completed to the letter."

"That's good, you're paid well to make sure this is done. I can feel comfortable knowing you're using top workmanship and the highest quality in materials. Correct? Considering I'm told you're the best in the world, and for your price, you best be."

118

"Mr. Baskov, you're getting more than your money's worth." A resentful expression crosses his face.

"Shall you escort me on a grand tour?" I wait for his movement.

"Please, this way."

Walking on a red brick path to the right, we pass through Palm Trees, entering an opening where the event's action will be held: the fighting cage.

"Sir, we sat the cage on the beach in back of the island to prevent uproar during the fights from disturbing guests not watching the events."

"Good. Oh, I've decided to keep this permanent. I'm coming to find out this fighting thing is popular, so don't pull the cage or spectator stands. I will find another place for the tennis court."

We continue to the temporary dining facility and sleeping quarters for the guests, then to the servants' quarters. Finishing my tour, we head back to the dining area where aerial maps of the island are laid out on a table. They've been marked up with what's completed so far and the other with what still needs to be done. Viewing these, I'm impressed with his accomplishments.

A cute young girl brings a pitcher and two glasses. "Please have a glass of cold tea." Placing the tray on the table, she looks deep into my eyes before leaving.

"I've hired ten workers from a nearby island to assist in the feeding and bedding of the construction workers and others staying here during the prep work."

"That is a good idea." Watching the backside of the girl walking away, I whisper, "I just may have other plans for these sweeties."

"Sir?"

"Nothing, just mumbling to myself." I need to be careful not to think out loud.

"Mr. Abdella, let's do another stroll. It helps me to think."

We begin walking and discussing the layout, making short stops to mark up the drawings. We spend the rest of the day searching and identifying all the unknown areas. Darkness covers the island when I call it a day, releasing him. I go to my room.

I'm working on the computer when a soft knock hits the door. Opening it, I find a young girl standing there, the one who brought the cold tea to the dining area. She's holding a bottle of wine and wearing a thin, light blue nightgown. I'm sure she was ordered to come. I'm not sure who sent her and really don't care, well maybe a little curious? But I'm not turning this gift away.

"Mr. Baskov, I'm Yoshe. I've come to make sure you're comfortable. Comfortable in any way that pleases you." Stepping in the door, she sets the wine on the table next to the bed.

"Did Mr. Abdella send you?"

"No, he's not aware of this. It's the woman in charge of customer relations who did."

She steps to the other side of the room to the Jacuzzi. Bending over, she turns the water on when her nightgown moves between her crack.

"Sir, please?"

Dropping my clothes in place, I walk over and climb into the warm water. Relaxing, I watch her lay out massage oils and silk sheets on the bed, spending the next fifteen minutes organizing her things. Without saying a word, she gives me a look of—I'm ready. Walking over to me as I stand, she dries me with a soft Egyptian cotton towel. Moving to the bed, I lie on my stomach in the center. She disrobes, climbing on my back; the oils feel great as she takes the next thirty minutes to cover my body. Done, I turn over.

"My dear, I have better plans for us. Call me—master."

Time to experiment. If this works for me, I can offer it as a luxury room option to my visitors, male or female. I roll her onto her belly and start giving her sexy bubble butt smacks watching them turn red; she doesn't resist.

"Master, I want to please you." She's letting out low groans.

I've always been kinky, which scares off most girls. I'm going to see how far I can take this before she resists, then until I'm satisfied. Damn, I don't have my box full of sadism and masochism toys, but I'm sure there are things in here I can use, laughing.

"My slave, we're about to find out just how much you want to please me."

I rip the pillowcases to use as bondage ropes before flipping her on her back and grabbing her wrists.

Fear crosses her face. "No. Please . . . don't hurt me." She's pulling her arms, trying to get free from my grip.

"Stay still!" I command, squeezing tighter.

Holding her wrists with one hand and binding them with the other, I get her wrists tied to the top bedposts. Tears come to her eyes. I tie her feet up next to each hand. Only her head and upper back are touching the bed. Last I gag her mouth; I don't need anyone bursting into the room, ruining my fun.

"So, you want to please the master?" Grabbing my computer, I search S&M websites, finding many interesting things to try.

Searching the bathroom, I find lotion to use as a lubricant; coming out with it, I see more fear than I have ever seen in other girls I've been with. I remove the cap off the lube and open her rear cheeks then fill her forbidden hole. Her eyes open wide as I watch her bite down on her mouth gag.

"Let's begin." Damn, I love seeing girls like this.

Deep into the night until early morning, I jump from one S&M website to the next, trying all the ones without toys.

By morning, Yoshe lies untied with her arms wrapped around me, covering my chest with passionate kisses. I've either broken her spirit, or she found the true desire missing in her life.

"Yoshe, you have done well. I am on the ultimate high. The power to bring pleasure or pain at will is the ultimate feeling. I believe it's one and the same."

Eating breakfast, thinking of last night, bondage may be the edge I need to pamper rich guests; it will attract the very wealthy. They will come and come again spending obscene amounts of money. It will be a secret society for the rich, equal to none. I would pay obscene money for that type of experience. That's it!

The island's specialty will be extreme sex with beautiful girls from around the world. I will advertise.

"Come and fulfill your fantasies. Anything goes next to death," I'll say. I snicker thinking, maybe some exceptions. "What happens on Andrey's Paradise Island stays on the Island."

I need a plan to keep Frank's girls here after the grand opening without his knowledge. Having girls from Frank's five and the locals here gives me six different countries, which is a good start. I'll have to think this over a bit.

I have an excellent plan; I just have to fine-tune the details. I finish my meal, just as Mr. Abdella walks up.

"Hey, I've got a question for you, why haven't you shown me the office? I would think there's one in the design."

"It will be done soon. I feel it is a low priority compared to the rest."

"That's fine, just make sure it's luxurious. I may need to conduct meetings there in the future."

"You ready to go, sir?"

Continuing where we left off the day before, we review what items are completed and discuss what needs to be done and how. Everything's coming together; I'll take a break.

Calling my secretary: "Arrange an afternoon boat ride, I want to check out some of the local islands."

"Will get right on it, sir."

I'm told the closest island is over an hour away by boat. It's nice to know if a bomb exploded here, no one would hear it. I need this isolation for my plan. My secretary calls to tell me the boat's ready. I head to the dock. The captain takes me to the nearest island.

I'm enjoying the fresh air; the smell of the sea and the sea's animals coming to the surface helps time pass.

Arriving, I find this island is small and isolated too. It seems be primitive; walking about, I notice there's no electricity, plumbing, running water or anything else as my island once was.

"Captain, it must be tough living like this?"

"If you're born and raised here, it feels natural. They never experience anything else, except your island."

"I suppose. I was raised in difficult times, but not this bad."

"The girls working for you are from here."

"Really?"

"They're being spoiled with the simple luxuries they have at your place: they feel blessed."

What luxury? It's like camping out, but then, comparing this to mine, I understand. Maybe the willingness from the girl who visited my room could have been due to hopes for a better life, even though the submissiveness brought her pleasure in the end.

Spending the afternoon walking the island and meeting locals, who all seem to know my name, is entertaining. I share my need for young females willing to work and live on Paradise Island. When the sun sets, I tell the captain, let's go. I don't want this guy getting lost in the dark.

Returning, I'm hungry. I sit at the dining table when a girl brings a hot plate full of shrimp and steak. Eating dinner with the construction workers and help, I'm amused at their simple conversations. I don't have any desire to chat with people far beneath my intelligence, but it makes them feel important speaking to the owner.

Letting the underprivileged rattle, I notice an old woman walking around talking to the girls. She seems to be giving orders, but I don't understand the language. I stand and walk over to her.

"Are you one of the managers?"

"I'm Tomoko, presently the one and only. How can I help you?"

"Thanks for the gift last night."

"You're welcome, boss." Her eyes smile. "If you plan to stay another night, she can return, or maybe you desire another?"

"The girl last night accommodated my needs. But what I would enjoy is a second girl of the same age and beauty to join her."

"I can arrange for two. I'll have them arrive after dark."

"I'm sure you're aware my evening activities need to be kept low-key?

"Oh, but of course," she says.

"The problem is, I can't have them going back to their island talking of what happens here."

"Sir, I see no reason for them to go back. I can keep them here for the rest of their lives; you're giving them a better life?" She looks at me for approval.

"I like your way of thinking."

"Thank you, I'm happy you're pleased."

"Your willingness to do anything I want or need puts you in a position for a permanent job here as their manager, and of course you'll be moved to better quarters. One last thing: put Yoshe aside as my personal slave."

"I will be happy living here and being loyal to you for the rest of my life; I have nowhere else to go, boss."

"I am staying another night. But I'm too tired for fun, plus I need sex toys for next time. If you know what I mean?"

"Of course." She gives a wicked grin.

"Make sure any of the girls willing to submit their bodies to please men or women with no limits are moved to special rooms as an incentive."

"I'll have that arranged before you leave." Leaving her with that thought, I mosey back to my room.

In the morning, Mr. Abdella joins me for breakfast to discuss different topics and last minute ideas.

"Mr. Abdella, I have promoted Tomoko to permanent manager of the girls. She and the others picked as top girls will be assigned special rooms until I return."

"Whatever you say, sir."

"Second, I've been thinking and decided on having a wine cellar, as most of the guests of my class drink wine."

"Sir, being this is an island with water underneath, I'll have to check if it is even possible."

"Well then, find out, got it?"

"I'll get some designers out in the next couple of days. If it is possible, I'll get it done."

"Quit sniveling and make it happen, geez." Why do I pay these guys to snivel?

"One of these days," he says, staring at me with hate in his eyes.

"What's that?"

"One of these days I'm going to make you happy, boss." I like that response, but I know what he meant.

"Make it as big as possible, I want to use it as a multi-purpose room for wine, storage and other things."

"No problem. If it can be done, I will have it completed by the time you get back."

124

"Sounds good. I need to get going." Grabbing my bag, I hop on the jet and we're off. Switching on jazz, I kick back in the main cabin falling asleep.

Sammy

All The King's Men
*** Chapter Fifteen ***

Chatting to Frank during our hour or so ride to Bangkok keeps my mind busy while watching out the windows. Entering the city the streets are full of motorcycles and bicycles converted into cabs. After checking in, we decide to spend the day sightseeing before splitting up to work on our projects.

"Frank, I'm going to drop my stuff in the room. I'll meet you back here in thirty." The hot girl behind the desk hands me the room card.

Throwing my things on the bed, I open the curtains to let the light in, then the window and pop my head out. Wow, being on the 15th floor gives an awesome view of the city; this is going to be exciting. Leaving my things laying on the bed, I take a two-second shower and quickly dress. Grabbing my phone, I'm out the door. Spotting Frank sitting in the lobby, he's bug-eyed staring at the girls coming and going out the main entrance.

"Hey Frank, when you get your eyes put back in your head, I'm ready to go."

"Huh, what was that you said?"

"Okay, let's go."

We step into the sunshine. There's all kinds of things going on, so I figure why take a taxi when walking can be more fun. I love the taste of Thai food.

"Hey, Frank, you ever eaten Thai food?"

"No, but it sounds good to me, let's go."

Looking around, there are all kinds of Thai restaurants, but American too, like McDonald's, Pizza Hut, House of Pancakes, Kentucky Fried Chicken and vendors filling the streets selling food and everything else.

Seeing a little restaurant with only a few people, we drop in. The menus have plenty of pictures helping in our choice. I focus on the seafood dishes. Ordering a spicy seafood Platter, Frank does the same except requesting it mild.

"Thai tea?" the waitress says.

"Never had it, but willing to give it a try," I say.

"Me too," Frank says.

Waiting for our meals, I say, "I'm somewhat familiar with this country and an art called Muay Thai. It's a sports fighting art that I want to see at the Grand Stadium before leaving Thailand. I've trained in Muay Thai and used its different strikes in competition fights. In fact, it helped me win the World Championship Fight before I retired."

"That's great. I've never had a fight in my life."

"For years I've wanted to come here to see these the professional fights." Responding to Frank, I said, "You should come along. I'm sure you will love it."

"Let me know when you're going. If I'm free, I will be happy to join you for this event."

"That'll be great, I know you'll surely enjoy it. Thanks."

When the food arrives, I change topics, explaining Muay Boran. "Muay Boran is the mother of Muay Thai and other Thai arts; it's the art used by the ancient warriors and still used today for self-defense and the military. Although Muay Boran is a

128

great art, I picked an art called Muay Lerdrit. This art has many awesome strikes and can be very deadly."

"Wow! Fascinating, I have never heard of all these martial arts. It's like a secret world. You're lucky," Frank says.

Finishing our meals, we're on the street walking about town. I say, "Look at all these statues."

"Yah, I have been noticing lots of men and women wearing these colorful dresses with shaved heads."

"Me too, I'm getting thirsty. Let's stop for a drink?"

Seeing a restaurant with outdoor benches, we sit and order drinks, escaping the sun. An old man sitting at the next table begins chatting with us.

"Sir, what is the deal with all the statues and these men and women in the beautiful dresses with shaved heads?" I say.

"These people and statues are to be well-respected. The people you speak of are Buddhist monks, and the statues are of Buddha. Many of our people follow the teaching of Buddha. You and your friend should visit the many Buddhist temples in our country; I am sure it will bring you both much pleasure," he says.

"I'm sure we will," I say.

"While there, be very respectful as these places are held in high regard, and it would not be wise to offend them," he says.

"Sir, I wouldn't think of offending anyone, especially them. We will be extremely careful in what we say or do." Finishing our drinks, I say, "Thank you for sharing with us."

Frank and I get up, continuing our walk. Approaching a huge Buddhist Temple, it is unbelievably beautiful; with all the carvings and small detail, it must have taken a long time to build. A monk sees us and walks up.

"You're interested? This temple is eight hundred years old. Would you both like to see the inside?" Frank and I agree and follow him. He says, "Please remove your shoes before entering."

On our tour, we see more beauty inside. This place is spotless. Coming upon people praying, we keep quiet, passing them. Many of the monks are everywhere, busy mopping floors, cleaning windows and on ladders polishing. I guess that's why this place is so clean. Completing the tour, we're escorted outside. Feeling grateful, I give a donation to the monk before walking off.

We continue sightseeing until dark, and then wave down a couple of bicycle taxis asking for a ride back to the hotel. Arriving, Frank and I say good night and go to our rooms. It has been a long day with longer ones coming up. Stepping into my room worn out, I lie down and head off to dreamland. My dreams are full of Thai fighting and arts I can't wait to see.

Waking refreshed from an awesome dream, I'm eager to get going, starting off in search of Muay Thai camps, Muay Boran camps, and other places that may lead to Lerdrit fighters. I wonder if going to the palace, I'll be allowed access to the king's bodyguards? I'd better check if it's cool first; I don't have a desire to get locked up in some dark dungeon at the bottom.

I'll focus on the Muay Thai first, and might get lucky and end up with leads for Lerdrit camps. I need to get advice on the ins and outs around here to keep out of trouble.

I google and create my list of places to visit. I respect Muay Thai fighters, as they are badass. I've trained in the art while being a fighter, so I'm one to know. There's a big difference between sports and street fighting, but I still want to check them out.

Excited, I'm on a roll getting invitations from many of the camps I'm calling. Most places say the training is informal with the ring and equipment outside. I know all too well how hard the training is in the U.S. and can only imagine how it is here. When I first started Thai training years ago, I recall many nights with the Kru who trained me, having me kick a rock-hard, four-foot-long bag hundreds of times. I'd go home with my shins swollen and bleeding, and I had flashbacks of yelling for mom to come help me climb the stairs to the apartment.

Finishing the calls, I get dressed and off to catch a taxi to the first camp. Standing on the street corner next to the hotel, I wave down a motorcycle taxi. I hop on back and show the driver the address, then we're off. About twenty minutes later, he swerves to the side of the road and stops. Jumping off, I pay him and walk up to the camp.

A well-built guy with grey hair meets me at the door. Putting his hands together as if praying he says, "Sawadee Kap," while bowing. "I'm the one you spoke with on the phone. I'm the lead trainer. You can call me Kru. Please follow me."

Escorted to the back everyone in the camp is wearing boxing shorts with some wearing sleeveless shirts, and others shirtless. There's two rings set up with a canvas over the top. This makes sense as it does rain a lot in Thailand, and these guys train everyday year round in hopes of someday fighting in one of the two Grand Stadiums.

He takes me over to a ring where two boys about eight years old are going full contact. A trainer stands outside the ropes yelling pointers to them. These kids are fighting like pros. Watching, one kid jumps up, kicking the other in the side of the head knocking him down, as blood begins dripping from his mouth.

"Get up. The round isn't over," the trainer says.

The kid jumps back up exchanging kicks, punches, knees and elbows with the other.

"Wild! I bet these kids can kick my ass." I laugh.

After watching a couple more rounds, I'm taken to watch adult sparring matches. Checking out the training equipment, I notice the bamboo being used by students to kick with their legs.

"What's up with that?"

"It is used to harden the fighter's shins."

"Man—that's got to be painful."

"Only until the skin hardens, and the nerves die: care to try?"

"I think I'll pass; thank you very much! Kru, I'm interested in checking out Muay Boran and Muay Lerdrit camps, is there any way to chat with the Royal Guards or the Royal Family's security teams?"

"I advise you to stay away from any government places. If they take your intentions wrong, you could end up in big trouble."

"Yeah, I understand."

"Follow me."

After I follow him into the building, he prepares and gives me a list of contacts for Muay Boran Instructors. He also writes his info.

"Here, you can use me as a reference."

"Thanks, I'm grateful," I say.

Getting outside, I catch a taxi and continue visiting one place after another until the list is done, then head back to the hotel. Arriving, I pay and climb out.

"Let me go, you bastard," a female screams by the trees across the parking lot.

Running to the sound of the screams, I see two guys are trying to force a young girl into a limo. Seeing me, one guy punches the girl and shoves her into the back of the car. Both guys come at me. I punch the first guy in the throat; he drops to his knees grabbing his neck and gagging. The second man pulls a small bat out of the front seat and strikes at my head. I duck to avoid getting hit, then reach up, grabbing the back of his head and slamming it into the side passenger window. Unconscious, he falls to the ground.

Stepping to the rear door the girl jumps out and hugs me, saying, "Oh, thank you, sir, you saved my life. Those two guys are Mafia and were trying to kidnap me. I have to go, thanks again." She runs off.

I walk back to the hotel going to my room disappointed I couldn't find Muay Lerdrit or anyone who could help me. Calling room service I order a double chicken salad and iced green tea. Hoping to beat my salad delivery, I jump into to the shower, finishing just as a knock comes on the door. I throw on a bathrobe before opening it and getting my food.

While I eat and watching TV, the news comes on with an image of the palace in the background. Damn, I've got to try. I'm going to find a way to get inside the palace and speak with the bodyguards.

Waking early, I get dressed in all black, determined to sneak in. I have the taxi drop me off a few blocks away in front of a

132

McDonald's. Sitting in McDonald's eating a fish sandwich, I'm shaking. I know I should just get back in a taxi but can't force myself. Damn it, I've got to do it. Finishing, I throw my trash away and walk out the door towards the palace.

I blend in with a group of tourists standing in front listening to the escort talking. He's saying the king doesn't live here anymore but does visit. Disappointed, I might as well check it out. Getting inside, walking around, a group of plain-clothes men yell that we have to leave and push everyone out the door. Trying to hide I'm knocked off balance by the rush and fall backward into a small opening in the wall hitting my head, feeling dizzy.

Opening my eyes, it's dark and no one is around. Stepping out, I walk down the corridor, finding myself surrounded by four guys in commando uniforms. They push me down three flights of stairs. We enter a cold, dark, concrete room. I'm chained to the wall. The men leave, locking the door. Two of the men return with another man. They're carrying a battery and two cables with alligator clips.

"We will only ask politely once. If I have to ask a second time, it will be with the help of this battery," the new guy says.

"What . . . what? I'll tell you anything. Just ask."

"Why are you hiding in the palace? Did you know the king would be staying here tonight?"

"I don't know anything. I was knocked out, honest."

The two men standing in back grab the battery and sit it on the table next to me. Ripping open my shirt they connect to cables to the battery and clamp the other side to my nipples.

"Aaaah, my God; please take them off."

"We haven't given you the juice yet." He shows me a device with a knob connected to cables between me and the battery.

The electricity shooting through me hurts so badly. I watch him turn the knob. Feeling extreme pain, I cry out loud.

"Brother stop this now, please." Opening my eyes, I see it's the girl I saved.

The guy calling the shots says, "Turn it off."

Running to her brother, she says, "Khemkhaeng, this is the man who saved me. Remember I told you?" She pulls on his arm with a pleading expression on her face.

"Pull off the nipple clamps and bring him down," he says.

"I'm so sorry." She runs up and hugs me.

"You're a lucky man that my sister showed up to get me."

He and his sister help me to a conference room upstairs where I explain what happened. He tells me he is the captain of the King's bodyguards, and will kill, without thought, to protect the King.

Finding out who he is I introduce myself, and explain why I was there. I ask if he and others on his team want to be part of it. He agrees but wants his team to meet me, so we exchange contact info. He escorts me to the front gate.

"Sammy, in the future, don't do something stupid like this again: promise?" He gives me a look like I'm a total idiot.

"Promise," I say.

Turning, I wave down a taxi and go back to the room. I call down to have a salad delivered; after eating, I fall asleep working on documenting my notes.

My sleepy eyes open to a new day, my nipples are still sore. I get ready for breakfast when I find a message waiting.

"Hey, this is Frank, can't make it for breakfast. Got too many things going on this morning. Catch you later, and have a fun day."

"Hmm! What a surprise, guess I'll be eating alone."

Returning from the restaurant, I start digging into the best fight dates at the Muay Thai arenas. I find there are two popular arenas that every Thai boxer dreams of fighting. Their dreams start while training from a boy up through the years, until becoming a pro fighter.

Lumpinee Boxing Stadium's Muay Thai contests are held on every Tuesday, Friday and Saturday. The fights usually start around six o'clock. Ticket prices range from two hundred to two thousand baht.

Rajadamnern Boxing Stadium's Muay Thai contests are held on every Monday, Wednesday, Thursday and Sunday. The fights usually start around six-thirty. Ticket prices range from five hundred (third class) to two thousand (ring-side)

134

Now I'm getting excited and don't care whichever I attend, as long as I'm able to get two tickets. The one thing good about this is that fights are nightly switching between stadiums. If I'm lucky, I can get tickets dated before Frank gets our airline tickets.

Dressed, I'm out the door in no time, heading to catch a taxi. From the back seat, I check the calendar on my watch. Noticing it's Tuesday, I say,

"Please, take me to Lumpinee boxing stadium." I hand the address over his shoulder.

He laughs. "What's this? Everyone knows how to get to Lumpinee boxing stadium."

"I didn't know the stadium's that popular."

"Anything Muay Thai is popular in this country."

Hitting the gas, the driver speeds off. Arriving at the stadium's ticket office, I'm told ringside is sold out, but there's a couple in the very back.

"I'll pass. If this is going to be a one-time deal, I want it up front and personal."

Returning to the taxi, I say, "What a bummer!" The driver takes me to Lumpinee boxing stadium. Getting to the ticket counter, I say, "I'd like to get two ringside seats, please."

"Sorry, sir! All the seats except in the far back have been sold. It's best to come buy tickets a few weeks out."

"I don't have two weeks. Sorry, didn't mean to yell." I walk back to the taxi frustrated.

The driver looks in the mirror at me. "Hey, what's with the long face?"

"I tried to get two side-by-side ringside tickets for either today or tomorrow as I'm leaving Thailand, and I'm told they're sold out. My once-in-a-lifetime chance is gone."

"Actually, I know people for the right money can get anything in Bangkok. Let me call one of my scalper buddies and see if I can help out, for a small fee that is." He is laughing as he picks up his cell phone.

"I'm on a tight budget, but if I can afford it, we have a deal."

The driver starts making calls, about a dozen later he says, "He wants two front row side-by-side." Turning back at me, he smiles. "The tickets you want are five thousand baht, plus my finder's fee of ten thousand; is it a deal?"

"Argh, makes it about three hundred fifty US. Okay, you got a deal."

He turns back around. "Lock the tickets in for me. I'll drop by and pick them up within the hour."

He takes me to pick up the tickets then to the hotel. "I want to thank you. You made me the happiest guy alive."

I pay the fare plus tip and walk into the hotel. "I'm on top of the world," I say, holding my tickets.

Khemkhaeng calls to meet. A few hours later, I'm sitting in the hotel restaurant with the team.

"I'm Khemkhaeng Boonliang, but you can call me Kevin. Being the captain, I'll also be the team-lead."

Finishing the meeting, I tell Kevin I'll let him know the date soon, and my partner Frank, who handles the finances, will meet with him to arrange the expenses.

"Guys, thanks for joining and train hard. You'll be going against some highly skilled fighters, so don't underestimate them."

I call Frank but get voicemail; I decide to leave a message.

"I got my team. Please meet up with Kevin as soon as possible. I put the info under your door. Oh, by the way, I got the tickets." He's chasing girls, I'm sure. I laugh.

When I turn on the TV, a news channel pops up with English subtitles. It's police roping off an area in Patpong. Shit, this is where Frank's been hanging out.

Reading the subtitles, it's about multiple homicides. "Damn! What if—"

Frank

Red Lights Of Patpong
*** Chapter Sixteen ***

"This restaurant is a great pick. My seafood dish is delicious," I say.

"Yap, I love Thai food, I eat it all the time in the states. Oh, speaking of Thai, how about going to a Muay Thai fighting competition with me?"

"I don't know anything about martial arts and violence scares me." The frown on Sammy's face gets the best of me. "Okay! If it will make you happy, and if we have the time." It does sound exciting.

I walk into my room finding the mess picked up, the bed's made and a couple of chocolate Kisses are lying on the bed's pillow. Grabbing the Kisses, I sit at the laptop and key in "Thailand young hot girls." The search returns, filling the screen with "Bangkok's red light district is the place to be." I'm convinced. First stop, the red light district for some bar-hopping and girl-hunting.

At six in the evening, I pull a T-shirt over my head and slide into jeans. Slipping on sandals, I'm out the door and onto the streets, hopping into a cab. "Take me to where all the go-go bars are at."

Turning on his meter, the driver looks over his shoulder before pulling away from the curb. "You want to go to Patpong, my friend." He winks turning back toward the windshield.

We pull up to a narrow street full of bars, clubs and massage shops. "It's still kind of early, so there isn't activity. If you're lucky, you'll find a go-go club with dancers open." Paying the driver, I walk up the street.

Strolling the empty streets, most places are closed except a few outdoor bars serving tourists. Homeless people sleeping in doorways reach out their hands begging for money.

"Hey, *farang*, come inside for a good time." Two topless girls with big nipples yell, leaning out of the back door of an old building.

I'm getting hard. "Hey girls, I'll be back later." Waving bye, I step into a restaurant.

After eating a plate of fish and relaxing until the sun goes down, I step into the night. Neon signs light the streets and the street markets fill the sidewalks, full of shoppers. Male foreigners whistle and yell catcalls when beautiful Thai girls pass carrying shopping bags. There are so many people it reminds me of Bourbon Street during Mardi Gras.

It's time for a little club-hopping. Strolling the main strip, club doors are open with dance music blaring out. Hundreds of beautiful girls wearing sexy outfits flirt standing in front of club doors. They yell at the foreigners, "Hey, handsome, sexy girls inside." Grabbing men as they pass, they try and pull them in.

Walking past the Hot Lips club, someone grabs my arm; scared, I turn to pull away but freeze in place. A goddess has me. Her eyes are as black as coal, peering through deep slits. Her stare passes through my eyes, taking my soul hostage, putting me into a trance. I'm unable to control my thoughts.

"Sir, please come in and have a drink with me?" I have no will to resist, and she pulls me in.

Putting her soft hand in mine, she leads me into the club. Adjusting to the loud music, I see a large stage in the middle of the floor. It's full of beautiful girls dancing in tiny G-string bikinis; there're badges pinned to their bottoms with a large number on them. Bangkok's getting more exciting by the second. My girl leads me to a table in the back with a loveseat for two.

She sits next to me, wrapping her arms around my neck, when a girl in a short black dress steps up.

"Sir, what will you like to drink? And what about my friend?"

"Bacardi and Coke, and whatever she wants."

My new companion says, "A lady's drink, Lawan." A few minutes later, the girl returns setting our drinks on the table, along with a small wooden club holding a slip of paper.

"Hi, my name's Frank."

"I go by my club name, Princess." She takes my hand.

Other girls are laughing and guzzling drinks as men grope their bodies. I'm not sure the costs of those drinks, but believe it is a fair trade for what they put up with. I'll keep my hands to myself.

"You like what those boys are doing over there?" Pointing at the Octopuses.

Feeling Princess' hand between my legs the sound of my zipper follows. Pulling it out, she softly strokes as I become rock hard. Lifting her right leg, she puts her hands on the table and slides onto my lap. I smell the lustful scent of her neck. She frees her opening, her wetness feels awesome as she moves me in.

My eyes are focused on the G-string girls on stage as she slowly rotates her hips in a small circular rhythm. I am unable to control myself and let go. Princess looks over her shoulder, giving a playful grin. Sliding off, she takes napkins from the table and cleans up the mess. I finish my drink and she walks me back outside, where I give her a generous tip and she gives me a shy look, saying,

"Cum again!"

Walking away, I think, if Princess only knew she just laid a virgin. This is one fantastic night. I continue hopping club to club; at each one, a hot girl pulls me in. Some clubs I leave quickly as the girls down their drink in five seconds asking for another. I do meet some with hearts of gold who become my friends. It's sad our friendship will only last for days. It's getting late, so I hit the streets. Girls patrolling for drunken men in search of a good time approach me.

"Sir, come to my room and I will make you feel good."

"No thank you." I smile.

Getting late the streets are still full, but the girls are now sitting and the foreigners are stumbling between clubs. Tired, I yell at a cab passing.

"Hey, stop." The cab pulls over and I climb in. "Take me to this address," I say, handing him a hotel card.

Getting to the room and sitting on the bed, my head's spinning. Standing, I stumble to the bathroom and take a leak; wobbling, I piss all over the toilet seat. "Wow, what a night." Stumbling back, I trip on a suitcase, falling on the bed and off to sleep.

Ah, so thirsty. Damn, it's already ten in the morning? I pick up the hotel phone. "Please bring me an American breakfast and a large black coffee." Hearing the knock, I hop out of the shower, wrapping a towel around me, before answering the door.

"Set it on the table next to the TV, there by my computer." After handing her money, she bows and leaves.

Sipping coffee and eating toast, I search for more ideas to find my girls. What can I do differently this time? The red light district having thousands to choose from, surely I can find five. Plus it gives me a reason to go again.

Stepping out of the business center with my finished pamphlets, I notice it's still early. Outside I breathe in the morning air.

"Taxi." I wave and one swings over. "Take me to this boarding house," I say, showing him the address.

He drops me off in front of a two-story home. I'm surprised there isn't a fence to keep people from stepping in the beautiful garden. I walk up and knock on the door.

"I'm looking to rent five rooms, do you have any available?" I say to a tiny grey-haired woman balancing on a cane.

"Sorry young man. Women only . . . no men allowed inside."

"That works for me. Only girls will be staying in the rooms and don't want men around."

"In that case, I do have five that come with meals."

"Here's your deposit, I'll pay the rest as I bring the girls." I hand her cash.

Back in the room, I slip on a tank top and a pair of knee-length shorts, watch a Jay Leno rerun until seven-thirty. Grabbing the pamphlets and a handful of business cards, I'm off, stopping at the hotel restaurant for a burger and fries to coat my belly for drinking.

I jump into the back seat of a cab parked in front. "Take me to Patpong please." The driver nods, looking in the rearview mirror, then speeds off.

The taxi driver drops me off at the same corner. I pay the fare then rush into the packed street. Going into the first open club, I sit on a bench seat along the back wall and sip on a Bacardi and Coke listening to the song; what does love got to do with it. A dancer comes up and sits next to me.

"I love the smell of your perfume." This girl smells great.

"Sir, I don't use perfume. It's my natural body scent."

"Wow, getting me horny. I'll tell you what, get a refill on my Bacardi and Coke and I'll buy you a drink."

"Deal." She waves a waitress over ordering our drinks.

"I'm working on an international project and need to hire some girls. Interested?" I hand her a business card and pamphlet.

"I grew up living on the streets with no family. I don't like working here, but it's hard to find a job with no education. I want to go with you, okay, Frank?"

"Really, I'd love to know more about you. Call me in the morning. Let's see if we can work something out. Oh, if you know anyone else who may be interested have them call, too."

I hop club to club, as I did last night, my head's spinning and needs to sober a bit. Outside the clubs, I chat with girls on the street. These street girls keep trying to take me home, while I hand out business cards and pamphlets, but stay focused on the job or try, too.

141

There are two hotties standing in front of a fruit stand. "Hi, girls. Having a fun night?"

They look at me with fear in their eyes. "Sir, if you're not buying, please go away, before we get punished." The girls turn towards a dark alley across the street.

"I wouldn't want to do that. Here, take, and look at these, you can call anytime." I hand them cards and pamphlets.

"Please go . . . hurry!" One puts the card down her pants.

Two Thai men walk up. "What are you doing here, farang? I hope it's to spend money on our girls," the short, muscular one says and steps inches from my face.

"I'm just looking for girls to hire for a project," I say, stepping back.

"So, you want to hire our girls? Then you must pay us for their use," the tall, tattooed one demands.

The short guy pulls a knife. "These girls and others on this street belong to us and we don't like you interfering in our business, understand? If you're not here to use our services you best leave these girls alone. If you know what's good for you?" the short one says.

"It is bad for business to kill or wound a farang. It'll bring police in our customer area, but before letting some farang tap into our cash flow—we will," the tall one says.

"I didn't know and don't need any trouble." This is not fun.

"Smart," the short one says, pushing me.

Turning I get out of there quickly. Standing down the street pissed, watching them, if I had fighting skills like Sammy, I'd kick both guys in the balls.

Better stick to clubs to find my girls. Still shaking, I go bar-hopping and drink until around three. Getting back to the room, I fall asleep still in my clothes.

Waking late with my head pounding, I'm hoping to get enough girls from last night.

"Hello?" I say, answering my phone.

"It's Sammy. I got the team pulled together and slid the info under your door earlier. Can you meet with them this morning?"

142

"I'll get right on it." This is perfect timing. I call Kevin. "This is Frank, Sammy's partner. Can we meet this morning?"

"Yeah, the team's available in the next couple of hours."

"Let's meet at our hotel restaurant," I say, giving him the address.

Noon arrives and so does Kevin with his team. I sit in the hotel restaurant by the front entrance when five tall guys with rippling muscles in tank tops step up to the entrance.

"We're looking for Mr. Capper?" one says to the lady.

"Over here, please," she says, pointing at me while walking them over.

"Have a seat. Who's Kevin?" I say.

One with a shaved head says, "It's me."

"Hello, Kevin. Here's the contract for you to read over and sign. I will give funds to help out before Sammy and I move on to our next country. Oh, here is my business card with my cell number. If you have any problems or need anything, just call." I had him the papers.

"You're alright, Frank, I expected to meet an asshole, but you're alright." He introduces me to his team, then reads and signs the papers.

"Well, It's nice meeting you guys and can't wait to see you fight." I escort the guys to the lobby door and see them off.

When I enter the room, the phone's blinking. Putting the receiver to my ear, I hit the play button and jot down the messages on the hotel notepad on the desk. As I write the names and numbers of multiple girls, the one with the good smell comes on. Damn, this is great. Writing her name and number, I underline it. The next one is the girl who stuffed my card down her pants before the two jerks arrived. I also underline her name. She needs to get away from those bad guys.

I arrange to meet the two I underlined and three more at the boarding house.

Arriving, all five girls and the house lady are standing out front waiting for me. Getting out of the taxi, I walk up to the group. "Here's the full pay for a month," I say to the lady, then exchange phone numbers.

I get the girls' photos and personal data, then set them up in rooms. It's a good day. Sammy and I both completed our parts.

I call Sammy, "Hey, we're both done, let's party tonight?" I'm so hoping he will.

"You know I'm not into that. I'd prefer to read up on some cool martial arts I've just heard about."

"It's okay, I'll have a few drinks for you. Hey, one more question. Are we still on for the competition you asked me to go to?"

"The fights are on for tomorrow night."

"Great, I will arrange our travel for the following morning." Martial arts have become more fascinating after what happened last night. I'm ashamed there was nothing I could do. I felt so helpless. Enough with the negative feelings: Patpong tonight and Muay Thai fights are tomorrow night.

Eight o'clock rolls around. I finish eating and am out the door hitting the streets of Patpong again.

"Frank, over here," the girls in front of the clubs yell.

"How do you girls remember my name?" I really don't remember their names or even them.

"You are favorite customer, Frank, come buy us drink."

"Sure, if I'm your favorite customer, let's go inside." The girls scream and jump in place.

"Come on, Frank." Two pull me into the back corner and yell for the waitress.

"This is my last night, so I'll buy you two the big-size drinks." Screaming, they grab me around the neck and kiss my cheek.

"Frank, we going to show appreciation for big drink and going away present," I hear my zipper first, then feel hands stroking me. The drinks are delivered. One girl puts her head under the table and with her tongue, she massages my shaft for a few minutes, then the other one takes over. They trade back and forth until I explode.

Walking out of the club, I cross the street to a small coffee house empty except the owner. I sit on an outside bench drinking coffee and watching the girls hustle guys.

"Farang!" Standing before me are the two guys from last night with a grey-haired man. There's a scar across his left eye down to his lip. He's wearing a designer pinstriped suit.

"We warned you not to interfere with our cash flow. We know you have one of our girls, now either buy her or return her. Either way, you'll pay us big for the money we lost not having her on the street," the muscle guy from last night says.

"Get the girl," the old man says.

The short guy walks into an alley on the right side of the coffee shop. I start looking for an opening to run when he returns; he's pulling the second girl from last night by the hair. She's crawling on her hands and knees to us.

"Stand before I break your neck," he tells the girl.

Standing under a street light her face is beaten to where it's hard to recognize her. Wobbling, she falls to the ground on her scraped and bleeding hands and knees.

"It had taken some doing, but we got her to talk. She told us her friend is with you."

"I'm sorry," she says. She's looking up at me with her swollen eyes.

"Shut up—Whore," the old man says, kicking her in the face.

"Come up with the money now, or your face is going to look like hers," the old man says.

I hate these guys; I wish I had a gun to kill them. Scared, I take off running, pushing the old man to get past him. Confused, I don't know where to go. Looking back, all three are running after me, holding knives. Panicking, I turn right, going down a side street, finding it to be a dead-end alley.

Small street lamps at each end give little light to its emptiness. Red brick walls line the three sides. Up against the back wall, I watch the three shadows at the far end slowly come at me.

"You had your chance, farang. Now we're going to carve you up."

I watch them come closer, wetness runs down my leg, creating a puddle.

"Are weak and defenseless people the only ones you can pick on?" I yell.

Stopping, they turn, looking back. In the dim light, I see Kevin the team-lead for the Lerdrit fighters standing at the alley opening.

"I know who you are . . . Khemkhaeng Boonliang, and the skills of the King's elite bodyguards, but this is none of your business. Be on your way or we will cut you up too," the old man says.

"Unfortunately for you, it is my business," Kevin says, walking weaponless into the dark towards the men.

The three men walk into the dim light towards Kevin waving their knives. Barely able to see, the sound of screams echo off the walls. From the darkness, I can hear the sound of beating. I want to go help Kevin, but I'm too scared.

"What the hell is going on?" I yell.

Kevin steps out of the shadows, limping over to me. He's lightly bleeding on his arms and chest from knife wounds and there's some minor swelling on his face.

"They may be looking out for their investments, but so am I. Get out of here quick, go hang out in a club for a while. The police will be looking for their murderer." Kevin vanishes as swiftly as he appeared.

Running from the alley, I trip and fall. I've fallen on three grossly mangled bodies; I almost throw up. I stand and run towards the light of the street. Shaking, I step out to the mainstream of partiers. Dashing for the closest club, I order a double Bacardi and Coke. Downing the drink, it's hard to believe, Kevin—the king's bodyguard. What the hell is Sammy doing? Calming down, I go bar-hopping with my emotions under control.

Still tense, I shoot a couple double Bacardi 151s, and then I'm feeling much better. Now light-headed, I party and flirt with

146

the girls until daylight. Riding home the crazy night goes through my mind like watching a video. Thinking, I could be the one the police find in the alley instead of the bad guys, if not for Kevin. I owe this guy: I owe him my life.

Waking around noon, I run the events through my head again. Best I act surprised as everyone else when the news comes out. I eat lunch with Sammy in the hotel restaurant.

"Did you see what happen in Patpong last night while you were there?"

"No." I start getting nervous.

"Three thugs were killed, and the police are saying it is gang related due to a turf war over prostitution. You need to be careful, Frank."

"You're right. Maybe if I train in martial arts I won't need to worry as much. Sammy, when are the fights tonight?"

"Around six-thirty, but I want to get there early, so we can quickly get to our seats. I don't want to wait in a long line."

"Sounds good," I say.

When it's time to go, I wait on the black leather couch by the indoor waterfall for Sammy. I'm still thinking of last night and how amazing it was that Kevin destroyed those guys with knives in seconds. It's made me interested in seeing all the things martial artists can do.

"Frank, let's go." Waking out of my daydream, I stand and follow Sammy.

Reading billboards on the way, I see that many of them use Muay Thai fighters for their advertisements. It's strange how just a few days ago, I was bored hearing Sammy talk about fighting, but now I'm excited too. The taxi stops in front of Rajadamnern stadium.

"Sammy this place is gigantic. The size reminds me of baseball stadiums back home."

"Hurry, that crowd is getting bigger. Look at that line."

When we walk to the front aisle, a security guard is standing in front of the closed-off front seats. We show our tickets, and he lets us through. Flopping into 11A, I scan all the rows of seats to the far back, I'm so glad Sammy got ringside. I'm happy to be up close and personal for the action.

"Frank, take this."

"What's this handkerchief for?"

"It's for the blood that might get splashed on you by the fighters."

When I look up in the ring, the fighters are climbing in. Music's playing as each is doing a unique dance. The sounds and watching them are hyping me up. When both fighters finish, they're called to the center of the ring and I guess told the rules.

The fighters go back to their corners, and each removes medals, a ring of flowers around their neck and a special headpiece. The bell rings as both fighters move to the center of the ring and start fighting. They're both very aggressive. This is nothing like the boxing matches I've seen on TV. These guys are pushing with their feet, and then all of a sudden go at it with all kinds of things, like punches, kicks, knees, hands, and elbows. They are jumping in the air to punch: it's unreal.

One fighter becomes airborne, flying through the air connecting with his knee to the other's face. Blood's going everywhere; the guy falls to the canvas not moving. This fight has got to be over as they carry the fighter out of the ring.

The second fight starts with the same special dance before they begin fighting; they're really going at it when the crowd starts yelling. It sounds like "Huaw." I'm not sure.

I'm thinking these guys are going to kill each other when one comes running and steps on the other's bent front leg, boosting him above the fighter; coming down, he strikes the top of his head with an elbow. Damn, that's it; this guy's head must have split in two. He falls to the canvas and is carried out.

Fight after fight, this goes on. I am totally into it now and doing the yell, "Huaw." Sammy looks at me and slaps me on the back. This is awesome, and now I know why Sammy is so into it. Once it's finished, people start leaving, I can see the younger ones play-fighting as they follow their parents to the exit.

On the way back to the hotel, I ask Sammy, "Am I too old to start training?"

"Only for competition. Most start at a very young age and train very hard to become a pro. But for self-defense, being in

148

your mid-twenties is fine. Training to protect yourself can last a lifetime." Returning to the hotel, I tell Sammy, "We need to catch a taxi by nine to make our flight, so meet me in the hotel restaurant at eight for breakfast."

"Works for me." I head to my room and go right to sleep as I had an exhausting night.

The next morning, I meet Sammy in the restaurant with my bags. Eating breakfast, we talk about the night before; I listen to Sammy tell me he has extensive training in Muay Thai. He'd never had a chance to see an authentic fight at the elite Bangkok stadium either, so he was just as excited.

Finishing breakfast, we jump into a cab and head to the airport. Arriving at ten-thirty, we go through the security inspections, then head for the business lounge. We watch TV and snack until we hear the boarding call come over the lounge speakers. The airplane lifts off and enters the sky; I watch out the window.

"Goodbye, Thailand, you're definitely one crazy place."

Assassins In The Mountains
*** Chapter Seventeen ***

The Tokyo city lights at night are like Las Vegas on steroids from the sky. Hitting the ground, I'm eager to get out of the airport. It's crazy having thousands of people pushing and cramming with what seems no consideration for others. The strange thing is no one seems to care; it must be the norm.

When I hop in a taxi, the steering wheel and driver are on the right side.

"It feels kind of weird seeing you on the wrong side of the car."

"Do me a favor then: don't scream in my ear when I drive on the wrong side of the road."

"No problem, just came from Thailand and they do the same thing. I just never got around to asking anyone."

"Yeah, well it happens all the time with you foreigners, yelling in my ear that is."

I give the driver the hotel address, and we're off. Watching out the window, I see that this place is more modern than any place I've been, including the US. The live video billboards make it really a state-of-the-art country. I finally get to my room on an upper floor. I open the curtains viewing the city's beauty; its neon lights brighten up the sky.

I call Frank, and we decide to hit the streets to stroll around, and enjoy all the cool lights and neat places. I'm far from being a nerd, but most of this stuff is unbelievably cool. These Japanese must have IQs bouncing off the top of the scale to think up the electrical gadgets we're finding in store windows.

My next challenge will be reading signs, same as had been with the others. It's kind of special how each country uses its own unique style of characters.

"Hey, Frank, feeling the jet lag, I'm about ready to start back."

"I agree, my body feels weak and my eyes are getting heavy."

Turning around, we take a different path back to the hotel and call it a night.

I start my search for Ninjutsu, the art of the ninja. This one's going to be interesting; it has a unique history, including the reputation for being assassins. Spending the day searching for Ninjutsu schools, I find many other types of martial arts and many flavors of these arts to including Karate, Jujitsu, Aikido, Kendo, Judo and Sumo. These are great martial arts in their own right and well respected, but my desire isn't just people training in martial arts: it's true ninja.

Who knows, maybe I'm chasing ghosts and the ninja are now only in storybooks. I've got to find out and will do my best before turning to another art. The Internet isn't doing its thing for me; the searches are coming back dry. Who would hire these types of assassins: governments wanting to eliminate terrorists, the wealthy offing their spouses or other undesirables in their lives, powerful global corporations dealing with rivals or people who know too much? There is still a need for them, even in this 21st century.

Trying desperately to get a martial arts grand master to speak to me over the phone, I begin to lose hope of getting clues when I'm surprised by one agreeing to talk to me. He offers a dinner invitation at his home. I accept, feeling a bit nervous; all my years in martial arts, I've never had the honor of meeting someone of high rank and skill.

Arriving at his home in an upscale neighborhood, I knock on the door. A young girl wearing a kimono opens.

"Sir, please come in and follow me."

I follow her through this large home. The walls are covered with oil paintings of samurai and warlord battles. The rice paper doors and everything in between puts my mind back thousands of years (back to 1200 A.D.). Kind of makes me wish I lived back then.

"This place is neat."

"Yes, sir." She leads me into an isolated room. "Sir, please sit and rest. Master Isao will be with you soon."

In the center of the room is a dining table built for midgets, standing about fifteen inches off the ground surrounded by small pillows. Taking a seat on one of the pillows feels a bit uncomfortable. I check out the room while waiting; the door opens, and in steps a well-built man having short hair, a long beard and a colorful silk robe extending to the floor.

"Welcome, Sammy, I'm honored to have you as a guest in my humble home!" Bending forward, he bows.

"Thank you, master."

I was expecting a dangerous-looking old man who could tear your head off. But I find an intelligent man with perfect manners, keeping in mind he does have the skill to put some serious pain on me.

"Miki."

The same girl comes in. "Yes, master?" She keeps her head down while speaking to him.

"Please bring our food and drinks."

"Right away."

"Sammy, tell me why you're so interested in ninja?"

"Sir, my interests are for a world-class competition and the ninja are the elite of Japanese fighting arts."

"The ninja vanished a very long time ago." He's staring into my eyes as if he's able to read my thoughts.

"I feel they're still here, master. I will try my best to find them."

Miki brings food and wine. "Master, and Mr. Nelson, please enjoy!" She sets it on the table, then bows before stepping out the door.

Eating, we continue talking; he seems to start opening up to me. "Sammy, if I were ninja the best place for me would be high in the mountains where I can train and stay hidden. If you ever do run into them be careful: they're to be taken very seriously."

"Master, I will give them the utmost respect."

"Yes. After spending this time with you, I believe you would. There are things I must complete this evening, so please forgive me." We stand and bow before he leaves the room.

Miki returns. "Sir, please follow me."

She takes me to the front door allowing me to leave. "Sir." Turning back, she hands me an envelope. "From the master."

"Thank you, Miki."

She smiles, closing the door. Returning to my room, I open the envelope, only to find numbers. Confused, I'll show it to Frank in the morning.

During breakfast with Frank, I'm still confused about master's note. "Hey check this out," I say, handing it to him.

"What's this, Sammy?" Taking the note with a strange expression.

"I got this last night and don't know what it means."

Frank looks at it for a few minutes. "You know, Sammy, this looks like grid coordinates to me."

"What?"

"Yes, you know I've traveled internationally over the years. I've seen this number format many times."

"Yeah, I guess it does at that."

Getting excited, I tell him the story of the master and how I got the numbers. Finishing breakfast, I eagerly go back to the room and search on the grid, hoping to find the location. I get a hit; it comes back some place in the mountains. Printing it out, I set it on the table then start planning, I need to get a compass to help find my treasure: ninja assassins.

This all seems so surreal or maybe something from a fiction story, but I need to know. Grabbing the printout, I head to the sporting goods store and purchase a compass, outdoor clothing and survival gear like a water canteen. Returning to the room, I view the grids to the map putting me into the Fuji Mountains. Maybe I should hire a guide, but then, I don't want to put anyone else in danger. Packing, I get ready to leave. I call Frank letting him know I'm heading to the mountains and may have issues with my phone.

Hopping into a taxi, I hand the map to the driver. "Please take me to the bottom of Mount Fuji where it's marked on the map."

"It isn't any of my business, but you really should hire a guide as people get lost up there all the time. Some never return."

"Thanks for your concern, but this is something I have to do on my own."

The driver turns, hitting the meter button and squeezing into traffic. Pulling up to the bottom of the mountain, I pay the driver and get out of the taxi. Within minutes, sweat drips down my forehead from the morning heat. Putting my jacket in the bag, I pull out the compass and map. Sitting on a rock under a tree, I play with the compass and grid coordinates on the paper. Hoping I figured it out, I start up the side.

Hiking upwards for hours, I take water breaks and rest the legs; even with the great shape I'm in, this is still a workout. When I finally get to where the grid directions point, it's empty except for an old log. I guess it was a waste of time; I'll take a short break before heading back down. Well, I guess I can look at the positive side, being it was an enjoyable hike and I do need the exercise.

Sitting on the log resting, I keep getting this eerie feeling that someone's staring at me. I hate this feeling as I watch and listen to every movement and every sound, putting myself on guard. Finding only little creatures wandering, I relax. It must be my mind playing tricks on me being out here alone.

I reach into my backpack, putting the water back and getting ready to leave when I see two feet next to my bag. Slowly bringing my head up, I see an old man standing inches from my face. Shocked, I jump back, falling off the log.

"Are you okay, young man?"

"You scared the hell out of me, mister."

"I'm sorry . . . didn't mean to catch you by surprise." He reaches his hand out in an offer to help me sit up. I take it in respect and slide back on the log.

"You must be Sammy Nelson?"

"I'm surprised, how do you know my name?"

"I've been waiting for you. Master Isao and I are old training partners and friends for many years, that is all I can say without having to kill you," he laughs.

"This is isn't a good day to die, so I'm good with that."

"Master Isao got word to me letting me know you two had a long chat. He's pleased with your manners and respect, and thinks you're an honest man."

"Wow, that's great and an honor."

"I'm surprised he gave you the location; in all the years of our friendship you are the first. You've must have really impressed him. We need to get out of the open."

The old man turns, and puts his hand on my shoulder, as I bend over to pick up my stuff. I feel his hand slid to my neck, then a small pinch. I wake finding myself lying in a room of a cave. A beautiful Japanese girl walks in carrying a glass of water and a bowl of fruit. She sets it on a small table.

"Please enjoy," she says before leaving.

Returning shortly, she escorts me to another part of the cave where there's an underground hot spring. Reaching for my shirt buttons, she says, "Please." She undresses me. Glancing into her eyes I'm helpless to resist. Within moments, I stand naked.

She then drops her robe with nothing underneath. She stands before me naked with a submissive expression. Reaching out, she softly grasps my hand and leads me into the water; I'm led to a rock about two feet underwater.

"Please sit."

This beautiful girl bathes me using her hands; I become totally relaxed and would be happy enjoying this forever.

"This is the only sensual massage bath I've ever had and I'm glad it's with you."

This has got to be a dream and I'm still out there sleeping by the log on Mt. Fuji, this is too surreal to be happening.

"It's my pleasure, please stand." She dries me off, then dresses me in a black outfit lying on a rock.

When she leads me out the door, there's someone standing waiting for me dressed in all black including the hood. He doesn't speak, but waves for me to follow and I go to another room in the cave.

The old man from the log is sitting at one of those short tables, drawing what look like Japanese characters.

"Sammy, you have a questioning look to your face. This is Hiragana, Japanese writing. I know your purpose for being here, please sit. I just don't fully understand why, so please explain?"

I explain everything in detail while he continues to paint on large sheets of what look like rice paper, and listens to me talk. Finishing, he looks up.

"It is time, follow me."

Following the old man, I hope he isn't going to torture me. Traveling down different passages, we come to a large cave lit only by candles in wall-mounted holders: we step in.

"Sammy, please take a seat here at the wall," he says, pointing to our right.

He then hits a metal plate hanging from the ceiling with a short bat. Within seconds, human forms dressed in black appear out of nowhere. I'm not sure, but it seems they're coming through the walls. But that's impossible, or is it?

Each one is armed with swords, knives and other medieval-looking weapons, ten total in two rows kneeling facing the old man. They bow until their heads touch their hands, which are placed in a star shape on the ground. This old man must be more than I thought; maybe an elite member or maybe the leader of these ninja-looking guys.

The old man says a couple of words in Japanese; they rise and move to the back walls. He says a few more words, and dummies drop from the ceiling, hanging a few feet off the ground. Then one of the ninjas steps towards one, pulling his sword; lightning fast, he demonstrates advanced skills compared to mine. One by one they step up, demonstrating skills with different weapons.

157

The old man continues when two ninjas come face to face using unarmed techniques on each other. I wish I could put them in slow motion to see their lightning-fast moves. Next, one throws a small chain connecting and wrapping around the other's neck, then releases. One thing I know is that this isn't sports fighting; it's easy to tell how extremely dangerous each move is.

The old man bangs the drum, and the demonstration ends. Standing, he escorts me back to his room where we sit and talk.

"Sammy, my clan is for hire only, and by people or groups with big money who need one or many people assassinated: clients who are unable to do it themselves. We're paid for our services to make people disappear forever."

"Sir, with all due respect this is hard to believe."

"Yes I know, people only think of us as in fairy tales, and that gives us a big advantage. Which reminds me: I like you, Sammy, but if you ever speak of this place, we will know. One of us will come for you!"

"I will keep it a secret." A shiver runs down my spine.

"Please stay seated, I will return." Standing, he leaves the room.

A short time later, he comes back and sits at this table.

"Sammy, I spoke to the clan, and we decided to let five of our members attend the competition. It'll give us a break from practice and contracts, and give us entertainment eliminating other skilled fighters. Let me know when and where. When it's time, we'll enter the ring to fight."

"How will I contact you?"

"Master Isao knows how to contact me. I enjoyed our time together, but this will be the last time we meet."

Feeling someone behind me, I black out. I wake at the log on the mountain, wearing the clothes I arrived in. Still wondering if it was a dream, I return to the bottom of the mountain and waving down a passing taxi.

Back in the room, I call Master Isao. "Master, I have returned and will let you know the competition date and time soon."

I call Frank in the morning. "My team's complete, but you will not be speaking with them, tell you later."

"Okay, I'll book our travel to leave in the morning. Meet me for breakfast, and we'll leave afterward."

Frank

The Geisha Await
*** Chapter Eighteen ***

My heart's racing in this Tokyo hotel room knowing my dream girls . . . Japanese girls are beyond these four walls. Can I get past shying away from them? My experience in Thailand's red-light district gives me some courage, but geisha have brought pleasure to my dreams on many of lonely nights. Here is my chance to fulfill those dreams: I'm terrified!

I must push these fantasies aside and do what I came here for, recruiting girls. Powering up my laptop, I search the Internet for poor girls in Japan. The screen shows one in three single girls in Japan are considered poor. It's amazing; I've always believed Japanese people are the rich of the world. Okay, how to find them? I'll start with searching small villages throughout the countryside, for young adult orphans. It'll also give me a chance to see the beauty of Japan and the true culture of these people and gorgeous girls too.

Stepping up to the hotel's business center viewing through the glass wall, I find a computer on a small desk next to an HP all-in-one printer. Happy it's empty, I push the door open entering. I step up to the printer, sliding my thumb drive into the USB port.

I select and print maps and directions to a dozen villages then print the updated pamphlets. Taking the stack from the printer, I exit the glass door and up the hall towards the restaurant entrance in the lobby to meet Sammy for breakfast.

"Good morning, sir, will it be dining for one?" She bows.

"No. I'll be eating with my friend Sammy."

"You must be Frank, please . . . follow me." She sets her clipboard on the podium.

I love seeing these girls in kimonos, how erotic. I watch her walk as she takes these tiny little steps: it's so cute.

Getting to the back, I'm led to a closed rice-paper door of a private room. She kneels to the side of the door, gently sliding it open. Sammy is sitting on a cushion at a table with legs two feet long.

"Sir, someone will take your order in a few minutes." Leaving the door open, she's gone.

"Hey, Sammy, how is it going?"

Sammy tells me of his meeting and the note, asking for my help. I share with him everything I know.

"I'm going there," Sammy says.

"I'm also going away, but to the countryside for a few days. If you need me call my satellite phone."

After eating, I go back to my room and grab my suitcase off the bed, then out the hotel into a yellow taxi parked in front.

"Good morning, sir. I'm off to the countryside. Please take me here," I say, handing him directions to the first village.

Drivers honk and yell at each other as we creep along the crowded streets to the outskirts of the city.

Leaving the city's border, the driver picks up speed, and it becomes peaceful on the empty road. The taxi flows down the curves of the two-lane highway; I watch out the window at the rice fields and bamboo huts while explaining my goals to the driver.

"I'll help you find these girls. Trust me . . . my heart is honorable and I know where to find them. Oh, just call me Joe as most tourists do."

"And my name is Frank."

Watching the old men and women working the fields using oxen and old wooden plows, I'm amazed at what shape they're in.

Pulling into a small village, Joe gets out, while I wait checking out the little bamboo huts spread across a large dirt area, surrounded by rice fields. These huts stand a couple of feet off the ground on poles. Each hut has a cute little porch poking out the front. Watching Joe disappear into the front of one, I climb out to stretch my legs; villagers are watching me through their windows.

A few minutes later Joe appears with an old, short, stocky man with facial hair touching his belly.

"Frank, this is Katsuo, the village elder. He'll let us stay here a couple of days and arrange interviews with suitable girls for your project."

"Hey, happy to meet you, Katsuo, and thanks for your kindness!"

"Follow me," he says. Grabbing our stuff, we follow Katsuo to the back of the village.

"Frank, take the one on the right, and Joe, you're on the left."

"This is great." Inside a small room were a straw mat on the floor; large foam pads for the bed; no chair, just an ancient Japanese style table with cushions surrounding it; and a small dresser. While I was putting my things away, a knock comes on the door.

I open the door finding a tall girl possibly in her late teens stands holding a tray. She balances a teapot, cups, sugar bowl, teabags and a spoon on it.

"Tea, sir?"

Inviting her in, she follows me to the table and sets the tray down, then prepares tea for two.

Wearing a faded old dress a bit big for her skinny body, she bends forward handing me a cup. The front of her dress moves away from her body displaying braless breasts, causing an instant hard-on. What a pervert I am or is it the Japanese-craving lust in me? I laugh. This girl is sexy with her hair wrapped in a bun on top her head.

"My name is Frank, tell me about you?" I raise my cup to take a sip.

"Aiko, meaning love child. My mother died during my birth. My father left the village that night and never returned, eighteen years ago today."

"I'm sorry. Happy birthday." Watching the tears forming in her eyes makes me want to cry.

"Please don't feel pity. I've lived in this village all my life and have my own hut in the back. My job washing clothes and other tasks to serve the people here pays my way. I'm happy for my life as it's the only one I've ever known." Finishing our tea, she put our cups back on the tray and walks to the door.

"Aiko, I truly enjoyed having tea with you. Thank you for your company, and I hope friendship?"

Smiling, she bows and closes the door behind her.

Lying back, I watch out the window as the sun sets when a knock comes on the door. I open it.

"Frank, get ready, the village people are throwing a party in your honor tonight. They'll introduce you to all available young girls who desire to work on your project."

"Sounds perfect, let me get ready."

"I'll come back for you when it's time."

Damn, only outdoor bathrooms. What's this? I find a bucket of water, sponges and a soap bar in the corner. I'm sure hoping this water's clean. Taking my chances, I use it to wash.

"Frank, party time." Going outside, I walk with Joe to the front.

"Joe, I'm amazed everyone speaks English here."

"They all do, a missionary lived here for a few years and gave classes."

Getting to the party, there's a large bonfire with villagers of all ages. Adults are standing around the fire joking and kids playing. I feel a bit out of place but try not to show it. I step up to the fire, and all eyes turn to me as the village elder says,

164

"Village, this is Frank, the international traveler looking for people to hire."

"Hi, Frank," they say.

Some of the villagers begin playing musical instruments, others singing and the adults drinking homemade alcohol. Girls interested in the job line up to my side.

"Girls, let's enjoy tonight. We can do business tomorrow."

Where is Aiko? I find Joe sitting and drinking with the old men.

"Hey, Joe, where's Aiko?" I say.

Joe gets up, pulling me to the side and away from the group.

"Village servants are not allowed at these type of gatherings. Sorry."

I guess there's unfairness everywhere in the world, even small communities like this one. I go back to the party and do shots with the guys trying to enjoy the party. A few hours later, I excuse myself, returning to my hut; having interviews in the morning, I don't want to get drunk. Lying down, I close my eyes, drifting off to sleep.

A soft female voice wakes me. Opening my eyes, I see a candle on the table with Aiko standing by it.

"Frank, I will feel shame if you send me away."

She drops her red with gold trim robe to reveal her naked body. With the candle's light reflecting off her flesh, she's an angel beyond any fantasy I could ever dream up.

She slides into bed next to me, I feel her body's heat while she slowly kisses and massages me. Pulling the covers back, she plays with my pubic hair while sliding my shaft into her mouth.

Reaching down, she squeezes my sack with her free hand while tickling the blood vessel on the back of my shaft with her tongue: it sends me into ecstasy. My body's shaking, and I'm about to explode when she stops. Taking a bottle of ointment from the table, she coats me then climbs on top, putting her hips over mine.

"Frank . . . Frank!"

Sliding me in, I watch both pleasure and pain come to her face. Feeling her push hard, I look past her pubic hair to find myself entering her rear love channel. Putting her hands on my chest, she slides up and down with a rhythm that's driving me crazy. Within minutes, I lose control and shoot my load.

"Aiko . . . I love you!"

Grabbing her arms, my body becomes stiff as a board. She lowers herself, leaving me inside; she takes my tongue into her mouth and softly dances hers with mine. Relaxing, I fall asleep.

Waking from what I thought was a wet dream, I feel the warmth of a hot sponge Aiko's using to pamper my body. The smell of fish and vegetables coming from the table gets my stomach growling.

"I have to go work now, but I have a special gift for you tonight." Kissing my lips, she takes a moment to suck on the lower one, then fades out the door.

I get up, dress, eat and get ready for the interviews. I step out into the fresh air, the countryside's cool breeze makes me feel alive.

Katsuo walks over to me. "Good morning, Frank, are you ready?"

"Yes, you have some place set up for me?"

"The girls will come to your hut. It will be more comfortable for you this way; we'll also keep fresh hot tea and snacks in your room."

"I'm good with that. You can start anytime."

I answer my mobile phone, and it's Sammy. "I'm heading to Mount Fuji looking for ninja assassins."

"Sammy, I don't have a clue to what you're talking about. But, it sounds exciting. Be careful."

Leaving the door open, I step back inside and get a stack of info sheets and the camera ready, then sit at the table. Moments later a short plump girl comes in carrying a tray and setting it on the table; she's wearing a brown dress with black stripes. Putting a tea bag in a cup, she pours in hot water and places the cup in front of me.

"I am the first one for the interview, sir."

"Here, please fill out this form and tell me a little about you?" I want to get a feel for her personality.

For about ten minutes, she talks about her life. Taking her picture, I thank her before letting her go. I continue this process throughout the day.

It's getting dark when Aiko steps in.

"I'm happy to see you. I was wondering when you would show up for your interview."

"Sorry, Frank, I'm not here for an interview. Me and the other servants were told we are not allowed to interview."

"They have no right to stop you. Sit down quickly and complete the info sheet, and I will take your picture."

With her hand trembling, she takes the silver pen and completes the form. "Don't worry, I will take you with me. I promise no harm will come to you." Her eyes smile along with a wishful grin on her lips. "Have the others servants come for a quick interview too. Here are some info sheets to take to them."

"Frank, they are afraid more than me. These people are kind, but if we servants anger them the punishment is painful."

"I don't understand, what do you mean painful? They seem so nice."

"We're tied up on crosses in the back of the village naked, then beaten by any villager in the mood, sometimes for days. If you don't believe me go to the back of the village and look at the crosses. You'll find blood all over them and the straps."

"You will be safe," I say.

Cheerfully, she grabs the dishes and hides the forms in her dress, rushing out the door.

What a day, having so many beautiful girls in my room one after another, then finding out this place is out of a Stephen King novel. I laugh.

"Frank, let's go eat. I'm hungry and it's ready," Joe says, standing at the door.

"You surprised me. I was in deep thought. Okay, great, I'm hungry too." While eating, I say, "We will need another taxi to fit all the girls. Please arrange it for noon tomorrow. I'll give you the girl's names in the morning, so you can let them know to pack."

"No problem, I'll take care of it."

Curious, on the way back to my hut, I walk behind the village. There, in an open area stands two wooden crosses, each about seven foot tall with hand and leg straps. Dry blood is covering most of the wood. Whips, rocks, and broken bottles lie at the bottom of each, covered in blood; shocked, I go to my hut.

Going over the info sheets, I hear a noise outside the door. Glancing towards the sound, someone pushes papers underneath. Going to the door, I find seven completed info sheets; I'm sure they're from the servants. Looking them over, I decided to pick Aiko and four of the youngest servants, realizing Katsuo may try to stop me, maybe with force. I hope Joe will understand: he's our ride out of here. Best I let him know now and get his reaction. I go to his room and he lets me in.

"Joe, I've picked Aiko and four other servants."

"That's not funny."

I sit and explain what's going on and why I picked them, hoping it will change his mind.

"You may get us killed, but I will stand with you, Frank. If it is all true what happens to these girls, then you picked the right ones. I will deal with Katsuo."

"I'm scared for the girls, I have to do this, Joe. Good night." Getting back to the room, I make sure the door is locked.

"Hello . . . who is it?" I wake to a soft knock on the door.

"Please open up!" A young female voice whispers.

When I open the door, there is a girl maybe ten years old standing there with fear in her eyes.

"Follow me . . . please, be quiet."

Confused, then thinking the girls are in trouble and need my help, I follow her willingly, hoping it's not a trap. She takes me to the far back where a hut stands alone out of sight. The little girl pushes me towards the door.

"Go in. It's okay." She then runs off.

Reaching down, I pick up a rock; holding it in my hand behind my back, I step into the hut.

Two girls I've never seen are wrapped in colorful kimonos, their hair and faces are done up just like geisha, just like the girls in my fantasy dreams.

They put a finger over their lips and ease their way up to me. One of the girls has a small metal bucket with steam rising from the top and the other a basket of white sponges. Feeling safe, I set the rock on the table. The girls set their stuff on the table, each one takes an arm to move me next to the bed; together they slide my shirt over my head, then my sweatpants down my body.

"Who are you, girls?"

"We're twin sisters and two of the servants."

Sexually removing their kimonos, they reveal two perfectly matched handful-size breasts and well-toned, pure, white, hairless bodies. I have always been attracted to small women, guessing them to be both under five feet and less than eighty pounds; I've been blessed.

Leaving me standing, each takes a sponge, dipping them into the hot water then moving to opposite sides of my body: they bathe me. Finishing, they lay me on the bed. With one at my feet and the other my face, they give me a tongue massage. I don't know what is making me crazier—the girl sucking my toes or the one sucking my ear lobes—but it is definitely affecting the middle.

Each girl slowly tongues her way to the middle as if searching to find erotic spots at each lick. One gets to my nipples sucking and biting, sending a sexual charge shooting through me. Both girls get to the middle at the same time, sending fireworks through my brain. There is no turning back: I'm lost in lust. Letting it shoot, the girls give cute little giggles and lick it up.

I start to sit up. "Sekushi, we're not done yet, please stay down." The girls begin to kiss and play with each other, then lie on each side of me and suck my neck and earlobes. I instantly become hard again.

The sisters get back up, kissing each other again, when one moves over my hips, sliding my rod inside, and the other sits on my face. Both gently move their hips in circles until I shoot the second time. They climb off and clean me up.

"Sir Frank, you have to go now. One of the village men will be here soon to be serviced." Quickly dressing, I'm out the door.

Early the next morning, I walk to Joe's hut, giving him the list of girls.

"Frank, I'm proud and respect you for making the right choice knowing it can cause you some real problems. I spoke to Katsuo, and he said losing these five servants is fine; he still has enough to do the chores. Plus the younger orphans are growing up fast and can take their place. Oh, the second taxi will be here around noon."

"Thank you, Joe."

"I'll let these girls know so they can get ready."

I keep busy searching for anything and nothing on the Internet to help calm my nerves. It seems like forever when Joe pops his head in.

"Frank, time to go, the girls are loading their stuff into the cars," Joe says.

"Okay, be there in a minute."

Getting out front, I put my things in the trunk of one then thank everyone and say goodbye.

Coming off the ground, my head slams the windshield. With my head spinning, I hear, "Our servant isn't going anywhere. She's been our house slave for years."

Through blurry vision, I see some teenage kid coming at me, fast; I'm too dizzy from my head hitting the glass to get out of the way.

I begin wishing Sammy was here. I start praying when a leg comes flying across my sight, hitting the kid's stomach. The kid's expression turns to pain; she bends over and kneels to the ground. Turning to see where the leg came from, I see that it was Katsuo the village elder.

As I lie on the hood of the taxi, my girls come running up to me. "Our Frank, are you okay?" While they pamper me, I think maybe this is a blessing in disguise.

Recovering, I see the girl who attacked me stand and run off. "I apologize for the youth," Katsuo says.

Katsuo helps me climb into the taxi. We speed off towards Tokyo.

170

Arriving, I have the driver's of both taxis take us to a boarding house I arranged for earlier. After briefing the house manager, I go to the hotel.

Stopping in front, I say, "Joe, thank you so much, you're a good man. Hey, I want to give you a bonus for helping me find the girls." I pay both men for the taxi fare, then give Joe a generous sum of money for a tip; it brings a shocked expression to his face.

"Joe, can I get one of your business cards? Just in case I can use more help."

"Take this one," he says, handing me a card.

Drained from all the action, I stop at the hotel bar for Bacardi & Coke, then I'm off to my room. I receive a call from Sammy.

"My team's complete, but you will not be speaking with them. Tell you later," Sammy says.

"Okay, I've completed mine too."

I decide to book our travel to allow us to leave in the morning, before taking a nap. At breakfast, I tell Sammy. "I was able to get airline tickets last night, and we're leaving in a few hours." Heading back to our rooms, we get ready, then we're off to the airport.

Sammy

Danger In The Jungle
*** Chapter Nineteen ***

Coming into Philippine airspace, I see there are islands everywhere and wonder how long it would take to visit them all: Maybe a lifetime? Landing, we jump terminals, catching a domestic flight to an island called Cebu.

"Frank, why Cebu?"

"From what I can tell on the map, it's the centermost island of them all. It seems the best place for our command base."

"That's a great idea."

Touching down in Cebu, we exchange some dollars for pesos, then walk to the taxi stand. The heat is making me dizzy.

"Frank, this has got to be the hottest place on earth."

"Yeah, I'm from the East Coast with similar weather, but this is unbearable."

Getting to the room, I crank up the AC to full throttle; the cold air blasts out, chilling my skin. Powering up the laptop, I realize it's going to be much easier here with almost everyone speaking English. Okay, let's see how to deal with these islands, hopping around them and to stay safe.

Eww, got to remember to avoid Abu Sayaf, one of a few terrorist groups located mostly on the southern islands. It scares the shit out of me just thinking about them. I'm told they kidnap people for ransom, and if not paid will kill them. I'll need to keep Frank and me far away from that type of situation. Hmm, I think we need to consider getting escorts to watch over us during our stay in this country.

I put that thought aside for now. Next, there seems to be as many flavors of Filipino martial arts as there are islands. The goal is to find my Serrada Escrima fighters; like Japan I'm sure all the arts here are great, but I need to pick one and this is the one that interests me most.

Early in the morning, I decide to do the bodyguard thing first, so I go searching for the local police station. Finding it, I say, "Guys, I just arrived and plan on traveling to many of these islands. Can you recommend legitimate bodyguards or bodyguard agencies? I need to keep myself and my partner safe while traveling."

"Well, most places in our country are safe, but we do have some bad elements out there giving the Philippines a bad name. If you plan on wandering off into the southwest, it can be dangerous. There's a Philippine and American commando joint task force hunting these terrorists down, but they can't always protect you," the officer sitting behind the desk says.

"We're not sure where we will end up. I'm thinking bodyguards are a safe idea."

"There are a lot of beautiful and safe places in our country, but like all countries, there are bad too." He hands me a map. "I don't recommend going in the areas marked in red, as even a group of guards can't protect you. But if you're determined, here are a couple of names, these guys are badass. You can entrust your life to them, but keep in mind they can't defend you from a squad of terrorists. Please be careful."

174

Back in the room I call the guard company, arranging to meet this afternoon. Then I get Frank on the phone.

"Frank, I want to hire some escort protection."

"Are they cute?"

"No, quit playing; this is serious. I'm talking bodyguards."

"You're for real?"

"Yes. I arranged a meeting to get a feel and decide whether to hire them. I hope you will join me at four this afternoon?"

"It sounds like this means a lot to you, I'll be there."

I focus on my research until I get a call from the reception desk.

"Mr. Nelson, there are two men here asking for you."

"I'll be right down."

When I arrive in the lobby, the receptionist points towards two men who look like they've been taking steroids for years, standing by the front entrance.

I walk up to these clean-shaven guys. "Hello, I'm Sammy Nelson, follow me." Escorting them to the pool area bar, I say, "Please have a seat."

Hearing girls scream, I notice Frank playing in the pool with them. I give him a yell. A moment later, Frank honors us with his presence.

"This late arrival is my partner Frank."

"Hello, Frank, Sammy. I'm Manny; this is my partner Efren."

"I don't know how much you guys have been told, but we need bodyguards to travel with us. Possibly to many different islands."

"We're okay with this. What are your goals?" Manny asks.

"Frank and I have separate ones. I am searching for Serrada Escrima fighters and Frank girls."

"Frank's job sounds more fun, I pick him," Efren says.

"Sammy, I'll help find Serrada Escrima fighters. I'm trained in multiple arts and have martial arts friends on different islands."

"Sounds great. If you accept the job, I'm fine working with you."

175

"Frank, I'm bodyguard trained too," Efren says, "but also a ladies man. I'm sure you and I will be a good team." He laughs.

"Sounds good to me, Efren."

In the morning, while printing business cards, I get a call. "Hey, this is Manny. I'm ready to go anytime you are. Call this number thirty minutes prior to you wanting to leave. And pack for a few days, we will be on a boat going to an island called Mindanao."

"That sounds fun, I'm excited."

"I know many good fighters there, who train daily to survive and protect their families. We can talk more on the way, it's a long boat trip."

"How should I arrange transportation?"

"No worries, I will book and arrange everything and just bill you later for it."

I spend the rest of the day catching up with my documentation then organize everything to bring it up to date. Finishing, I go for a walk, finding a mall; strolling over to the entrance I walk around inside, window-shopping.

Coming to a movie theater, I check out what's playing. Cool, a Jackie Chan flick. Buying a ticket, I grab some popcorn and soda then search for Theater Four. Getting into the dark room, I flop into a good seat and ready to enjoy my favorite action star. After the excellent movie, I go back to the room and pack before sleeping.

In the morning, I meet with Manny in front of the hotel where he takes us to the boat dock; climbing aboard, we're taken upstairs to the outside first class area. Moments after we find our seats, the boat pulls out into the ocean: we're off to Mindanao. Sitting side by side, we talk most of the day while enjoying the ride. Manny discusses how the locals train, the different Filipino martial arts and how they're closely related.

"Wow! Manny, this is an interesting place."

"Most of these remote islands don't have much of a police force. There's no money to pay them so the locals have to protect their own villages. That's why their martial arts kick ass. They have no choice but to take it deadly seriously."

The boat docks at port where trikes are waiting for customers. Hopping into separate ones, we have them take us to the bus station, where Manny and I hop on a VIP bus. Within ten minutes of waiting, we're off. A guy walks down the aisle punching small holes in a booklet, giving us tickets and asking for five hundred pesos.

"Sammy, get some rest; we'll be riding this bus for the next four hours."

Manny kicks back, closing his eyes, and I do the same. We fall asleep as the bus pulls out of town and into the jungle. Hitting a pothole, the bus wakes me; glancing at my watch, I've been sleeping a few hours. I stare out the window, wondering just how dangerous it's out there. Could these bad guys stop this bus and take us to their camp? Maybe torture us until ransom is paid?

I gaze out the window between the few stops, throughout the long ride: finally.

"Last stop, everyone off."

Getting off, Manny and I grab our things. It's late afternoon, and we're standing at a bus station in the middle of a tropical jungle.

"We need a trike to get to our final destination," Manny says.

"Wow! This is really cool, but a little scary."

"No worries, my friend, this is my home province. I will keep you safe."

Following Manny to the front of the station, there's a group of those motorcycles with side-carts. Manny says a few words in Filipino, then says, "Sammy, jump in one," while he's jumping into another. Riding down the bumpy dirt road, I notice the driver stuff a gun back into his pants that was slipping out.

A short way into the jungle, we come across what looks like a camp but turns out to be a small village. There're tiny huts placed everywhere, children are playing and women washing clothes in a nearby creek.

An attractive young girl takes us to a hut. "I'm told this is where you'll be staying." Walking in, there's a single bed on each side of the room; we each set our things by one before going back out.

The girl shows us the outdoor bathroom. "Sirs, here is the bathroom, we use the creek over there to wash up and bath. We are very open here, please don't be shy." Looking at the creek there's a group of naked people playing in the water. After our tour, we walk back to the main compound area.

When we reach the central area, a man comes up, giving Manny a joyful hug while speaking Filipino to him. Suddenly he stops and looks over at me.

"I'm so sorry, how rude of me not to speak English in front of a guest."

"It's okay."

"Amado, this is Sammy. The one I spoke to you about."

"Glad to meet you, Sammy."

"Amado and I are friends from childhood. He's been training in martial arts from a small boy up. His father is a Filipino military commando and been passing on his skills to his son. These classes were two hours every night when possible, starting from the age of six. Now he teaches the locals to defend their families."

While eating, we continue to talk. "With the intensive training over the years, the men, women and children of the village have become very skilled in martial arts," Amado says.

"What style do the villagers train in?"

"We train in one called Pekiti-Tirsia Kali. This martial art was taught to my father while in the Filipino Special Forces fighting terrorists in these jungles. My father then passed it down to me."

"This is neat. I have never heard of this art Pekiti-Tirsia Kali."

"After eating, I'll be conducting my nightly class; you're welcome to watch or join in."

"I will watch at least for the first one and join in for the second one."

Finishing our meal, we get up from the table. Amado says, "You two guys be careful while here. The last couple of weeks strangers been hanging around our small villages. We don't know who they are but feel trouble is coming."

178

"Thank you." I go back to the hut.

A couple of hours later, I hear Amado's voice outside the hut. "Guys, class is starting in ten minutes." Leaving the hut, there's a bonfire in the main area with a dozen guys stretching out around it. Amado comes up. "Take a seat, guys. Class, we have a special guest, so training will be different tonight. We're going to put on a demonstration for him."

I see Manny keep glancing towards the trees. He steps over to me as if to show me something. "Sammy, keep your guard up. We have visitors." Curious, I look that direction, noticing two men trying to hide.

Walking up to Amando, as if to ask a question on the training, I whisper, "Look just past the huts to the north, there're two men hiding in the tree line. I'm not sure how many more are out there."

"Thanks. Just sit back and watch for weapons. I'll take it from here. I want to show our hidden guests these villagers are well trained and not to be messed with."

Amado gives a demonstration that even shocks Manny and me. He spends the next couple of hours going through advanced weapon and hand-to-hand combat demonstrations. I'm amazed at their skills. I then decide that even though I haven't seen skilled Serrada Escrima fighters yet, I'm so impressed with these guys I decide to make them the offer.

After training, our uninvited guests are gone. Everyone sits down to eat, and the women bring out the food. While eating, I say, "You guys have a unique art that is extremely deadly. I'd like to have a team of five join in a competition." I explain everything from sponsor funding and travel, to the winner's purse and how the teams are made up.

"This competition is an exciting idea. I'll be one of the members and team lead," says Amado. All the others want to join too.

"Amado, this is great; please pick the others." Tired, I get up to walk to the hut.

"Sammy, wait," Amado says. "I have a bad feeling about those guys in the trees today." He hands me a loaded pistol. "Please keep this under your pillow."

I leave Manny and Amado talking by the fire after giving him my phone number and email address. He gives me his.

The next day a group of villagers take me on a tour of the local town and other beautiful areas; we're told to travel in groups for safety. I have lots of fun, and it's an entertaining break, much needed.

Getting back to the village, Manny and I get ready to leave in the morning back to Cebu.

Leaving the hut in the morning, Manny and I are surprised as all the villagers are sitting outside by two trikes waiting on us. "Thank you for being so kind," I say grabbing my bags while getting into the trike.

Arriving at the station, we hop on a waiting bus with a port sign in the window and grab a seat. Thirsty, I reach into my backpack for water, finding Amado's gun. "Damn." I'll ship it back from the hotel. Sliding it back in, I put my backpack between my legs.

The horn blows as the bus rolls into the deserted jungle on its four-hour journey to civilization. I'm woken from a deep sleep. "Bang . . . Bang . . . Bang . . . Bang." People scream, and luggage flies across the bus when it crashes into a tree.

"What the hell—" Startled and dizzy from my head hitting the side window, I gaze, trying to see what's happening. Out the window, four masked people are running towards the bus when the bus door slams open and two of them climb on. One shoots the driver while walking down the aisle with the other following.

Not thinking clearly, I reach into my backpack, feeling for the gun. Wrapping my hand around the grip, I put my finger on the trigger. Holding the gun, I watch as they come closer.

"They're here for you," Manny says. A nervous look comes over his face. "I'm going to get you out of this or die trying!"

180

Jumping up, Manny pulls a gun from his side, and fires a round into the chest of the terrorist closest to us. Screaming, the masked man falls in the aisle when the second one shoots Manny. Manny falls backward into his seat, bleeding.

Confused and shaking, I pull the gun out from the backpack, aim and pull the trigger, hitting the second one in the face. He stumbles backward, splattering blood all over the windshield.

As I stand with the gun pointing toward the door, one from outside comes into the bus shooting. Horrified, I can't shoot or even move. Manny reaches up, grabbing my collar and pulls me into the seat. He grabs the gun out of my hand and shoots the third one. Aiming at the door, he waits for the fourth, but the fourth runs into the jungle.

Police and soldiers arrive an hour later with an ambulance right behind. It seems one of the passengers called them when the bus first crashed. I'm happy Manny only has a flesh wound; once bandaged, we board an arriving bus and leave for the city. Relaxing on the boat ride to Cebu I'm feeling much better, but I'm keeping an eye out for boats coming at us, or even scuba divers. I have no idea what these terrorists are capable of doing.

Arriving back at the hotel, I pay Manny with a big bonus knowing I could never repay him for risking his life to save me and the bullet he took for me.

"Manny, I can never express how grateful I am. Thank you!" I wave goodbye as he drives off.

After dropping my things in the room and craving a glass of cold green tea, I head down to the outdoor bar by the pool, finding Frank having a drink.

"Sammy, how did it go?"

"It was way too wild, but I am back safe and have my team. Here's Amado's cell to call."

"Great. I'm arranging for our flight in the morning."

The next morning I get up and pack my stuff. After breakfast we get our things; grabbing a taxi, we're off to the airport and back to the United States.

Frank

Girls Of The Islands
*** Chapter Twenty ***

 "Take me to the Grand Cebu hotel please," I say, slamming the taxi door closed.

"Your first time in the Philippines, sir?" He lifts the napkin covering the meter, pushes a button and lets it fall back over its face.

"Yeah."

"Well, lucky for you just about everyone speaks English. Do you plan on visiting all our seven thousand islands or just the two thousand populated by people?"

"I don't have a twenty-year visa." I laugh. Leaning my head back, I close my eyes.

The driver rouses me out of a dream. "Sir, we're here. That'll be eight-hundred pesos." He peeks under the napkin-covered meter.

"I want to see the meter . . . lift the napkin." Leaning forward, I peek between the seats.

"Sir, it's eight hundred pesos."

"I said . . . I want to see the meter, or you're not getting paid."

Lifting the napkin, the meter shows four hundred. I hand him the money and climb out. "You should be ashamed!"

As I relax in my room on the bed, the AC is creating icicles off my earlobes and the tip of my nose while I search the Internet. There're countless islands with many filled with people in poverty. I guess it makes sense; how much can one earn on some small island? It'll be tricky, but I'm going island-hopping in search of my girls.

My first plan of action is to find the girls a boarding house here in Cebu. It's the perfect place, being central to most islands, and I can fly the girls directly to Manila International Airport from here. After I arrange the boarding house, my mobile phone rings.

"Frank, I keep hearing how this place is extremely dangerous. I'm considering hiring bodyguards and want you to be at a meeting with me and them at four today."

"Well, if this truly worries you, I'll attend. See you at four." If he only knew what happened in Thailand.

It's time for a cold drink; I hit the power button on the laptop and am out the door into the heat.

Perfect, the outdoor bar near the swimming pool's open. Standing at the bar, I lean on the counter.

"Sir, Bacardi & Coke please . . . what's this?" It's a pool full of beautiful young girls.

"Bartender, where did all these girls come from?"

"This hotel has a go-go club, and the girls work as dancers there." He sets an ice-chilled glass in front of me.

Leaving my drink, I run back to the room and jump into my thong swim trunks. Sprinting back, I do a belly flop into the water, knocking the wind out of me. The girls all laugh before attacking me: splashing water, jumping on me and tickling me under water. Now this is the life.

After hours of playing the girls, they say, "Frank, you're lots of fun, but it's time for us to get ready for work. Can we meet in your room sometime soon?" They put their hands down my swim trunks and squeeze.

"Anytime. Anywhere." I feel it getting hard again.

The other girls notice the bulge and giggle, climbing out of the pool. I watch their beautiful, dark, tanned rear globes as they drift towards the main lobby door, making me rock-hard.

"Hey Frank, over here," Sammy says, seated at the outdoor bar with two bodybuilder-type guys dressed in silk shirts and slacks. Thinking about the ugly girl from the Israel bar helps to get me soft before grabbing a hotel towel and walking over. Sammy introduces everyone; I talk with one guy named Efren while Sammy chats with the other.

"Efren, I had a bodyguard in Israel, and am open to having another. My goal is to find sexy girls to support the fighters Sammy is rounding up," I say, sipping my, now watered-down, drink.

"I can protect you and help you find the girls. Me being Filipino, the Islanders will feel more comfortable trusting you."

"I want to start in the morning; can you be here? Oh, one more thing. I'll be island-hopping for them, so plan on being gone for a few days."

"Sounds like fun, see you in the morning," he says, shaking hands.

He walks over to his buddy, talking for a few minutes before they both walk off, waving goodbye.

Early the next morning, I get into Efren's car parked in front of the hotel. "We're off to an island called Laythe," he says, speeding off.

Paying for our tickets, we follow the long line boarding the super shuttle boat for our two-hour ride. It is full of wooden beach seats packed with families shifting around to try and get comfortable.

"Frank, follow me upstairs. We have first class seats." Climbing the stairs, I find that it opens to an outdoor area full of lounge chairs. The boat moves out into the ocean, and the rocking from the waves puts me to sleep. I wake to the sound of the captain.

"Welcome to Ormoc City, folks," he says over the speakers.

Getting back on land, we push through hundreds of people before squeezing into a side cart attached to a motorcycle, and we're off. Ten minutes later we stop in front of a beachside restaurant, climbing out.

"Efren, is this a taxi?" I stretch my body.

"Yeah, this is a Filipino countryside taxi called a trike. You'll find many of these while hopping islands."

"Neat." Another trike pulls up, and a young girl climbs out coming over to us.

"Hi, I'm Analyn." She kisses Efren on the cheek.

"Hi, I'm Frank." We shake hands. "Let's take a seat and get something to drink." We all sit down at a plastic table on plastic chairs.

"Efren and me are long-time friends. He knows I became homeless when robbers killed by my family. I was twelve, but now I'm twenty-three. Efren said you could help me with a job. Oh, I have other starving friends who need help too."

"I'm scared—you're younger than you say and I don't want to hire minors."

Analyn laughs, pulling out her ID, showing she is twenty-three. I give it an unsure look.

"It's a legal ID. You're going to find most Filipina girls look very young for their age," Efren says.

"Frank, please check other girls too! I can have them here in the morning if that's okay?" Analyn says.

"That's fine, but no promises." She hops back in the trike, and we're off to the hotel next door.

It's getting dark, so I turn on the lights to keep working. After a few hours, I'm finished and power down the laptop when the phone rings.

"Frank, let's go have some fun? There's a karaoke bar near here; we can have some drinks and listen to the singing, whatcha think?"

"Deal." His timing is perfect. "I'll meet you in the lobby in twenty."

Coming around the corner into the lobby, I see Efren's chatting with the young counter girl. "Let's go?" I say.

When we walk in the bar's front entrance, it's full of girls with only a couple of guys. We get most of the attention all night, I guess because of me being a foreigner. The fun lasts until two o'clock when the bar closes. Two girls in short skirts come over and begin rubbing their hands between our legs.

"Hello, boys . . . lonely? We need some fun cuddling tonight . . . you want?"

"Girls, it wouldn't be right to deprive you of your needs. Please come with us, we'll escort the two of you to our rooms. Being the gentlemen that we are." I grin.

Joking around on the way to the hotel, we walk by four guys standing around a trashcan on fire, drinking beer. They grab at the girls as we pass. When the girls scream and try to pull away, the guys slap them. Picking up a board, I move to help the girls when two of the guys cut in front of me.

"You best stay out this unless you want to get hurt," one says.

"Girls, if you go behind the bushes for a little fun, we'll let you go," another says.

All four men are now around the crying girls, pulling them into the bushes. Scared, I pick the board back up and walk towards them, hoping I can protect the girls.

Efren grabs my arm and in a low voice. "Let me take care of this," he says, pushing me aside he turns towards the guys. "Let the girls go now, or your families will be buying coffins by morning."

Knocking the girls to the ground, they laugh, moving towards Efren. Efren bends and pulls a gun from his pant leg.

187

"Who's first?" he asks, cocking the gun's hammer back.

It goes silent, with the only sound from the crackling of wood burning in the trashcan. The men stare at the gun, then stumble over each other as they run off.

The girls and I also stare at the gun in disbelief when Efren grins.

"This is a perk for being a government-certified armed guard. Let's go to our rooms for some fun."

We all laugh while walking to the hotel. Going inside, each girl grabs a hand of one of us and follows.

In the room, I check out her body: it's a fantasy come true. She's short and skinny with big boobs: a body of perfect form. She steps up to me smiling with her full lips, big brown eyes and soft low voice.

"Hun, go for a shower. I will give some body tongue massage when you finish."

I'm about to go crazy.

"Don't go away, I'll be right back."

Stripping, I dash to the bathroom with my rod bouncing like a wobbling diving board. The thought of being naked with her gets me even harder; this is awesome. Doing a quick shower, I step out of the bathroom still wet. She meets me in the middle of the room.

"Let me take a shower too. Go lie on your stomach, and I'll massage you when I come back." She grabs my hard-on and slowly strokes it.

"Wow . . . I can't wait," I say.

Leaping on the bed, I drift to sleep waiting. Woken by the bed moving, I feel her legs on both sides of my hips, then the feeling of hair over my shoulders as she kisses my neck. Umm, she has a great natural smell. Nothing beats a geisha girl, but I'm enjoying this. I feel hardness push between my rear cheeks as she sits putting her weight on me.

"What's that?" I ask, pulling my hand free from under my chest.

"It is okay, hun, just enjoy," she says.

I move my hand around my back and between her legs. I feel her manhood.

"What the hell? Get off me! Are you crazy?" I ask, squirming.

"What's wrong, hun? You were horny for me before. Knowing I have little extra meat for you to play with should make you happy," she says, speaking to me in a sweet, calm voice while holding me with strong arms.

Twisting with my entire strength, I'm able to throw her off. I quickly slide off the bed and jump to my feet.

"Why?" she says, staring with sad puppy dog eyes.

Glancing down, I see she has one twice the size of mine. "Please get dressed and leave, now." I'm still trembling.

After dressing, she sadly wanders out the door with tears dripping down her cheeks.

Peeking out the door, I hear her voice echo: "Ladyboys need to feel love too," as she vanishes down the dark hallway.

Eating breakfast, Efren keeps staring with a smirk.

"I know about last night in your room; I have a brother who's a ladyboy. I'm not into them, and it doesn't bother me being around them. Sorry for not warning you, but I didn't know if you're into them. I guessed not when I saw you push her out the door and heard what she said. I was at the ice machine in the hall. Glad mine was real." He snickers.

"It's not funny, in fact, it was freaky. How can I tell in the future?" I ask, drumming my fingers on the table.

"Things to look for are an Adam's apple on the throat, large hands and large feet. Or you can reach down to see if there's something to squeeze. If so, say, no thank you, please." He snickers again.

"I'm doing inspections from now on. Shit."

"Grabbing between the legs is sure proof," Efren says.

Moving my empty plate to the side, I sip on my coffee when I get a call. It's Analyn. "Hey, there are six of us girls. It'll be easier if you guys come to where we are, okay?"

We agree and get the address. Taking a short trike ride, we pull up to an abandoned-looking house with no windows or doors. Analyn is standing in the front opening, waving at us. Climbing out, we walk up to her.

"Hi, Analyn, is this where you girls live?" I say.

"Yeah, we pay five hundred pesos each per month and sometimes we don't have the money, so we pay secret way. We don't like that way, but it's better than sleeping in the street."

"I understand."

"Guys, come this way."

We follow her in a large room; holes fill the walls, no windows or furniture. The concrete floor has only a piece of cardboard. I join Analyn, Efren, and the other girls sitting on cardboard.

"Hi, girls, glad to meet you. Let's get started."

I pass out data sheets and take pictures of each one then interview them. Finishing with the last girl, I take Analyn out to the front to discuss options.

"Analyn, I'm sorry, but you're the only one I can take. I feel sad for them, but I have to stick to the boss's rules. If you want to go, we're leaving at noon, so be at our hotel with your stuff on time."

"Yes, Frank, I want to go, but wish the rest could go too."

Stepping back in, I give the girls the bad news. I hurt seeing their sad faces. I tell Efren "Let's go" and walk out to the trike. The girls follow. Reaching the trike I turn around; each one comes up giving me a hug and kiss, tears dripping down their cheeks. They wave goodbye as the trike pulls onto the road.

"Sorry." Looking back at the girls almost gets me crying.

Just before noon, Analyn shows up, and we hop on the boat to Cebu. Arriving, I take her to the boarding house and get her settled in.

"Let's go to our next stop, guy, Inampulugan Island," Efren says.

We're off in his car to the boat for our long trip. Sleeping all the way, we pull up to the dock at a small, old-looking resort with only cabins for guest rooms. When we get on land, this place seems really cool with plenty of sexy girls everywhere. We book cabins for the night, then Efren goes to work mingling with the girls and me to my room to escape the heat and work on the computer.

A few hours pass when a knock comes on the door. When I open it, Efren is standing there with four awesome girls.

"Frank, I sought out all the girls and found these to be the best. I brought them for you to inspect, check and interview."

"Perfect. Girls, please step in, sit down and relax," I say, moving aside to let them pass.

Efren leaves, pulling the door closed behind him. A sexy, short one with perfect-size breasts, for my taste, comes up, putting her arms around me.

"Frank, Efren says we should spend the night here with you. We're happy to stay if you want us," she says, pressing her breast against my stomach as she squeezes.

"You girls are here for the night?" I ask, feeling it get hard.

"Yes, sir."

"Really. Well then, let's pull the mattresses off the bed and put them side-by-side on the floor so we all can fit."

I remove my shirt, and some of the girls follow my lead stripping, when a cute chubby one, now topless with delicious oversized breasts, comes up, putting her arms around me.

"Frank, we're shy. Can we turn down the lights?" she asks, rubbing her breast on my stomach.

"Sure," I reply, thinking that I'll turn them back up when we're all naked.

We pull all the mattresses to the floor, then throw sheets on them. I'm the first one completely naked and jump on the mattress. Excited, I slide back to the wall leaning against it, hoping there's still enough light to see the naked bodies when they strip.

Watching four girls getting naked at the same time is making me crazy, even in this dimly lit room. When the last of their clothes drop to the floor, they hop on the mattresses and under the covers; there are two girls now on each side.

"Ready, girls," one says.

As if planned and rehearsed, two girls move to my feet sucking my toes with the other two suck on my ear lobes. They joyfully giggle while sucking on me.

"Frank, how does this feel?" They continue giggling, going between my legs and taking my sack into her mouth.

Another says, "I can do better then that Frank, how about this?" She takes my shaft into her mouth, circling her tongue on the head.

I can't help but whimper out loud.

"Girls, do you hear Frank? We're making him crazy. We need to quiet him down."

The chubby one sits on my face, putting her backside over my mouth.

Muffled, I say, "I'll teach you a lesson." Reaching up with both hands, I grab her hips to hold her in place then stick my tongue between those soft rear cheeks.

"Frank!" she screams and laughs, trying to lift off my face.

"You're going to give her a heart attack," the girls yell.

Two move up and pull on their friend, trying to help her escape from my tongue. Throughout the night, we pleasure and tease one another, doing everything we can think up. The sun rises, finding all five of us tangled together and in a deep sleep.

Waking, I move their arms and legs off me and climb off the mattress. Standing, I see all those beautiful naked bodies across the mattresses. Efren said they met the standards; I will bring all four with me back to Cebu.

Kneeling down on the mattress, I say, "Girls, wake up, I have good news." All those sleepy eyes pop open, glaring at me. "All you girls are hired and coming with me in a couple of hours."

The girls go crazy, screaming and pulling me back down on the bed for another around. An hour later, I reluctantly have to stop them so we can get ready to leave.

Getting dressed, they go back to their rooms to pack. We only have an hour left before the noon boat leaves to Cebu. As I walk to the dock, the girls are approaching from the other side, happily talking and joking. I buy everyone an upper-deck seat, and we board the boat. The girls surround me as I take a seat, and we all enjoy the beautiful boat ride back to Cebu. I love being around these girls.

Arriving in Cebu, Efren and I take them to the boarding house, introducing them to Analyn. She seems to fit right in with them.

"Girls, you'll be staying here until I send someone to pick you up and take you to the airport." They all come up and give me hugs and kisses.

"We love you, Frank. Please take care yourself!"

I leave with a warm feeling in my heart, wishing I could take them home, but I know it is impossible.

Efren returns me to the hotel where I give him my mobile number. "Efren, I'll call once I'm ready, and thank you for all your help!"

"Thanks, Frank, I will be waiting for your call."

I stop at the outdoor bar, ordering Bacardi and Coke, then daydream of the night before. Sammy walks up.

"Frank, you okay?"

"Yeah, just resting."

"Hey, I've pulled my team together. Here's the info."

"Great, I have mine too. I'll book flights for the morning to the U.S."

"Alright. I'm going get ready, see you in the morning, Frank."

He walks away. Getting to the room, I book the flights and arrange everything with his team before heading out to the pool in search of the wild girls.

In the morning, we hop into a taxi and off to the airport. This has been an adventure of a lifetime and I hate that it's over, but it's time to go home.

Andrey

Pulling It All Together
*** Chapter Twenty-One ***

Looking at cars and people rushing to go nowhere from the office window, it's sure a different world from the relaxed one of the island. Sitting down at my desk and sliding a notepad over, I get to work writing my immediate need-to-do list. Paradise Island is a perfect plan. The top priority is to get with the architects and check on the status of the wine cellar, also to make sure the special design is correct.

Leaving my office, I step past my grinning secretary and through the hall to the makeshift island command center. Four guys huddle around a blueprint talking.

"What do we have going on, guys?" I ask, walking up to the table.

"Good morning, Baskov," they say.

Going over the phase two drawings and a miniature island model they created, I'm impressed with how they laid out the servants' quarters, far to the back of the island and out of sight.

"Guys, when can I expect this to be completed? The staff is on the payroll, and I need them on the island ASAP earning their wages. Second, have you received the special wine cellar requirements?"

"Andrey, we did receive notice of the cellar, and we can build a very large one. We found a designer who can build it under the island with water-sealed walls and floors."

"Excellent, I want it as large as possible. Start building now. I want a twenty-four-seven crew with as many men needed to have it completed a couple of days before the grand opening."

"We can do it, sir."

"Next, I want fifty small cages built six feet wide by eight feet deep. I plan to use them to secure some of my expensive wine and other items; I don't want the help stealing. Also, I want a large area in the back to put a hidden casino for my special guests."

"Gee, anything else?" Tim grabs a pen, taking notes.

"Make sure the entrance is facing the back of the island, I want to sneak special guests in without them being noticed. Last modification, I want a large incinerator placed close to the wine cellar entrance door. I'm not sure about international laws and gambling, but if I'm ever raided, I want the ability to quickly destroy evidence. Have it enabled for one thousand eight hundred degrees, or better."

"Anything else, sir?"

"I'm assigning a special team to handle the gambling area, skilled in setting it up the way I like. Once the cellar's completed, turn it over to them. From that point on they'll be the only ones allowed in the cellar. I need all this done quick and will spend whatever it takes to accomplish it, just don't disappoint me."

"We're on it. Oh, almost forgot, all the guest rooms are ready."

Nodding my head, I walk out and back to my office.

Sitting in my custom leather high-back chair, I ponder what's next? They better get the servants' rooms ready; I might as well get the girls there to help setup, I can keep them in the guest rooms for now. Picking up the phone, I speed-dial Frank.

"Frank, Andrey. I bought an island in the middle of the ocean and will use it for the venue. Construction is at a point where we can bring the girls. I want them all brought there now."

"And the fighters?"

"I want them there at the last minute. If they see each other train, it will take the excitement of surprise out of the fighters. Better yet—send all the information on the girls. I want where they stay and contacts for each group. Call and let the contacts and guesthouses know someone will be calling for more girls. If needed."

"I'll get right on it."

What is third on my list? Call Mark Jacobs and arrange to meet. I've worked with Mark, and for the right money he's loyal. He has done prison time for me and didn't snitch me out for a break on his sentence: I can trust him. I'm sure Mark will stick with me as long as there's money. He knows I have his back from past experiences; I bankrolled his prison account when he took the heat for me.

"Hello, my friend, this is Andrey. Long time no chat."

"Wow, it has been a long time. It's delightful to hear from you. I know you're not the type to call to say hi: what's the scam?"

"I guess there's no fooling you." I snicker. "I'm glad you're not back in the big house. I need your services."

"Well, I do my best to avoid the feds. Never doing time for the same thing twice."

"Ready to fill your pockets? I've got a job offer for you. If you can pull this off and I know you can, there's a big payday in it for you. It will require some international travel."

"I've got nothing going on at the moment, and out-of-country travel sounds fun. What's up?"

"I have two tasks for you. One is to customize a special room for me on an island I bought."

"Wow, moving up in the world. Special room? I'm all ears. Lay it on me."

"Second, I need to bring groups of girls to this island in secret. For a special event."

"Same old Andrey." Mark laughs.

"Quiet and listen up. Each country's local contact is aware I'm transporting five girls for the tournament. But we're going to arrange for an additional five, informing them that we need more help. The second five will be kept a secret from everyone on the island. It's a must."

"I'm with you so far."

"All the girls will be flown to a small country that's only a few hours by boat from the island. Late at night we'll transport them to the island on a small boat."

"Andrey, this sounds like you're up to your same old shit."

"Can you handle the job?" This guy is pissing me off.

"Sorry, sorry, already. Yes, you know I can do it."

"Make sure to wait until the first batch of girls arrives on the island. I don't what anyone seeing the second ones. I will have a special place to store them until I put them to use. I'll call you in a few days with how I want it done."

Two items down, I need to get a place to house up the twenty-five girls all together before sneaking them onto the island. Wow, this is going to be tough. Once this is set up, it'll make all our future international slaves easy to import and store. I know Mark will kill if asked; he's done it before. It's foolish to throw away my investment if I can avoid it, but I will kill them all to avoid prison. Okay, let's get my global real estate buddy on the phone.

"Good morning, Mr. Biden's office."

"This is Andrey Baskov, I need to speak to Mr. Biden?" I'm hoping this guy can come through for me.

"Hey, Andrey, how's life been treating you?"

"Jeff, I am doing well, and you?"

"I'm doing well too, international real estate sales are filling the old bank account."

"For me, the legal loan shark business put me into a Manhattan penthouse office."

"You've always have been one for backdoor action and in more ways than one." Mr. Biden laughs. "When are we going for drinks?"

"I want to drop by this evening. I need to lease a mansion in a country near an island for a couple of weeks, it's to hold some workers."

"Great, let's meet at our old strip club hangout."

"Okay, see ya about eight, later."

I need this guy's help to pull this part of the plan off; I have no other contacts that specialize in this field. I kick back in the office catching up on emails until it begins to get dark. I hit the intercom.

"I'm ready to go home, get my limo pulled to the front."

"Yes, sir."

When I arrive home, the servant prepares the hot tub and lays out clothes for the evening. Dressed, I splash on Clive Christain cologne, wondering what's in it for two thousand plus a bottle.

The limo drops me off in front of the club; this place still looks the same after all these years. A woman dressed in a suit and tie approaches me.

"Mr. Biden's table," I say.

"Mr. Baskov?"

"Yes."

"Mr. Biden is waiting." She escorts me to a table next to the dance stage.

I walk up to the table finding Jeff sitting with a couple of very attractive girls. I grab the maitre d's hand.

"Sweetie, have a margarita with Jose Cuervo 250 Aniversario brought, and whatever they're drinking."

Chatting with Jeff about the old days brings back fun memories. We continue to chat while drinking and dancing with the girls. A few hours go by. Jeff glances over at them.

"I have some business to discuss with Andrey, you girls go have fun on the dance floor."

"Yes, Jeffrey." Giggling, the girls get up and stumble off.

"Jeffrey?"

"Hey, as long as they give it up, they can call me anything." Jeff laughs.

"Okay."

"Anyway, what can I do for you, my friend?"

"Well, I bought an island and converting it into a hangout for the rich. I'm almost ready for the grand opening, which includes martial arts fighters for the kick-off."

"I'm impressed. But where do I fit in?"

"I have staff arriving and don't want to clutter the landing strip; I want it available for paying customers. I will bring the staff in by boat."

"I'm with you so far."

"My plan is to jet them to a local country, which happens to be only a couple of hours away by boat. Then I'll transport them at night into the back of the island with the supply delivery."

"That sounds like a plan; I'll look into it and see what I can do. Call me tomorrow with the country and what accommodations are on your mind."

"Sounds great, should we invite the girls back?" I ask, watching them dirty-dance with each other on the dance floor.

Jeff motions to the cocktail waitress, then points at the girls. Moments later, the girls show up, sitting down with sweat running down their faces.

"Boys, care to lick our sweat off?" They down the remains of their drinks in one swig.

"Hey, another round of drinks for our table," Jeff says.

We continue to party until the club closes. Stumbling out the door, Jeff takes the girls in his limo, and I'm off in mine speeding home.

The next morning, sitting at my desk drinking coffee, I read emails when the phone rings.

"Sir, Jeff is on the line, transferring."

"Good morning, did you sleep well?" Jeff says.

"Yes, thanks. Have good news?"

"In fact I do, I found the perfect place. It belongs to an old man who lives in China; he only hangs onto it to use as a business tax write off. If you're willing to pay cash and not report it as an expense, the old man says you have a deal."

"This works perfect, a match made in heaven. Get a deal, do the papers and have a courier drop it off. I'll sign and send them back with a cashier's check."

When I step into the reception area on the way to lunch, there's a courier handing my secretary a package.

"I'll take that," I say, reaching my hand out to the courier.

Sitting at Le Bernardin eating lunch, I examine the documents. With a currency exchange, the cost comes out to about one hundred a day, not bad for a mansion. I love third world countries; that's as long as I don't have to live in them.

Signing the document, I drop them on the secretary's desk returning from lunch, telling her to carrier them back with a cashier's check for the amount on the first page.

Next, getting Frank's girls, Sammy's fighters and other staff to the island. I forgot jet parking for the guests. I need them to drop and fly off to allow for the next guest. Maybe? I speed-dial Jeff.

"I have another problem. Maybe you can help?"

"Sure, what is it?"

"I need additional sleeping quarters and lots of room for jet parking for the guests."

"It's your lucky day Andrey, it so happens the old man with the mansion also owns a large private airstrip on some property. It was once owned by the military."

"You're awesome, Jeff, let's make a deal. Oh, don't forget all these people need a place to sleep before transporting them."

"I have that covered too. The military barracks were never taken down, they're fully functional with a working dining facility. You can staff the place with cooks and housekeepers for almost nothing."

"That's a good idea. It will help move the flow of people more quickly, send a fresh contract over."

Later in the day the contract arrives. I sign and give it to the secretary.

Hitting the intercom, I say, "Come in with your notepad."

She steps through the door and swiftly moves across the room, sitting on the other side of my desk.

"First, get the address of the airstrip from Jeff. Second, create pamphlets on getting there for the pilots. Third, add to the pamphlets how the food and sleeping arrangements will be for the works. Hire local staff to do the cooking and cleaning. Hire a firm to manage the staff and so on. And get it done now. That's it."

"Yes, sir." In another swift movement, she's at the door.

"Wait, forgot something. Arrange for a private company to pick up Frank's girls, and drop them off at the island within a week. I want them on the island before my guests start arriving."

"Yes, sir."

I review the list and find two more major steps that need to be completed. First I need Frank on the phone.

"This is Andrey. I want the girls on the island within a week. Call my secretary, she'll brief you on how the arrangements will be. You can brief your local contacts. Let them know a guy named Mark may call if more help is needed."

"I'll get right on it."

Finishing the call, I hit the intercom. "Come back in."

The secretary opens the door and again speeds to her seat.

"This will be quick. Frank will be calling you to make sure you have things ready for his group. Second, contact everyone I know, business, friends and anyone else who has a lot of money. Tell them about my grand opening and send them all invitations. I'll give you a special list for an after private competition party; only the ones on this list get the special invite." Shaking her head in agreement, she leaves the room.

The only thing left is getting to the island early to entertain guests. Once again speaking on the intercom, I say, "Let my pilot know we will be leaving back for the island in a couple of days and will be staying for a few weeks. He will stay the whole time in case I need to go somewhere."

I keep busy for the next few days catching up on other work. I need to get ahead; there'll be no free time once I'm on the island.

Frank

Servants Of Paradise
*** Chapter Twenty-Two ***

Getting back to the U.S. is bittersweet. It feels good to be home, but I already miss the excitement and the love of traveling throughout the world. Setting my bags in the corner by the door, I stumble across the room, falling on the couch, where dreamland takes me. My cell wakes me a few hours later.

"Listen up, this is Andrey. I have an isolated place for the competition on an island. I want the girls there now; get with your contacts, as someone will be arriving to escort them to a waiting jet. Also, call my secretary and give her the names of your local contacts in those countries; she needs to link them with the escorts."

A bit shocked at Andrey's urgency, I want to question it, but let it go.

"I'll get right on it, sir."

"I want you on the island now to help prepare for the competition and arrival of the girls. Second, work with my secretary validating that there'll be enough rooms for the guests.

I don't want to be embarrassed with them showing up and no place to sleep."

Going into the kitchen, I fill a large chilled glass with more Bacardi, then Coke, before making calls to contacts. Going through my list, I speak with everyone, letting them know it's time; they need to get the girls ready for someone to call to pick them up soon.

Hours later, my cell begins ringing off the hook. The contacts are calling; they say the girls are scared to go with strangers; they want me to go get them. I explain it's impossible. I tell them to give each girl my satellite phone number and to call collect anytime if they're scared or feel something is wrong. Second, I'll be at the airport waiting when they arrive. This seems to relax them a bit. Finishing speaking with the last one, I call Andrey's secretary.

"I'm done and faxed you the list of contacts and phone numbers."

"Good work, Frank. I'll be sending the company jet for the girls and others traveling to the island. I'll also email your travel info once I receive it."

A few hours later, the fax machine kicks in, printing out the travel documents. I page through them, finding Andrey has my flight leaving at ten tomorrow morning. It's from a small airport close to here; excited, I rush to pack enough stuff for a few weeks.

Waking, still sleepy, I hurry to get ready. Getting a call from the taxi out front, I grab my things and lock the door behind me. I jump into the taxi arranged by Andrey, and it speeds off towards the airport. Arriving, we pull onto an airfield and up to a small jet.

I board, listening to some of them grumble they've been waiting on me; I take a seat with the other nine passengers. When I sit, the door closes, and the jet takes off. The cabin remains quiet except for the occasional passenger asking for drinks or food. I drift off to sleep, to dream of visions of seeing my girls once again.

Snapping out of my dream, I hear, "We are now over the island and will be landing in a few minutes." The sounds of mechanical doors fill the cabin as the wheels lower under the jet, just before it skids down the airstrip to a stop. The exit door swings open; I follow the others down the stairs noticing the island full of construction workers hard at work, stepping off the stairs, I stretch my legs when two men approach.

"I'm Mr. Abdella. You're Mr. Capper?"

"I am," I say. Reaching my hand out, we shake.

"Daren, take care of the other passengers and their belongings," he says.

Mr. Abdella escorts me to the dining area where the other passengers are in a buffet line. "Let's eat," he says. I grab a plate and follow the others through the line, selecting a large helping of sushi and miso soup, grabbing wooden chopsticks and a plastic spoon. I take a seat next to Mr. Abdella.

"Mr. Baskov has had a double crew working twenty-four-seven since we begun, and recently doubled the crew. It's difficult to manage all these guys, to include keeping them from stepping over each other. But he set a deadline, demanding we don't miss it."

"Trust me, Mr. Abdella, I know all too well Andrey's personality."

"On a call with Mr. Baskov, he mentioned your arrival. He said to make sure you're in a decent room in the servants' quarters and to work with you getting things ready for the competition."

"That sounds great. I'm ready anytime you are."

After we finish our meals, Mr. Abdella takes me to my room. I find the help has placed my things on the bed. Leaving it there, I shut the door and follow him to the competition cage.

"This is Sammy's area of expertise; I bet he's going to love this big cage."

"Can't wait to meet him. Let's talk about guest seating for these bleachers. I'm concerned about everyone getting a good view, so let's have a meeting with staff supervisors who'll handle the event's support," Mr. Abdella says.

"Let's go," I say.

We go to the servants' quarters where I'm introduced to a middle-aged woman with the same accent and complexion as the servants, but who talks and acts like someone educated.

"Frank, this is Nancy, our support supervisor."

"Nancy, this is Frank, one of the event owners." We exchange smiles and handshakes.

Mr. Abdella walks off, leaving Nancy and me to our tasks.

"Nancy, I am not aware what you've been told at this point, but I have twenty-five girls arriving in the next few days. I'll be managing them for the most part but could use your help. Twenty-five girls are a lot to keep an eye on."

"Sure, Frank, what else do you have?"

"Give me a little time to get settled and organized, I'll get back to you."

"Sounds great . . . I'll be waiting."

A couple of days pass. I'm sitting by the water in back of the island, sipping a Bacardi and Coke. Enjoying the breeze, I see a boat from the distance. Standing from my comfortable spot under a palm tree, I wander over to the dock; getting closer, I see the girls.

They're screaming, jumping and waving as the boat docks. They come running off, squeezing past the others; each one gives me a big hug and kiss on the cheek.

"Frank, Frank, Frank, we missed you!"

This continues for each group of girls, making me feel special.

I swear I won't let anything bad happen to them. Nancy walks up behind me, saying, "Wow, Frank, any man would be jealous to get this kind of attention. Shall we get them settled in?"

Nancy places each group on cots in a conference room; I let them know it's only until I assign rooms. Once all the girls arrive, I speak to them as a group with Nancy.

"Girls, this is Nancy, a supervisor. She'll be helping me take care of you while you're on the island." Turning to Nancy, I say, "Please take good care of them, they are very special to me."

206

"It'll be my pleasure, Frank. Let's get them off these cots and to rooms where they can clean up and rest for today." She waves to the girls, and I follow them towards the servants' quarters. Nancy assigns each group to a room, letting them know it is not just to free up rooms, but for their safety it's better to sleep in groups.

Once I know they're safe in rooms, I go to mine and work throughout the day. At lunch, I notice all the girls eating at the buffet. They're happily chatting with one another. It seemed all the groups have become friends, or possibly like sisters.

Returning to my room, I doze off, running all the things completed and the things needing to be done through my mind. A few hours later, I'm awakened by the sound of knocking. I open the door to find one of the Thai girls staring up into my eyes.

"Mr. Frank, dinner is ready." She holds out her hand, and I take it.

We walk hand in hand to the dining area. Filling our plates we sit at the table. I chat with the girls while eating. One thing they have in common is they're all enjoying themselves; it's the happiest they can ever remember being.

They're learning to understand the difference in each other's cultures as the groups bond. But this causes arguments at times as the girls become closer: like sisters, they seem to be looking out for one another.

We finish just as a loud horn blows, alerting the construction workers that it's chowtime. Waves of men come storming the chow line. Fear hits me like a rock in the head.

"Girls, listen up. None of you are allowed to be outside your rooms alone at night, better stay in groups of three or more. Second, make sure your room doors are always locked, and don't open them unless you know who's on the other side. Got it?"

They all say, "Yes, Frank." Now I realize why Nancy put groups of girls to a single room: to discourage any horny men from trying anything.

"Well, girls, we're about to be overrun, let's get the hell out of here." Standing, we run towards the servants' quarters laughing.

About an hour later, scanning emails, I find one sent by Andrey's secretary; it's the guest list in a spreadsheet. Opening and working it, I match names to rooms, deleting non-priority ones and assigning rooms to the rest. Deciding to check them out, I run into Nancy watching a couple of the girls sweeping sidewalks.

"Nancy, I need these two to help me, would it be too much of a burden?"

"No, I'm okay with it. These girls' priority is supporting you and Sammy. As a courtesy, please inform me when you're taking them; I feel better knowing where they are at all times."

"Fair enough."

After I exchange phone numbers with Nancy, the girls follow when I step away, walking towards the front building. Mr. Abdella comes walking in our direction and up to us.

"Is the guest suite list done? I need to know so I can finish assigning them."

"It's good timing. My crew finished the last of them this morning."

Mr. Abdella hands blueprints to me with master keys for all the guest rooms. Thanking him, I hand the girls the prints, then we make our way towards the suites.

"Girls. Here is what I need you to do as we walk. I'll tell you what rooms to put an 'L' or 'S' on the blueprints while we are inspecting them, L is for luxury and S for standard, understand?"

"Understand, Mr. Frank."

Stepping into the first suite, it's amazing how beautiful and luxurious it is with expensive paintings, leather chairs and extra large beds with silk sheets and giant pillows. The girls kick back on the bed watching the big screen TV.

"Mr. Frank, can we stay in this room . . . please?" They giggle playing with the bed's vibration remote control.

"Girls, calm down and get off the bed, you're going to get me in trouble."

Realizing it's hopeless, I check out the custom Jacuzzi in the far-right corner surrounded by a marble floor and mirrored ceilings. The room's lights go out; colored light-beams are blinking all over the place. Looking over at the girls, they're still playing with buttons on the remote control and laughing.

"What else are you going to find on those buttons?" I ask, laughing at them.

"Mr. Frank, if you come play with us on the vibrating bed, we'll give you some tongue," they say, flashing their breasts.

"I wish, but we've got work to do. Turn the other lights back on, and let's go." I hate being responsible.

Moving on to other sections of the building we find ones of lesser quality, but still better than I've ever stayed in. Finishing our walk through and marking the blueprint, I release the girls, telling them to report back to Nancy.

I stop by the chow line on the way to my room, grabbing food to take with me. Back in the room, I create the girl-to-fighter assignment list, taking all afternoon to complete it. Printing out copies for each girl and a couple extras, I put them on the desk by the door. During dinner, I hand them out.

"Girls, one of your tasks is to wear sexy clothes when escorting fighters to the ring."

"Nancy gave us some very sexy clothes this morning. If you come by the room, we will model them for you. Okay?"

"Maybe. That reminds me, I forgot to tell you. Guys are not allowed in your rooms, and you're not allowed in theirs. I don't want you girls getting hurt."

"You're an awesome guy, Frank. We're blissful you're our boss. Thank you!" They all get up surrounding me, trying to hug me at the same time.

"Please be on your best behavior and work hard."

The phone vibrates in my side pouch. It's Andrey. "I'm preparing to leave to the island, I'll see you tomorrow."

"See you then, Andrey."

Sammy

Arrival Of The Warriors
*** Chapter Twenty-Three ***

I've been home close to a week when the phone rings.

"Is this Sammy Nelson?"

"Yes, who's this?"

"Andrey Baskov. You've forgotten your boss's voice?"

"Honestly . . . yes. And you're not my boss. What's up, Andrey?"

"I have an island for the competition, be there with the fighters within a week. Oh, this is your competition, so make sure you get it right."

"Don't worry about me, Andrey. It's my life dream or I would tell you to . . ."

"Tell me what?"

"Nothing, I'll give the best show the world has ever seen."

"Good. Frank's been on the island for a week doing the prep work for you. Call him if you need help."

"Will do."

"Hang on, transferring you to my secretary who has your travel arrangements. Just ensure the fighters get there, enter the cage and give a bloody if not deadly show."

That's one thing we agree on: a bloody battle.

"Hello, Sammy," she says.

Her voice sounds so sweet. Hmm, wonder what she looks like, or maybe not, being Andrey's secretary. "Hello," I say.

"You'll be riding on Andrey's private jet with others going to the island from Los Angeles. Your teams will be picked up on leased private jets. I have taken the liberty of getting the leads' names and numbers from Frank. I've made arrangements for you for getting the fighters to the island. Don't take it as if I overstepped my boundaries?"

"No, I appreciate you taking care of it, thanks."

"If you have any issues, please call me right away, so I can deal with it. Best wishes for your competition!"

"Thanks." She and Andrey are like night and day.

Reading emails, there's one from the secretary. She must have gotten my address from Frank. When I open the email, it's filled with all the info for the fighters and my travel, which happens to be tomorrow morning. After I finish packing for the two-week stay, I hop in bed, drifting off to sleep.

Waking early, I receive a call from the cab driver waiting out in front for me. Riding to the airport, I think that that secretary is really on top of things. Pulling up to Van Nuys Airport, I'm relieved there're no lines. How cool is this? Entering, I walk up to the security counter.

"Good morning, I'm getting on a private jet owned by Andrey Baskov."

"Yes, you must be Sammy Nelson? Your ID, please."

Whipping out my passport, I hand it to him.

"Thank you, follow me, please." I'm led to the door; security scans his badge on the reader to let us out, and he walks me to the jet.

When I get on, there's only one seat left, so I guess it's mine. After I sit and strap in, we taxi down the airstrip; after getting airborne, this sexy girl comes out from the back, serving us drinks. I spend my time reading eBooks on competition fighters and napping until we land at a small airstrip where a van is waiting. We're taken to what looks like old Air Force bunkers surrounded by concrete; this place seems to have been abandoned years ago.

We're dropped in front of beat-up buildings turned into makeshift hotels, where fighters are outside kicked back on benches. Getting off the van, I walk over, taking a seat, and chat with them until dinner. Before eating, I stroll over to chat with the guards at the gate.

"I'm Sammy Nelson, manager of the fighters. Where are we, and what's going on?"

"Mr. Baskov had this set up as a staging area to help keep track of who enters and leaves the island. By tonight, all your people should arrive. We'll be moving you and them in groups to the docks, where a boat will take you to the island."

"Thank you."

"No problem. Here's the list of names and departure times. The list has not just your fighters but many others. Please help by grouping them at the right times."

"I'm here only for my fighters, but that's fine. I'll help out."

When he hands me the list, I scroll down it finding I'm the last to leave. In the morning, an outsized bus waits outside with a guard standing by its door. I send groups out, and the guard checks them off the list as they board. This continues until late afternoon. I'm distracted by a call.

"This is Andrey. I'm told no fighters boarded in Japan."

"They're not here; I'll have to check what happened."

"Where in the hell are my ninjas? You better find out and fast. This violates our contract, and you know what that means. Right?"

"You better watch how to talk to me. Contract or no contract I'll go there and kick your ass."

"You just better find my ninjas." I hear a click, and our connection drops. Damn. I call the master.

"Master, the ninja haven't shown, and I'm being harassed for an answer, please help."

"Relax, Sammy, if my friend says they will be there, please trust him."

213

"Okay, but without them I have some serious problems." I hang up.

The last of us board the bus for a short drive to a waiting yacht. Some hours later, we're hopping off at the island's dock.

"Sammy, wow, it's great to see you again. This is so exciting," Frank says.

"You too, but my ninjas didn't show and Andrey called threatening me."

"Screw Andrey. Everything will work out; all my girls did arrive, including the Japanese sweeties."

Sitting in a lawn chair by the pool, it gets dark and still, no ninjas. Calling the private airline company, I ask for their status. I'm told they never showed up at the airport. Falling asleep in the lawn chair, I wake to voices of people going to breakfast. Buzzing sounds are coming from my phone. Glancing at my watch, I see that it's nine.

"Hello," I answer the phone.

"Sir, please listen, this will be quick. I'm told to relay this message. There are no concerns—the Japanese ninjas are on the island—put them on the fight roster. Each will be in the cage when called."

"That's great. Thank you so much!"

"Second relay. Frank's Japanese girls are taking care of the ninjas. Do not interfere with their instructions. Do not question them about the ninjas or their tasks. Any information they reveal may cause their death." The call disconnects.

Curious, I look at the phone's call history. No number. The last incoming call was yesterday from Andrey. How freaky.

Frank walks up and sits beside me.

"Sammy, I wanted to show you to your room last night but was unable to find you."

"Slept outside. Listen, I got a call telling me the ninjas are here."

"That's great news. Come on, I'll take you to your room."

I follow him around the side of the bar to an area with huts and a pool in the center. We step into number four, which looks better than my place; it even has a Jacuzzi bathtub and wide-screen TV.

"It's one of the nicer ones centrally located by the fighters for your convenience. It's not where Andrey told me to put you, but so what."

I laugh. "I feel he gets on your nerves. Anyway, cool room, thanks."

"It's great the Japanese fighters are here, but the Japanese girls keep disappearing for hours at a time. I'm unable to keep control of them. I'm about ready to send them back for replacements. It's frustrating."

"Frank, I got a call just before you walked up. I was told the Japanese fighters are controlling the girls. I know we planned to manage them, but we have to make an exception for those five. We need to trust the ninjas will be honorable and abide by their word."

"If it works for you, then it works for me too. I'll leave it alone."

"Thanks, Frank. How about showing me around?"

Leaving my stuff on the bed, I shut the door and follow him.

"Okay, Sammy, ready for the grand tour?" he asks, slapping me on the back.

First we swing around to the servants' quarters where I meet a couple of Frank's girls. "Wow, you lucky dog." Then we're off to the fighter's cage.

During the cage tour, I say, "Ya know Frank, I've never battled to the death or even with weapons but have done a few cage fights. What fond memories, memories I'll never forget." Climbing in the cage, I walk around checking out the fence, floor, and padding.

"What are you doing, Sammy?"

"I'm checking to make sure it's done right. There's going to be enough blood between fighters without causing damage to them with wires, nails or other things poking out."

"I never thought of that, guess you're right."

While we stand in the cage, some of the fighters come by to check it out. We stand around chatting about the contest; a

215

couple of workers show up saying we need to leave so they can finish preparing. Strange, these two Japanese-looking guys are in exceptionally great shape for a cleaning crew. Frank and I exit the cage, leaving them to their work and head back to the dining area as the kitchen help is placing the food out.

We chat and eat, then go our own ways. Back in the room, I unpack before taking a shower and hitting the sack. Unable to sleep due to the stress of everything coming up, I go relax on the couch and work on the fighter lineup for the cage bouts. Man, what a pain. Five teams and five fighters per team brings it to twenty-five contenders.

Organizing the names, I get a creepy feeling someone's staring at me. Looking over my right shoulder—my heart almost jumps out of my chest. A Japanese girl is standing there watching me work. Turning my head, I glance at the door: it's still chained.

"How did you get in here?"

Speaking softly, she says, "I apologize for scaring you, Sammy. It's not my intention. Frank brought me here to help the Japanese fighters prepare. I have come to bring you a list of the five members who will compete, so you can add them to the roster."

This list uses NA1 through NA5 to identify them. I can work with this; I just hope they're in the cage when called. I guess these names will give a mysterious twist to the competition. I laugh.

"What amuses you?"

"Oh, nothing. Hey, if you want to hang out for a few, I can give you a copy of the roster for your team?"

"If it pleases you."

Working on the roster, she steps behind the chair placing her hands on my shoulders. Her fingers massage me, moving between my upper back, neck and head. It feels too heavenly to ask her to stop; of the many oriental massages in the past, I've never felt anything this awesome.

Finishing, I send a half-dozen requests to the wireless printer across the room. She has me totally relaxed and under her control. Moving me to the bed, she removes my clothes and lays me facedown. She proceeds to remove her clothes, climbing on my back; I feel her fingers press deeply into my flesh.

Feeling her hands working my body reminds me of the bath at the ninja lair. Oh, I'm remembering her face; this is the girl who bathed me in the hot springs.

I turn on my side to take a good look at her face. She isn't there, and it's now morning. Was I dreaming of the girl from the hot springs again, or was she real? I'm still naked, and my body does feel wonderful.

Jumping up I go to the printer, it's empty. Picking up the computer it shows I sent the print request two hours ago, and the request was successful. I laugh to myself: if this is true, I wish these Asian hotties would stop knocking me out. The security chain on the door is still latched. Lying back down, I doze off, making a mental note to have Frank introduce me to the Japanese girls in the morning. I'll remember her face.

Waking full of energy, I hear a knock on the door. When I answer, it's Frank with a pleasant expression.

"Good morning, Sammy. Hungry?"

"Yap, let's eat."

I follow Frank to the dining area; it's empty except for the girls. I guess the construction guys have already eaten and are on the job. Looking around, I notice the five Japanese girls have joined us but don't see the one from last night.

"Frank, where are the other Japanese girls?"

"Who are you talking about? These are the five girls I hired."

"No. There has to be one more. One came to my room last night and worked with me on the fight roster; she's not one of these."

"If she isn't sitting here, then she must have been a wet dream." He laughs. All the girls laugh too, embarrassing me.

"Hey, I'm serious. You girls see any other Asian girls running around the island?" I stare down the table at the Japanese girls, with a demanding expression on my face. "Where is she?"

"Please, sir, don't put us in danger!"

"Forget it. I'm sorry, girls. You're right. Let's drop the subject."

"Sammy, we need to work on the fights. Andrey will be arriving this morning and the guests shortly after."

"Yeah, I agree, it's almost showtime."

Everyone gets up, going their own way to finish their last-minute tasks.

3rd POV

Can Secrets Be Kept
*** Chapter Twenty-Four ***

Andrey finishes his work backlog to prevent distractions during the grand opening of his legacy.

"Andrey's Paradise Island for the rich," he yells out loud.

Tapping the intercom, he says, "Get the jet ready for tomorrow morning, and let the staff know I'll be gone for possibly two weeks. Prepare a laptop with satellite access."

"Yes, sir."

"Update me on the status?"

"Frank and his girls are on the island along with Sammy and his fighters. Mr. Abdella is doing the finishing touches to the island's construction. Your invite responses are overwhelming. Seems everyone desires to attend, sir. The headcount already exceeds room capacity. I'll send apology letters, including letting them know that they'll be at the top of the list for the next event."

"I hope you worded the response with respect."

"Sir, it states that the invitations are handled by a small team and told to book on a first-come, first-serve basis, as you have many friends and don't want to offend any of them."

"That's perfect. Everything is coming together, and an excessive guest list response shows I'm great."

"Yes, sir."

"This has got to be the grand opening of grand openings. I want the filthy rich talking about this event for years to come. This island needs to be the place everyone wants to be, with a waiting list years back filled."

"Knowing you, sir, that's how it'll be."

Almost forgot Mark. Now that would be a major setback, Andrey thought, picking up the phone.

"Hey, Mark."

"Good morning, Andrey."

"It is. Everything's falling into place. That's why I'm calling you."

"Really. And?"

"I'm ready for phase two of the project. The first batch of girls is now on the island. Use the list I gave you to get hold of the contacts. Tell them it's a huge success, and we need five more girls with the same requirements within a week. There's a large bonus for whoever can meet the deadline, not forgetting the conditions."

"Sounds great, where do you want them delivered?" Mark asks.

"Bring them to the same airstrip, but make sure they land on the far backside of the field, which is already prepared for their arrival. We'll transfer them by boat. The guards know what needs to be done; housing and food will be waiting. I leased the backside using a fictitious company name to deter suspicion."

"Sounds like you did your homework on this one," Mark says.

"I need you to assign someone else to handle that actual transport of the girls. I want you on the island to prepare for their arrival and handle them as they come off the boat. I don't want this screwed up and things to go wrong."

"Don't worry, Andrey, just pay me well and I will make it all happen."

220

"One last thing, the wine cellar is modified to handle their storage. We will slip them in at night into the back of the island directly into their cages in the cellar. I have told the staff you're Chief of Security and responsible for maintaining full control of the wine cellar. No one but you or your staff is allowed in there without your permission."

"Chief Security Officer of who?"

"I guess you better hire some security personnel," Andrey says, laughing.

"I guess you're right. I will see you on the island soon."

"Great, bring your security guys in through the front. We want everyone to see them as legit. In fact, they'll also handle island security."

"Got it," he says, hanging up.

That should cover everything. Hitting the intercom, he says, "Get my limo. I'm going home early. Also make sure it's at my home in the morning to take me to the jet."

"Right away, sir."

Packing his suitcase, it crosses Andrey's mind how busy it's going to be and that he could use some help on the island. Knowing how efficient his secretary is, and how she takes a great deal of pleasure in serving him, he says, "Hell, why not take her along on this one." He hits the intercom.

"Yes, sir?"

"The next few weeks are going to be a challenge, and I'm going to need administrative help on the island, for at least the first week."

"Shall I arrange for office temp to send someone with you?"

"No. You know this project well. You'll be perfect to help in making this a success, that's if you're available? I would like you to go with me for a week or two."

Waiting for what seems like minutes, she responds in an excited, high-pitched voice, "I would be happy to go and help make this a success for you, boss."

"Great. Pack and have the limo pick you up first. I don't want to have to wait on you. Also, make sure you have a laptop with a satellite wireless card. I will be leaving for home in a few minutes, make sure my car is downstairs waiting."

"Yes, sir."

Leaving for home, Andrey steps out of his office looking down at his secretary organizing her desk. She looks up giving him an ear-to-ear smile. She has a habit of always smiling at him, but this time it seems her eyes are smiling too. Andrey enters the open elevator and turns around. As the door closes, he can still see her smiling.

"One strange woman," Andrey says.

Exiting the front lobby, Andrey walks up to the open rear door of the limo and climbs in. The valet attendant shuts the door, and the driver pulls out, taking him home. Arriving, he packs for the trip then goes to bed early.

Early the next morning, a Bentley limo stops in front of an upscale condo building in Battery Park City, New York. Moments later, a female, about six feet tall with blond hair going down the length of her back, steps out. Having the body of a supermodel causes men passing to stop and gawk as she walks to the limo. The chauffeur stands by the car door, keeping an eye on the now group of men, with a can of mace in his right hand.

"Good morning, Savannah . . . I mean, Miss Calia," the chauffeur says.

"It's okay, Joe, but we better hurry—don't want to keep Mr. Baskov waiting."

His gaze locks on her huge breast with a low-cut dress showing a delightful view. His eyes wander up into her bright blue eyes having smiles of their own.

Giving him a pleasant grin, she bends forward, climbing in. The group of men yell, "Mwah," staring at her ass. She swings it in and sits.

"We're on our way." He shuts the trunk after two uniformed building employees put her suitcases in.

Speeding off, a short time later the limo pulls up to the ten-foot, black, wrought-iron gates of Andrey's home. Pushing the intercom button, the camera on top of the gatepost moves scanning across the car.

"Good morning, Joe, nice job washing the boss' car. One sec, I'll let you in."

"Thanks, Annabel."

The gates roll to the side, and the limo moves up the twisting driveway. Pulling to the front, Joe gets out walking up the red-brick path to the eight-foot, double-door front entrance. Walking, he watches the gardeners perfect the beauty of the yard.

Annabel opens the door in a tight-fitting maid outfit; she's braless, showing her breasts through the thin white fabric. The length of the outfit is just below her panties, revealing most of her eighteen-year-old legs.

"Where are the boss's travel bags?" He's getting aroused, as he does every time he sees her.

"Right here, Joe, what's wrong?" She asks, speaking in her British accent.

"Ah-ah, nothing, just in a hurry. That's all."

Grabbing Andrey's things, he quickly turns hoping Annabel didn't see the lump in the front of his pants. Putting the luggage in the trunk he closes it, stepping to the side of the limo, he opens the back door and waits for Andrey.

Andrey rushes out and hops in. "Good morning, Mr. Baskov," the chauffeur says.

Andrey slides in glancing at his secretary sitting towards the front.

"If we have everything let's get going, I have a party to attend."

The chauffeur hops back in, throwing the limo in gear and speeds off. Twenty-five minutes later, they pull to the side of Andrey's jet. Andrey and Savannah board while the chauffeur and pilot move the luggage into the cargo section, then the pilot returns to the cockpit.

"Good morning, Mr. Baskov, welcome aboard. The weather report indicates you will have a clear view and peaceful trip."

The flight attendant calls up front giving the pilot an okay, everyone's seated and strapped. The dual turbo engines speed up as the jet taxis down the airstrip. They feel the jet lift off, and then they're in open skies.

During the flight, Andrey sleeps in his bedroom while Savannah stares at clouds out the small window, wishing she had the courage to tell Andrey how much she loves him. If he only knew the reason she never married: the hope one day he would see something in her.

She feels she has been blessed. Her and Andrey are out of the office together; she can show him how she feels, but she's terrified he'll laugh, calling her silly. With hope and a wish, she dozes off in her seat.

"We will be landing in twenty minutes," comes over the speakers from the cockpit.

Savannah opening her eyes clicks the gold buckles of her seatbelt; she gazes around the main cabin in amazement realizing Andrey does live a luxury lifestyle.

Andrey appears from the back smiling, showered and changed. He takes a seat as the jet descends onto the island and looks out the window as his paradise comes into view. The jet rides down the airstrip coming to a stop, the door swings open. The pilot and stewardess stand in the jet by the exit door.

Mr. Abdella stands at the bottom of the jet's doorsteps when Andrey and Savannah exit; Mr. Abdella whistles at a woman and three men talking, and they come running over.

"Take Mr. Baskov's things to his room," he says, looking at the woman. "Take Savannah's things to her room, she will be staying in the room to the right of Mr. Baskov."

"Right away, sir. Please follow me, Miss."

"Mr. Abdella, has a man named Mark arrived?" Andrey asks, walking towards the buildings.

"Yes, he's in the wine cellar, sir. I'm not sure what he's up to, but he's been down there most of the time since arriving. Security prevents anyone from getting close."

"That's fine. He's following my orders."

"Yes, sir."

"I'm going to walk around to check things out. If you're needed, I'll call," Andrey says.

Mr. Abdella turns and walks towards the servants' quarters watching Andrey make his way to within a few feet of the wine cellar.

224

Andrey gets to the door; two bodybuilder type guys block his entrance. "Sorry, sir, but this is a restricted area."

"I'm Mr. Baskov. Owner of this island."

One pushes the button on his microphone hanging off his uniform. "Sir, a gentleman named Mr. Baskov is at the door requesting to enter."

A moment later Mark steps out the door. "Mr. Baskov or Andrey is the owner. You should have been briefed before coming on duty. He isn't to be stopped, or spoken to unless he speaks to you first. You best get the word out to the rest."

Mark steps back in with Andrey right behind. Walking towards the back, Andrey notices the wine shelves stocked, and stops to inspect. Pulling a bottle of Chateau Lafite (1869), he's pleased Mr. Abdella did his homework. He slides the bottle back in place, and they continue towards the back of the room, passing cages.

"These look perfect, how are the rest coming along?"

"Nicely. As you can see the cages are complete, and the cots have arrived. The only concern during construction was bathrooms. It's difficult to convince people you need bathrooms in storage lockers. I told Mr. Abdella I'm going to use the cellar for the security guards, and the storage cages will double as sleeping areas for them."

"That's brilliant, Mark."

"Almost forgot, I have your additional sweethearts at the private airstrip. I'll transport them when you give me the word. Oh, to keep them out of sight I leased a separate bus and boat to transport, and security to keep an eye on 'em. They won't give us a problem. I told them this country has lots of terrorists. That's why they're on a private airstrip. I said that to keep them safe, they'll be moved late at night to come to the island."

"What an imagination," Andrey says.

"It worked, fear filled the eyes of all the girls, they hugged and thanked me for keeping them safe."

"That's a perfect idea. As bad as I am, I don't think I'd thought that one up," he says, laughing.

Andrey continues to move towards the back. "Roomy, much bigger than I expected. I like what you did with the place. It'll be perfect for our after hours party. We'll have this set up so

225

awesome it will definitely please our special guests, having them, cumming, time and time again."

Andrey leaves the cellar escorted by Mark to the side of the building.

"Here's our so-called evidence remover Mr. Abdella built."

Andrey smirks. "Well, it's an evidence remover, just not the kind they believe it is built for." They laugh.

"I've forgotten how funny you can be, Mark. Hanging out with you for the next few weeks is going to be a blast."

"I hope to keep the island going for many years to come. Pleasure and money are a marriage made in heaven."

"Oh, bring the new girls tonight, let me know when they arrive. I need to check on Sammy and Frank to make sure they got their act together."

When Andrey walks to the dining area, both Sammy and Frank are sitting at a table, reviewing the agenda to make sure they are in sync for the competition. Andrey sits at their table.

"I've been walking around and only noticed three teams, where're the other two?"

"They're out training and don't want to be distracted," Sammy says.

"That's fine, but they better be in the cage when it's time for action, or it'll violate our contract. That means all my money back."

"They'll be there. Make sure you have my money ready when this is over." Sammy snaps the pencil he's holding in half.

"I don't know what's with the attitude. Business is business. Nothing personal," Andrey says, getting up and leaving.

"What an idiot," Sammy says.

Andrey returns to his room falling asleep. A knock on the door wakes him. When Andrey answers, it's a security guard.

"Sir, Mark told me to let you know the merchandise has arrived."

"I will be over in a few minutes," shutting the door.

226

When he walks up to the cellar, the guards open the door for him without question this time; hearing many female voices chattering brings a grin. At the bottom of the stairs, he turns right and walks the path to where the secret room is hidden by a temporary wall. Opening the door, he finds Mark talking to the girls circled around him. The room's full of them. Suitcases are stacked in a corner eight feet high.

Andrey moves up behind one of the girls and listens to Mark.

"Listen up girls—I want silence. The quicker you get organized, the quicker you get into your permanent rooms outside. These rooms are built for storage and for guards to sleep between shifts. You'll stay here for tonight while we finish construction on the staff rooms."

"Do we have to be caged up?" one says.

"I'm not sure why the complaint, we pulled all of you from sleeping on the streets. It's only for one night." Everyone turns around, watching Andrey.

The girls become quiet when Andrey stares at them, not saying a word. Hearing Mark, they turn back to face him.

"Girls, grab your stuff and step into one of the guards' sleeping areas. I want you all to keep your things with you, so there's no crying later something's missing. When I call your name, move into the one the guard will be standing next to with the door open."

The girls don't like the idea of staying in the cages, but they listen and do what they're told. Scared and confused looks fill the room as they move into them and sit on the cots.

"I'm adding a second shift of construction workers to complete your rooms by morning. It's been a long night, and you're all tired, let's get some sleep."

"Thank you, Mark," the girls say.

Andrey, Mark and the guards wait until all the girls have laid on their cots and the sound of heavy breathing comes from the cages, before walking to the front.

"You pulled off the hardest part Mark. I knew you could do it."

"Wow. What a long night, at least it's all done, and the girls are here and secured," Mark says.

"Almost forgot. Guard, when you're sure they're all sleeping, shut and lock the cage doors. No need to worry when they wake; being underground with concrete walls reinforced with iron, its soundproof. No one will hear their screams when they realize they're prisoners, and these cages are their homes for life."

Mark and Andrey walk up the steps and out the door. Standing outside, they continue to talk.

"Mark, I want these girls looked after. This means making sure they eat well and their needs are attended to. No one will want to spend big dollars on broken toys. These girls are valuable, I want to keep them this way." Andrey gives Mark a glare of seriousness before walking off.

3rd POV

Battle Of The Elite
*** Chapter Twenty-Five ***

Andrey stands watching the first private jet skid down the airstrip. The pilots were informed to get airborne as quick as possible to free up the strip for the next jet. Nancy's standing next to Andrey with a half-dozen girls; all dressed in short, island-style clothes. When the engines quiet down, Andrey steps over to them.

"Excellent touch of class with the girls' clothes."

"Thank you," Nancy says.

"Nancy, in my world, friends brag because limos drop guests off at their clubs, while private jets drop mine off." He smirks.

"Sir, I don't know what a limo is? But I have the girls escorting the guests and the construction workers taking their suitcases."

"I'm impressed with how you're handling things, Nancy. A permanent job here is beginning to fit you, keep doing your thing."

The first jet lands, and the door flips down. Andrey steps up to the stairs, welcoming the guests coming off. Nancy waves a girl over to take them to their room. As each jet lands, Andrew and Nancy continue their routine.

"Nancy, I feel like the guy from the old TV show Fantasy Island, just need a midget to stand next to me, yelling, 'Boss, the plane . . . the plane,' to make it perfect." He laughs. "I haven't had this much fun in years," Andrey says, thinking he should close his office and move here to run the place.

By mid-afternoon, the guests have all arrived. Nancy takes the girls to the rear dining area to eat before the night's events begin. Andrey takes an inspection walk to make sure the bar is open and the kitchen's serving a full menu of delicious food. He wouldn't dare feed the rich with a servants' buffet. Entering the bar, Mr. Abdella is inspecting a delivery of exotic beer.

"Sir, everything is in order. As you see, the bar's open, serving guests. The dining facility is full of happy people."

Nancy walks in. "The girls are fed, and I have them working throughout the island helping guests."

Andrey spots a girl sweeping the floor. "You, follow me." Looking at Nancy, he says, "She'll be back; I'm going to walk the guest areas and have her take care of any of their immediate needs." He walks out the door with her following. After spending the next hour helping guests, he sends the girl back to check in with Nancy.

Calling Sammy, he says, "The fights are beginning in the morning. You have everything ready?"

"No problem, got things to do, later."

Andrey decides to check on the extended entertainment. Heading back to the servants' quarters, he approaches the cellar door. The guards allow him to pass. Down the stairs and to the right, he walks to the back where the girls are locked in their cages. Mark and a group of guards are dragging two guards across the floor.

"What the hell happened?"

"I caught these two raping one of the girls, and I killed them to set an example to the others," Mark says.

"You hired rapists?"

230

"Andrey! All the guards passed extensive background checks, I don't know how these guys slipped past, but the rest of the guards now know the punishment."

"It best not happen again, Mark. I consider you a friend, but if anything else happens to my girls, you will end up dead." Andrey leaves the cellar and back to his room to deal with business emails for the rest of the day.

In the morning Andrey stops at the cafeteria for a protein drink, then off to the arena to entertain guests before the fights. Sammy and Frank are speaking with a group of men dressed in matching uniforms, with Andrey's Paradise Island logos on the back in big letters. Curious, he walks over.

"Frank, love the uniforms on these guys. What's their responsibility?"

"We'll use these guys to carry bodies out of the cage and other tasks needing to be done during the event," Frank says.

A short time later, three of the five teams arrive, but the Japanese and Israeli teams are missing. Sammy begins to worry, catching Andrey's gaze at him from a front-row, ringside seat.

At ten the fights are ready to begin. Sammy steps up to the podium picking up the microphone.

"Ladies and gentlemen, welcome to the greatest show on earth, presented by Paradise Island, hosted by . . . Andrey Baskov."

Standing, Andrey walks to the podium, grabs the microphone from Sammy's hand and pushes him aside.

"My dear friends, I'd like to thank you all for coming. You're very blessed to have this opportunity to be the first on Paradise Island. Please enjoy the island and the shows, thank you again." Stepping down, he returns to his seat between two Wall Street executives.

Moving back to the podium, Sammy continues, "There will be fights throughout the day for your entertainment. The battles will continue one after the other; as we drag each body out of the cage, the next fight will begin. As you can see, the only possible escape for a fighter is making it over the twenty-foot side or taking out his opponent. Now, let's introduce the teams."

"Welcome, Brazil's - Capoeira." They bow then sit.

"Welcome, Thailand's - Lerdrit." They bow then sit.

"Welcome, Philippine's - Pekiti, Tirsia, Kali." They bow then sit.

Stepping from behind the bleachers is the Israeli team. Shocked, everyone silently stares as the all-female team climbs the bleachers.

"Welcome, Israel's – Krav Maga." They bow then sit.

"Honored guests, there is one more team; Japan Ninjitsu who will be arriving soon."

"Each team is made up of five members; the team with remaining members in the end wins the grand prize. For obvious reasons, there is one rule: no guns. All other weapons are legal. The team leads will pick the fighter to represent them in each round; each fighter will have a number one through five identifying their fighting position. So, with no further interruptions, let the fights begin."

"Capoeira and Krav Maga leads, please send your fighters." The two fighters enter the cage; Sammy steps up and shuts and locks the door.

The fighters move around the cage keeping a safe distance, as they seem to be getting a rhythm and feel of each other. In a swift motion, Capoeira flips into a cartwheel striking Krav Maga's face with his heel, sending her off her feet and slamming to the ground.

Krav Maga immediately jumps to her feet and into a defensive stance, as Capoeira moves around the ring in deadly dance movements. Out of nowhere, Capoeira strikes Krav Maga's kneecaps with a low kick. Krav Maga drops to the ground. She squirms in extreme pain. Krav Maga tries to push off her good leg to stand but falls back down. Capoeira moves towards her. Krav Maga turns to her side, watching the fighter closing in. When he's only steps away, Krav Maga quickly slips her foot behind the heel of the Capoeira fighter's foot, then kicks the knee cap.

The sound of his knee breaking echoes through the cage. Capoeira falls to the ground, a bone now sticking out of the side

232

of his leg. Lying in pain, he moves into a defensive position and waits for Krav Maga to finish him off.

Recovering, Krav Maga stands and limps towards Capoeira. The spectators stand chanting.

"Kill him . . . kill him."

She closes in just out of striking range and looks down at the wounded fighter.

"You have some incredible moves; I've never seen such masterful techniques. You're indeed a warrior."

Stepping to the gate, Sammy opens it, letting her out; four staff members enter the cage, removing the battle-torn fighter.

The matches continue throughout the day; the teams continue to get smaller. As each match ends, there's one less able to fight—some no longer breathing. Outside in the servants' area are cots filled with wounded, lucky to fight another day, lucky to be alive.

Evening falls, and Sammy's a bit hesitant to call the next two fighters; the first ninja match appears on the roster. No one has seen the Japanese team, and he still wonders if the Japanese girl who mysteriously appeared in his room was a dream. Sweat drips down his forehead: he has no choice.

"Lerdrit and Ninjitsu, your teams are up."

The Lerdrit fighter steps into the cage, from the corner of Sammy's eye he sees something dropping as if falling from the sky. Now standing in front of Lerdrit fighter is a ninja straight out of a history book. The crowd goes deadly silent—Andrey leans forward in his seat—Frank steps up to the cage gripping it so tight his fingers turn colors. Even though Sammy recruited them from the mountains of Japan, his blood still runs cold from fear.

Lerdrit immediately strikes with a flying knee to the chest, followed by a palm to the chin, catching Ninja off guard. The powerful blows send Ninja flying backward. Ninja does a back flip, landing on his feet, creating enough space to give him a few seconds to recover.

A shuriken sails across the cage at the Lerdrit, striking his neck. Wobbling Lerdrit begins stepping in circles. Pulling out the shuriken, he attempts to throw it back at the Ninja. Ninja pulls his sword in one swift motion, slashing the fighter across the chest.

Spectators scream as blood gushes out, turning the mats red. Lerdrit fighter falls forward on his face while blood drips out the side of the cage onto the floor. Smoke fills the cage: the ninja vanishes.

Andrey stands while screaming, "That was awesome, I want to see more."

The spectators just stare quietly at the dead fighter. Sammy looks over at Frank, who looks shocked.

"I was hoping to see deadly fighters, but not sure if I'm ready for assassins," Sammy whispers.

Stepping up to the microphone, Sammy announces. "Honored guests, the fights are finished for this evening. They'll continue in the morning. Let's go enjoy the open bar; they're ready to serve your favorite drinks."

Guests step down from the bleachers and wander towards the bar whispering to each other. Sammy and Frank follow.

Andrey walks over to them. "Guys, that was great, you didn't let me down. The ninja thing is genuinely entertaining, an excellent touch for the last fight of the evening."

The battles continue in the morning, giving spectators exciting matches. In the end, the ninjas are victorious but did show mercy and let many live.

Sammy pulled off his dream and Frank's back in the money. Getting ready to leave the island, it's agreed to make sure everyone they brought is on their way home before catching their flights. Sammy arranges for a large enough boat to carry them all to waiting buses on the mainland. The private jets will leave toward the evening taking groups home.

"Andrey, I have arranged transportation for everyone to leave in a few hours," Sammy says.

234

"No, I want the girls to stay for a few more days to clean up this place."

"That is not going to happen; we brought them here, and we will make sure they get home safe. No exceptions."

"Whatever. Take them bitches." Andrey doesn't want to push it. No need to take a chance of them finding the other girls.

All are on the boat and accounted for except the ninjas, who disappeared, which isn't surprising. The boat pulls out heading to civilization. The bus arrives at the airstrip, and the group unloads and get comfortable.

Frank goes to town. Stopping at the bank, he gets cashier's checks to pay everyone before heading back. Returning, he passes out their pay, including the fighters, feeling they earned it even though it wasn't in the contract.

The jets didn't arrive on time, putting the flight off until morning. Sammy and Frank throw a special evening meal to thank everyone for a job well done, having pizza delivered. The project went well, as only a couple of guys died at the hands of the ninjas, and a couple seriously injured.

They all sit around enjoying the pizza and chatting. Frank, sitting with the group, calls their contacts to let them know the girls and fighters will not be arriving until the next day, due to late arrival of the jets. Each call to the girls' contacts comes back with the same response.

"Andrey called requesting five more girls. A guy named Mark arranged their pickup; they've been gone for over a week."

Hanging up with the last one, Frank tells Sammy and the people at the table what he was told.

"Does anyone know anything about this, or seen any more girls from their countries on the island?" he says.

The tables are full of confused looks and heads shaking. Sammy calls the martial arts master in Japan, who arranged the meeting with the ninja, telling him what happened. He says he isn't aware, but will contact his friend. After hanging up, Sammy tells Frank.

"I have to go back. I can feel something is wrong, something bad. I'm responsible for those girls. I gave Andrey their contact info," Frank says.

"I'm going with you: we're partners," Sammy says.

"No, I need you here just in case there's a trap. I'll call from the island to let you know if Andrey has the girls or not. If you don't hear from me in twelve hours, it means I'm in trouble."

"We're not leaving here until we know the girls from our countries are safe. We'll come for you if things go bad," one of the fighters says.

"Thank you."

Frank tells the gate guards he's on his way to town to pick up some personal items, passing through the front.

Speeding to the pier in a taxi, he glances at his watch hoping to find a boat to the island this late. Arriving on the dock, he's able to hire a private boat for double the standard fare. The few hours ride feels like forever.

Nearing the island, he says, "I need you to stop. I'm going to swim the rest of the way. I want surprise my friends."

"If you say, sir. Here take this life preserver to float on, we are still a bit out." He hands Frank the white tube; Frank takes it, sliding into the warm water.

On shore, he climbs out of the water, being as quiet as possible sneaking between the trees.

3rd POV

Chains Of Love
*** Chapter Twenty-Six ***

Andrey sits at an outdoor table, drinking carrot juice and watching Sammy and Frank load the boat, making sure everyone they brought is aboard. Once they fade out of sight into the ocean, it'll be better yet, knowing the two guys who would disrupt his one-of-a-kind party are gone. Okay, next on the list, seeing off the guests who aren't invited to his special after-hours event.

Standing at the airstrip excited, Andrey gives the guests a farewell and welcomes them back on their next vacation. Hours later he waves bye, as the last jet becomes airborne, screaming into the sky. Turning, he walks towards the guest lounge, unaware Frank is back on the island looking for the girls.

Frank creeps around from the beach doing his best to keep hidden. Coming up the back of the cellar, he slides along the wall, hearing the guards talk to one another.

"It's unfair, all them horny girls down in those cages, we ain't allowed to play with them."

"Yeah. The visitors get to play with them tonight, but we only getta watch."

"Well, maybe Mark will let us have leftovers."

"I heard Mark say when they're done there may not be any leftovers, the dead ones are gonna be put in that firebox over there."

Frank sees Andrey coming and crouches down as Mark comes from the other direction. Peeking around the side of the building, he sees them just feet away, standing by the cellar door guards.

"What's so funny?" Andrey says.

"Nothing, sir." The guards straighten up in a professional manner.

"Mark, get the merchandise ready, we're about to begin."

"It will be my pleasure Andrey. It'll take some time to set everything up, so give me a couple of hours?"

"That's it, text me when you're ready. Don't forget our special attraction," he says, slapping Mark on the back.

"This'll be one night I'll never forget," Mark says.

"How's our security?"

"We have twenty guards throughout the island; don't worry."

"I'm heading to entertain our guest at the bar, hurry up." Andrey walks off.

Hearing this, Frank creeps to the back of the lounge, finding an open window. Inching the curtain to the side, he peeks in. The bar is full of grey-haired men and woman laughing, joking and groping each other. Moments later, Andrey steps through the front door and up to the podium.

"Hey everyone . . . horny?"

Looking around at the senior-citizen-filled room, he continues to speak as Frank quietly listens.

"Welcome, all! This unique event is for the most perverted minds. If you're here, it's because, I believe you're a pervert. If not, it's a good time to leave." He snickers.

The room fills with cheers and laughter, "Andrey . . . Andrey . . . Andrey," they cheer.

Andrey raises his right hand over his head and waves as an expression of pride comes to his face.

"Please be patient. It'll take a couple of hours to finish getting things ready. But it will be worth the wait, believe me," he says, stepping from the podium.

238

Realizing what's about to happen, Frank calls Sammy. "I'm scared, Sammy, Andrey does have the girls here, and something bad is about to happen. Please bring help. Hurry before it's too late."

"What's going on? What did you say?" Sammy says.

"The cellar . . . the cellar." Frank's phone dies.

"I'm on the way with everyone that can fight," Sammy says, speaking to a disconnected call.

Frank watches and listens to Andrey while regretting the day he met him. How could he have fallen for this? It's his entire fault.

Andrey grabs a glass off the bar and walks around mingling with his guests. A few hours later, he looks at his phone as if reading a text.

"Listen up my loving friends, the girls and playroom are now ready for your pleasure. Please follow me."

Andrey steps towards the door with the group following, taking them past the cellar door and down the stairs. Frank slips in between the pack. Hoping not to get caught, he blends in from the rear.

The wine racks fill the walls on both sides, not an empty spot open to place a bottle. The group eyes the bottles while following Andrey deeper into this cave-like shelter. Within moments, the walls become cages, cages full of girls with faces full of terror, girls from the countries he had just been. They're naked and chained to the bars, cage doors open.

"Please inspect my harem as you wish, we'll talk price once you find one of your interest. If we agree, I'll bill it to your room as an incidental." He laughs. "The guards will take them to the playground in back."

Women, then men fondle the chained girls, squeezing their breasts, spreading their rear cheeks trying to put fingers in their holes, and pulling on pubic hair. Others smack the girls' breasts, leaving red marks.

Frank watches the pain and embarrassment in their eyes, the tears running down their innocent faces; he hates himself, it's his fault they're there. He wants to help but knows he doesn't know

239

how to fight; even if he did, he's far outnumbered. Watching, he prays that Sammy got his message and will come before they hurt the girls.

"Friends, let me introduce you to the playroom," Andrey says. Everyone follows, going to the back, entering a large medieval-like torture chamber.

"What do we have? Oh yes. Over here is a wall filled with shackles. Over here the sign displays 'Toy Wall' filled with different size whips, different kinds of vibrators, mouth gags and many more strange devices."

Frank's stomach turns, wondering what kind of sick man Andrey is and these people?

"And now for those who dare and have enough money. This one will be very expensive." Andrey claps his hands. "I give you . . . Savannah!" he says, pointing to the back wall.

The wall spins around, displaying Andrey's secretary chained naked with her arms and legs spread wide. She's wearing a spiked leather collar around her neck with a dog chain hanging off it. Her mouth is plugged with a red ball, held by a strap around the back of her head. Her eyes are wide open, full of terror and tears dripping down.

Frank's shocked finding how sick this man truly is. He can't believe Andrey would do this to the only one loyal to him. Frank's spoken to her many times on the phone. He could sense her devotion to Andrey. Yet, deep down he knows why Andrey did, as no sane or crazy people would deprive themselves of a taste of her flesh if offered. Andrey will make millions off her tonight and will allow these crazies to abuse her mind and body for that money; or is it for the pleasure of watching?

"You little bitch, bend over."

Frank turns towards the screaming. Mark's grabbing a girl chained in the cage next to him by the hair and begins slapping her face. Frank sees blood drip from her ears and nose; without thinking, he reaches out and grabs Mark by the hair slamming his head against the cage bars.

"You coward." He continues to slam Mark's head with all his strength.

"Help us," all of the caged girls yell and pull on their chains.

240

Frank feels someone from behind put their arm around his neck, choking him. He's unable to breathe and lets Mark go. Mark comes up swinging and hits Frank in the jaw, knocking him out.

Andrey smacks a twelve-inch rubber dildo he's holding on the table. "Guards, drag that man . . . tie him up naked next to Savannah."

Frank wakes nude and strapped to the left side of Savannah. The shackles inches apart allow his right hand and foot to touch hers. Glancing down at her body, he loses thought of what's going on. Being so close, the smell of her body scent, the feel of her flesh touching his. The sight of her breasts causes him to get hard.

"Well, ladies and gentlemen, we have an unexpected treat tonight, an addition to our auction, maybe even a two for one deal. Seems the guy's ready for action. Look, he has a hard-on. Tickle the sack to see if it gets harder." Andrey laughs. "Feel free to go play a little with them. The bidding will start soon."

Frank is now a victim of Andrey's sick party. Savannah and Frank look into each other's eyes; they reach over to hold hands, realizing this could be the end.

The senior citizens have stripped in the dressing room behind the podium and now all stand naked facing Andrey and the platform. Each one has an expression of excitement as if they just won bingo. Andrey stands on a podium at the entrance of the dungeon, hitting his mallet down to start the auction. The guards bring the first girl in from the cages, forcing her onto the platform.

"Shall we begin? This young beauty starts at one hundred thousand dollars, who wants to enjoy?"

"Hey, for that kind of money what are we allowed to do?" a woman standing in front says.

"Anything you want but if you end up killing one, there's a fifty thousand restocking fee."

The girl screams and tries to leap off the platform. Andrey takes a knife off the podium, sticking it to her throat.

"Stop, or I'll kill you now. With them at least you have some chance of living."

241

She stops, and the guests bid and continue to bid, making offers for the caged girls as the guards bring them in one by one. Andrey accepts the highest bid, and the girls are moved to a torture device of the winner's choice. The girls are stripped, chained or locked into place, in any positions demanded by the paying guests. The chamber's now full of naked girls in strange positions, screaming as their tormentors laugh.

Lining up at the toy wall, they joke while picking whips and other toys off the wall. Returning to their areas, some grab a tube of KY of the lubricant table while others prefer to dry insert. In one area, a woman is forcing the girl to lick her pruned up snatch, as the men insert Viagra-filled rods into the girl's holes.

The girls are now screaming in pain. Savannah and Frank stare at each other, now worried for themselves as a group walks towards them with evil smiles on their faces.

Frank gives a muffled yell, "No, this can't be real," pulling on his straps trying to break free. The group slowly moves closer when one reaches out and yanks on Frank's balls while others poke at Savannah.

A guard comes running in. "Andrey . . . Mark help." He's soaked with blood. His eyes roll up, and he falls to the floor.

Screams are coming from the front, "Help, we're under attack. We're overpowered. Ninjas, they're coming out of nowhere."

The guests drop their toys, pull out of the girls or whatever sick thing they're doing and run in circles. One runs to a cage, jumps in and shuts the door. Others see him and do the same.

Andrey grabs a metal bat and runs to the front. "What's the problem? There are twenty guards, kill the ninjas. They're ruining my party." Running up the stairs, he heads out the door.

Sammy storms the island with his team.

"Spread out! Let's help who we can, careful not to hurt the innocent. It's a battleground out here," Sammy says.

Flames from a burning building give enough light to show the dead bodies everywhere. Everyone is fighting everyone, and the ninjas are shredding guards like paper. The last guard drops dead, and the ninjas vanish as quickly as they came.

Sammy walks down into the cellar and towards the back, noticing the cages full of naked elderly people locked in them. He decides not to ask. Moving into the back room, he's shocked to see the torture chamber with all the naked girls strapped down to devices. But what shocks him the most is seeing his buddy Frank strapped to the wall, naked with a small red ball in his mouth, and Savannah to his side.

Seeing her sexy naked body up there gets his mind going; he is unable to control himself, and his rod gets rock-hard. Knowing this is not the time, he takes one last glance, hoping to keep the image forever implanted in his mind. He turns to Frank.

"Frank . . . to put you up for display they must seriously be hurting for money." He starts laughing.

Laughing so hard, he doesn't notice Frank and Savannah trying to warn him with facial expressions and shaking their heads that Andrey is coming up behind him with a metal bat.

"You ruined everything," Andrey cries, swinging the bat at Sammy's head.

Sammy feels a wetness on his neck and the side of his face. Turning around, he sees Andrey standing headless, blood shooting out of his neck hitting and dripping off the ceiling.

When the body drops, a ninja's inches away, gazing at Sammy with blood running off the end of the sword. The ninja bends and uses Andrey's shirt to wipe the sword then returns it to the shield strapped over the shoulder and along the back. The ninja turns to walk away.

"Thank you!" Sammy yells.

Slowly turning around, the ninja removes the head cover. It's the girl who bathed him in the cave on the mountain of Japan, the same one who massaged him in his room just days before. Looking at him with lust in her eyes, she smiles before turning and vanishing.

International police helicopters arrive. By morning, police boats appear. The caged, naked elderly and guards who survived are arrested. Mark somehow escaped in the night. A second boat arrives, taking everyone else to the mainland.

Frank and Savannah marry and take over the island. They must have bonded hanging naked together in the chamber.

Sammy goes back to Santa Monica to teach martial arts, hoping one day his special ninja will return.

The End

Acknowledgments

Dave Capper's been a close friend since 1985, and if not for him this book would never have been written. He not only gave me the idea to write a novel but also stuck with me until the end. Friends like Dave are truly rare, and I'm blessed to have one of them. Thanks, Dave!

I'm sure someday Dave will turn his authorial talents from writing books like *Silver Spoons* and others to help dialysis patients, to writing a fiction novel.

Cover Art & Graphics:
Custom ninja image and cover graphics completed by Illustrator – Reestah

Betareading and other contributions:
I want to affectionately thank friends and family who generously donated their time to help bring this novel to life:

Ariel Banzon
Chris Leyba
Dawn Perry
Henry Dinh
Kelly Banzon

www.ingramcontent.com/pod-product-compliance
Lightning Source LLC
Chambersburg PA
CBHW020318200626
46814CB00006BA/2309